I0685079

Telling Really Tall Tales

Copyright © [2016] by [Angel Berry]
First Edition: [March 2016]
Printed in the United States of America
ISBN: [978-0-692-65874-1]
Library of Congress Control #2016903825

Acknowledgement

"Pray to the Lord your God so that He will answer you in a way that you understand." – Walk the Path – God of Abraham

They sat around the campfire and stared at one another in boredom. Nancy looked over to her husband, Fred, and he sighed. Whose bright idea had it been to go on a camping trip anyway? I'm too old for this shit, he thought. He got up and went to the cooler for another beer.

Paula sat on a rock and roasted a marshmallow on a stick. She seemed to be the only one that wasn't miserable.

"Who's ready to go?" Isaac asked.

"Oh shut up, Isaac. This is fun." She offered him a marshmallow. "Let's do like when we were teenagers and sit around the fire and tell stories."

"Where's the pot?" Fred asked and everyone laughed.

"Like ghost stories, Paula? Really?" Susan asked. She got up from the ground and patted the dirt from her backside. "I'm going to bed." She headed for her recreational vehicle.

"Freeze! Sit your butt down." Paula told her, pointing to the spot that she'd been sitting in.

Susan rolled her eyes and frowned at her friend, irritated. She was forty-five years old. She was not going to sit around telling stories. As always though, Paula wouldn't back down, so Susan stumped back to her spot and sat down again.

"I'll start." Paula said to the annoyed faces around her. "If any of you move, I'll stab you in the eye with this stick." She threateningly pointed the marshmallow covered end of the stick at her husband, Andrew.

LACTRODECTUS

Ah, finally they were home. Once their ride had settled in for the evening, he climbed out, stretching his thin legs and broad body as his wife and son dismounted. They swiftly made their way home, glad for another safe trip. The weather was warm so they had enjoyed a most comfortable journey. The summer had allowed them extra hours of daylight, and to their absolute pleasure, they had been able to visit with their relatives a little longer than usual. His little family never knew when they would be able to make the journey across town to see their kin – visits were never planned, always spontaneous, and depended on their own ride's availability. If they got left behind unexpectedly, they never knew when they would be able to return home again. Nonetheless, they had been happy to see Mam and Pap after such a long time. Their kin had been surprised and overjoyed and little Jimmy had been excited to see his grandroaches.

Once his wife and son had settled in for the evening, he ran to the kitchen and enjoyed some sticky, sweet coffee that had been left to dry around the lid of an old, cracked mug. The night was his quiet time to enjoy the stillness of the house and to explore his surroundings. He crawled above the kitchen sink and onto the window sill then back down again and paused below to have a drink from a drop of water that hadn't yet dried on the faucet. He crawled over and inside of the cupboards, down the kitchen wall and into the living room and onto the carpet and stopped. He didn't like the way this tall carpet hindered his walking. Plus, the long hairs made his little legs itch.

He couldn't travel as fast over this new style of rug as he could over the beige, smooth carpet that they'd previously had before Dave had, had the bright idea to "modernize" the house. Mrs. Roach – his Harriet – had said that Dave was trying to erase anything that reminded him of Sarah, his ex-wife. He'd heard Dave's mother, Mrs. Montgomery, call Sarah a gold digger – whatever that meant. Hmm, he mused, he had never seen any gold around here and he'd been all over the house even inside the walls. Besides, he'd never seen her digging for anything and he saw everything that went on in this place. He dashed across the living room wall and onto the couch and then crawled around on the cushions before venturing within. Satisfied, that there were no new

2

treasures to be found and that all the springs were still in the right place, he raced out again and ran down the wooden arm of the sofa. He avoided Dave's old chair – he had kept that. There was nothing inside but loose coins and a few Cheetos that had been stale for so long that he and his son, Jimmy Roach, had long ceased to snack on them. Harriet was on a strict diet of vegetables. In spite of what he told her, she still felt that she needed to lose a gram or two. *Females*, he thought, as he used one leg to scratch an antennae, *will always find something to fret about.*

As leisurely as he wanted, he crawled about and eventually ended up in Dave's room. He silently crept onto the bed, being extremely careful to go around the side of the mattress. He had to avoid Dave's huge legs and arms. At any moment one could swing about and crush him. He'd learned the hard way that a simple movement of the sheets could send him catapulting into the air. Once Dave's hand had come down and swept him clear off the bed. He'd landed on his back and was forced to twist and turn about in that position for several minutes until he was able to turn over again onto his feet. He had been petrified while he struggled there on his back. He'd just known that at any moment Dave would wake with the urge to urinate and one of his gargantuan, bare feet would come down and crush him as he twisted about on the floor. That incident had darn near given him a heart attack, but he had counted himself lucky and had been much more careful during his future advances onto the huge bed while it was occupied.

Satisfied that his family's unknowing benefactor was sleeping soundly, he exited the bed and crawled towards the sliding glass door that led out onto the balcony that adjoined Dave's room. He knew a special way in and out and hastened to the spot, wanting to crawl around the window and in and out of that small opening before heading off to bed.

He got to the glass and then crawled up, up, up and then up further and froze – how had he missed it? He crawled quickly back down the glass the way he had come. Ah, there it was – a web. He peered at it through the window. Yes, indeed it was a web but he could see no poor, unfortunate critters trapped inside of it. He, himself, had been stuck in a web before but had been saved by his brother, Fellow Roach. That had been such a terrifying experience, of course, but that was just a regular house spider's web. This web

4

here was special because it was a black widow's web. He could tell by the irregular pattern in the weaving. It was woven underneath a lawn chair that Dave would sit on while he lounged around outside. Hopefully, it wouldn't venture inside, Mr. Roach thought as he proceeded to bed.

She crawled around the house, hissing as she went. She wanted inside. She had been watching the man who was asleep inside the house for days in an attempt to see if he was a viable mate. He seemed healthy and available. She planned to have with him what humans called a "one night stand." Her eggs would be laid in no time.

When Dave got home that evening he was as tired as always. There was a football game on tonight though and after a hot shower and a TV dinner, he planned to doze in front of the tube. He pulled into the driveway and shut off the car ignition then grabbed his briefcase from the back seat and got out of his car, a brand new Mercedes Benz that he'd purchased for himself after he and Sarah divorced. He'd needed something to cheer him up. He thought about his ex-wife and how their marriage had ended. His mother thought that Sarah had left him, but the truth was that he'd been the one to file for divorce. She wasn't a gold digger as his mother thought, but she was a trollop. He had known what he was getting himself into when he met her though. He had needed to have some fun in his middle-age and fun Sarah was. He distinctly remembered that she had promised to be faithful to him once they were married, but somehow his young wife had ended up pregnant. Even though he told her about the vasectomy that he'd had ten years prior, she still vehemently lied about the child being his. He finally had to threaten her with a paternity test to get the truth from her. That's what turned him off – not the cheating but the lying. Well, how did the saying go… ah, yes. You can't make a housewife out of a –

"Excuse me, sir. Is this your house?"

Dave turned and inhaled…goodness gracious. If it wasn't his house he would have lied and said that it was. *Red hair and eyes as black as onyx.* Well, her eyes were set a little far apart, but she was no less of a beauty because of it.

6

"Yes, it is." He said smiling.

"I'm sorry to bother you, but I just had a fight with my date and he put me out of the car. I need to get home, but I left my purse in his car and I don't have any money. Can I use your phone?" She asked him.

Oh, poor thing, Dave thought.

"Of course." He said, pulling his cell from his pocket and handing it to her.

"Thank you. I'll just be a moment."

She took the phone and went to the sidewalk to make her call in privacy.

Now what kind of guy would do a thing like that? Geez. Just throw the poor woman out in a strange neighborhood. Correction – who would let this beautiful, curvaceous creature escape. Dave could feel his mojo started to take off without him. This one looked like all types of fun. *Slow down, buddy*, he told himself, *this is the wrong type of woman for you. You know how it'll end.* But oh, how he loved the *click, click, click* of her high heels and the way her full hips swayed as she walked back to him and handed his cell over.

"Ride coming?" He asked.

"No." She said. "I couldn't reach anyone. It's fine. I can walk."

"I can't let you walk." Dave told her. *It's your lucky day, bud.* "I'll drive you home. No problem." He pulled his car keys from his pocket.

"No." She said hurriedly. "I, uh, live in a bad neighborhood and – it's embarrassing." She looked down at her feet as if ashamed.

Hmm, Dave thought. *A poor, pretty girl.* "Okay. How about I pay for you a cab. Here, you call." He said, smiling as he handed her the phone again. He didn't want to embarrass her. "And I'll be right out."

She nodded and Dave went inside, dropping his briefcase at the door. *What an odd young woman.* When he came back out, she was sitting on the porch swing. She clasped his cell phone nervously in her hands.

"Did you call?" He asked.

"Yes." She said. "They should be here any minute. Thanks again for your help." She said to him appreciatively.

"No trouble at all. I can't imagine how scary it must be for you to be in a strange neighborhood at night and all by yourself."

8

"Yes, it is." She whispered.

Dave sat down beside her and she lowered her eyes as he looked at her. It gave him an opportunity to admire the way her long, dark lashes swept her beautiful cheeks. Her red bottom lip quivered. As they waited for the cab they chatted about this and that, of course, and Dave became so engrossed in Lucy – that was her name – that an hour easily slid by without him even noticing. He was fascinated by a little black mole that rested on the swell of her left breast. The sight of her cleavage was such a treat. *I think you're going to get a little action, old buddy.*

"We've been waiting a long time for that cab." Lucy told him as she crossed a perfect nylon clad leg. She hadn't called a cab in the first place, but now it was time to go. She was satisfied that this man would be willing to mate with her.

"You know, you're right." He said to her. "I'll call for another cab."

Ten more minutes passed and then Lucy's cab arrived. The yellow neon sign glowed in the dark.

"Well, there's my cab." She said smiling.

"Lucy, would you like to have dinner with me tomorrow?" Dave asked her directly. No point in beating around the bush.

"I don't know." She said shyly.

He knew she wanted to say yes.

"I understand." He said. "If you change your mind then I'll be here tomorrow around the same time. Okay?"

"Okay. Thanks again." Lucy said as she provocatively pranced to her taxi. She climbed inside and waved to him as the car pulled away from the curb.

What a babe. Dave wondered why women always did this coquettish thing with their eyes when they were interested, but behaved coyly once you stepped up to the plate. He chuckled to himself as he went inside. She'd be back.

Dave stood in front of the mirror and adjusted his tie. Right on cue the doorbell rang. *Well, I wonder who this might be*, he thought to himself naughtily. *Lucy.* He opened the door and smiled down at her. Her beautiful red hair was upswept into a sleek chignon and she was wearing a black pantsuit and high heels. *Ah, there was his mole and that delectable, mouth-watering cleavage.*

10

"Come in." He told her, moving aside to allow her entry.

"Hello again." She told him, eying him boldly.

"I was just about to sit down for dinner. Wine?" He asked.

"Sure. Thanks." She told him as she looked around.

Lucy followed Dave into the dining room where he pulled a chair out for her to sit. The table was set for two and Lucy smiled to herself realizing that he'd known all along that she would be back. He exited the room and went into the kitchen. Lucy ran her hands across the table, smoothing the white table cloth where wrinkles remained in the folds. She stared at the dark veins in her hands and made a fist. *Maybe she should have worn gloves.*

Suddenly her head snapped up and she sniffed the air. She could feel eyes on her but Dave was still in the kitchen. She intently examined the room with her eyes, but there was no one else there. Lucy went back to inspecting the veins in her hands. They ran up the palms as well and she traced along them with her index fingernail. She needed to breed. Her head snapped up. There it was again. Then she heard it – a skittering. The sound of insect legs moving rapidly. She turned around swiftly in her chair and looked around again. *Where was it? What was it?* She closed her eyes and inhaled a deep breath and concentrated. Yes, the skittering had moved away, but she could still hear it. There was another bug in the house. That was okay but it sounded to her like a cockroach. She hated cockroaches. How bad she had to fight her instincts. Her eyes rolled into the back of her head. She wanted to find it and suck the delicious insides out of its –

"Here we are." Dave came into the dining room and sat a bottle of wine on the table. "Hungry?" He asked as he poured her a glass. "No." She shook her head as she sipped the red wine. *Drink up, Dave,* she thought to herself.

By the end of the night, Lucy was bored and frustrated. There was no seducing this man. He just went on and on about his ex-wife who he was obviously still in love with. He had become a big sack of blubbering drunk. She had to do something. There was no way she was coming back here again. She slowly sashayed over to Dave, her veiny hand trailed along the white tablecloth. She stood behind Dave and began to massage his shoulders, purposely leaning forward and placing her breasts against the back of his

12

neck. He turned and pulled Lucy into his lap and kissed her hard, his eager hands groped and tugged at her body. *Finally,* she thought. She waited patiently as Dave's mouth found its way to her chest.

Lucy threw her head back in mock pleasure and moaned wantonly. Dave moved her to straddle him and begin to pull the pins from her hair as his mouth found her neck. *There it was again!* That skittering was driving Lucy mad. She opened her eyes wide and desperately searched the ceiling above her. *Where was it? What was it?*

Dave picked Lucy up and carried her to his bedroom.

That night, Mr. Roach did his nightly survey of the house before climbing up into the chair where he'd seen the red haired woman sitting earlier that evening. The Roach family had listened as Dave mated with this new woman. Once Dave had fallen asleep, Harold Roach had watched the red haired woman run from the house barefoot in one of Dave's shirts. He couldn't figure out what it was about her that bothered him so much, but he knew that eventually he would be able to put an antennae on it.

He scurried into Dave's room and over to the sliding glass door. A breath of fresh air was what he needed. He went to the glass and crawled up, up, up towards the small, secret hole where he would exit and go outside. As quickly as he ran he came to a halt. Had it seen him? He wanted to run away even though he knew that it couldn't reach him through the window. Did it know about the opening at the top of the glass? He tried to crawl away, but it sped toward him and he froze. It was there on the other side of the glass, its eight eyes glaring at him hungrily. He knew what it was immediately by the red markings on its belly. He swallowed hard and began to back away.

Still on the other side of the glass she slowly stalked him. Harold panicked and he ran, he ran. He fled as fast as his little legs would take him. *Ahhh*, he screamed. A regular old spider was by no means worse than a centipede, which he hated profusely, but a black widow spider – and a female – and a hybrid -- oh, no. He would pack his little family up in a human's heartbeat if he had to. He ran, looking back as he went, and saw her there darting around on the glass as if the only thought in her evil mind was finding a
14

way inside. Quickly, he ran home screaming at the top of his little -- well, he didn't exactly have lungs, but in his mind he was hollering and screaming. Now he knew what had bothered him about the woman. *A hybrid*! He almost broke one of his tiny legs in his haste to get home.

"What is all this racket?" Harriet communicated to him as she came out of their small area. Why it looked as if Harold was getting their few things together! *What is going on!*

"Hurry up, up, up, up. We must leave at once!" He said to her as he moved about in a frenzy. "Go now, wife, wake the boy!"

"Posh, posh, Harold. Whatever is the matter?" She asked as she smoothed her leathery, brown wings.

"I saw it, it, it. I saw it, Harriet, and all its eight eyes looking at me."

"What dear? What did you see?" Harriet yawned.

"A widow, Harriet. A hybrid." He told her.

Harriet leapt an inch into the air in fright. "A widow!" She exclaimed. "Where?" She asked as she swiftly scurried about to help him pack.

Yes, now she understood. "There through Dave's window."

Harriet turned and looked at her husband. "Through? Through the window or inside of the window, Harold?"

"Well, outside, Harriet, but still, still, still a widow." He explained as he grabbed his cap. "We should get going."

She wasn't convinced. "Outside the window, Harold? You wake up the entire house because you saw a spider outside the window?" She asked him, feeling brave and secure again in her tiny home. Harriet impatiently tapped her tiny foot. There was no way that she was going to move. Dave had no idea that they were around and he had no pets to harass them. They had a really cushy spot here. What was Harold thinking? She rolled her beady eyes. Times like this made her wonder why she hadn't married Cocky Cockroach. A dumb spider never would have ran him home screaming at the top of his – well, they didn't have lungs, but that was not the point. She had once seen Cocky punch a full grown beetle right in the eye. But at the end of it all, and against her Papa's wishes, she had married Harold Roach because not only was he handsome and charming, but he was a notoriously smooth ladies roachman, and she had been the one to finally win his heart.

16

"A female, Harriet." He was saying. "What if she lays eggs around and Jimmy happens upon one?"

"Yes, yes. I know, dear, but she's outside. Now, now. Tell me, how many arachnids have we survived?" She said to him soothingly as she came over to him and rubbed her head against his own.

"I know, know, know, Harriet, but why was she there lurking that way? She wasn't hanging from a web, Harriet. She was sitting on the glass as if she were watching for something." He turned to her. "And there's something else. A hybrid, Harriet. I didn't want to scare you, but she was the one in the house with Dave earlier. They were mating." He whispered.

"Oh, no." Harriet exclaimed. "If she's in the house mating with Dave then you know what she'll do to him afterwards, right?"

Harold nodded. "We can't leave him alone, huh, Harriet?"

"Come to bed, Harold. Tomorrow is a new day. Sleep on it and if you still want to go tomorrow then we'll go."

She hissed as she thought about the roach that she'd just seen on the glass. He'd surprised her. She had been looking in that window for a while now and hadn't seen any insects inside. He was a smart one; she could tell. *How did he survive in the house alone? Where were the rest of the roaches?* Where there was one roach there were definitely others.

She had gone outside to make a meal of a fly that had been caught in her web. That's when she'd seen him. Lucy tipped back into the house and removed Dave's moist shirt before crawling back into bed beside him. He turned and embraced her and she tempted him again with her body. Dave pulled her beneath him and took her. She would be done with him by morning.

Lucy sat up in bed happily and listened to Dave in the bathroom brushing his teeth. She would lay her eggs soon. This was going to be the last egg sac that she would lay this year. She was behind anyway. She had been too picky when choosing mates. Out of the several hundred eggs that she would lay, only a small percentage of her cannibalistic babies would emerge from the sac. She thought about Dave. He had been so nice to her that she decided not to eat him. *What a sweetheart*! No, there was no reason for him to know.

18

She was so happy that she would soon have more babies that nothing could rain on her parade. Her kind of widow had to fight to survive. They were a special breed of widow, a superior breed. She lay down again and pulled the sheet over her head. She stretched her arms and legs across the bed and lay there quietly humming to herself as she ran her tongue over her teeth. She closed her eyes and hissed, loving the way her gums began to recede and her canine teeth grew into long, white fangs. She became preoccupied with piercing her tongue with her teeth and then sucking on the blood that oozed out.

There it is again, that skittering! Where is it? She quickly sat up and looked around. The sheets fell back to expose her full breasts. Her head swiveled around crazily as she searched for the elusive roach. She could hear the shower running in the bathroom. Slowly, Lucy eased from the bed and onto the floor. She began to crawl and slowly her body became smaller and smaller as she ran to the wall. She stopped again and listened. She heard it there! She raced for the crack above the door jamb of Dave's bedroom. Once inside, she knew she was on its tail. *There it is!* She saw its fat rump wobbling away as fast as it could go. She laughed to herself at how it swayed from side to side. She readied herself to shoot her web.

"Lucy?" Dave was calling her. *Damn it.* Lucy stopped her pursuit of the roach.

She turned and fled the other way toward the main bathroom. She jumped from the ceiling vent and her human feet met the tile floor as she landed. She strutted through the house and toward the bedroom where Dave was exiting.

"Hi." She said

Why does she sound out of breath? "You okay?" He asked.

"Sure. I'll get dressed so you can get to work."

"Hey, hey." Dave said grabbing her around the waist. "Why don't you stay for a while?" He nuzzled her neck with his beard.

Lucy tried to hide her disinterest. "I have to get going, Dave, but thanks for a good time." She moved towards the bedroom.

"When will I see you again?" He asked, following her. "I'm the perfect guy and I don't mind a no strings attached relationship. Hey, and you don't even have to worry about getting knocked up with me. What do you say?"

"What do you mean?" She asked, turning to Dave.

20

"I'd like to get to know you better is all." He said, putting his hands in his pockets and rocking on the balls of his feet.

"About being knocked up I mean."

"Ah. Well, I got fixed a few years back, if you catch my drift." He winked at her. "I was getting on and I didn't –" Dave screamed aloud in surprise as Lucy grabbed him by the throat and slammed him into the wall.

"You what!" She screamed in outrage.

Dave flew into the wall and hit the floor hard. Dazed, he tried to stand up but fell back against the wall stunned. He turned and looked over to Lucy. She had erupted in anger. *Had he said something wrong?* She ran at him. Veins, black and pulsating, covered her face and body.

"You what!" She screamed again. He braced himself as she grabbed him and threw him into the opposite wall.

Damn it, she was strong. He didn't want to hit a woman but this lady was crazy. Maybe she was on some kind of drugs. He mentally kicked himself as she kicked him with her feet. *You sure knew how to pick them, bud.* His head was pounding and there was

21

blood in his eye. He staggered to his feet and then was thrown wildly to the ground again. She jumped atop him and began biting him. He struggled with her, turning himself around on the floor as he lay beneath her and then screamed himself. She had fangs and she looked like a – *was that Lucy or a big ass spider?*

"Ahhhhh!" He screamed and fought like a hellion, ducking and punching at the spider as its jaws snapped in an effort to take a bite out of him.

He fought it until it was forced to back off of him and tried to crawl away. It lifted itself onto its hind legs and hissed and Dave kicked it in the center of the red hourglass in its abdomen and tried again to get away. He had to find a weapon or he would be killed. He could hear it coming after him again and he turned as it attacked him. Dave screamed as he felt the powerful sting in his leg and then another in his back. He gasped in pain. He couldn't move. He was exhausted and a numbing sensation began to move over him. He felt himself being lifted and wrapped in a stringy film. He was drowsy, and though he tried to fight it, he was unable to keep his eyes open. A heavy felling settled over him and he drifted into unconsciousness.

22

Lucy methodically lifted and wrapped Dave in her web, turning him speedily with her combed feet. Her silk was as strong as steel. The bristles at the back of her legs assisted in wrapping him in a perfect bind. He would be unable to move for a while. She would return to him after she got the roach. She could still hear him skittering about. She sensed that he was scared. She dropped Dave and ran up the wall and into the kitchen. Her body was taking too long to adjust so that she would be able to fit into the cracks and crevices of the walls quickly enough. She knew exactly where they were. She crawled to the refrigerator and then beneath it. They were there waiting for her -- three roaches. There was one little bitty one. *How cute. She would save him for last.*

"What are you?" The female asked her.

"I am a spider." Lucy hissed as she slowly stalked them. "Spiders crawl. I creep."

They backed slowly away from her. Lucy hissed as she approached them and snapped her jaws in expectation. Harriet held Jimmy to her as the widow drew closer to them. She purposely tried to divert the spider's attention away from everything but her and Jimmy.

The spider tried to leap for them, but suddenly couldn't move any further.

Lucy stopped and pulled at her hind legs. They wouldn't budge. She was stuck in something sticky. *What is it?* She looked up at the roaches and hissed, frantically trying to reach them with her front legs. Her jaws snapped angrily. To her chagrin, she slipped and her body spun and her abdomen clung to the floor. The more she tried to free herself, the more she became caught in the sticky mess *What is it?* She hissed in anger. She screamed and squirmed. The roaches ran swiftly around the back of her and she looked about as far as her small head would spin in search of them.

The sudden pain surprised her as much as becoming stuck in the sticky mess had. She looked to her right side and snapped her jaws at the silver needle that protruded from her side. Her body jerked in pain and she snapped and hissed at the roaches. She could see the small one running away. Lucy shrieked and her body enlarged. The refrigerator wobbled as she knocked against it. In her haste to get away from the roaches, she had enlarged and now the needle was stuck inside her body. She fell over on the floor and writhed in pain. It was stuck inside of her somewhere. *Where was it?*

She was in terrible pain. She knew that if she shrunk again the roaches would be waiting for her. *How had she been outsmarted by three house roaches? How had she been outsmarted by common prey?* She lay there on the kitchen floor and gasped for air. Her naked, shapely legs jerked as she struggled for breath. As a spider, she could not seem to push the needle out of her, and in human form she was unable to cough it out. It was stuck inside of her and somehow blocking her airway.

Lucy was furious. The roaches still would not let her die in peace. She tried feebly to hiss at them as they crawled upon her. Their little legs tickled as one crawled about on her face and then the other on an arm. She tried to swat at them and the fat one bit her. The small sting agitated her terribly. Infuriated and exhausted, Lucy took one last feeble swing at them and breathed her last breath.

Harriet crawled cautiously over the creature's eyeball and inside of its mouth. Yes, it was dead. Harriet was satisfied. She quickly ran over to Dave and looked him over. He was still unconscious but he was breathing. She stared at him lovingly. He would never know that his life had been saved by the Roach family. Harriet and Harold set off to find Jimmy. The poor little roach had been mortified at the sight of the vicious spider. *He has his father's disposition*, Harriet thought to herself. But she was confident that their little home was again safe.

AN URBAN MYTH

Toku was excited. He sprung upon his bed and jumped up and down on it with joy. He was wearing his favorite ninja pjs. His cousin, Henry, had come to visit for the weekend and they were going to play ball, mama was going to take them for ice cream and to play laser tag, and dad promised to take them to the movies tomorrow to see what? Ninjas! Henry ran into the room and jumped onto the bed as well.

"Look." Henry screamed as he did a somersault.

"Boys, stop jumping on that bed." Marie came into the bedroom and smiled at the children. "How about a story?"

"Yay!" They screamed together. Henry and Toku climbed onto the bed and got under the covers.

"All right now." Marie said, coming into the room. She pulled her long braids into a ponytail and then sat cross-legged on the bed across from the boys. "Listen here.

There was once a crocodile that lived in the jungle of the Philippines. He made his home along the Cagayan River. He was a cunning, deceitful predator. All this crocodile thought about night and day was how he wanted to sink his long, sharp teeth into a tasty human being, particularly a human boy. The only humans that lived nearby were the Ibanag people, and those little boys were too smart to get caught and eaten by the sneaky reptile. The crocodile was twenty feet long and this made it hard for him to sneak up on people. He was a vicious, carnivorous beast with hard scales that lay across his broad back.

'I sss-sss-sure wants-ss-ss me a human.' He would hiss. His long, forked tongue would flick in and out between his razor sharp teeth as he swam along the river. He was extremely aggressive but he had a small brain and –'"

"Mom, this is boring." Toku told Marie sincerely.

"Well, do you want a story from one of your books then?" She asked.

"No, Aunt Marie. Make up a good one about monsters." Henry said.

"How about Three Little Pigs with a twist?" Marie asked.

Toku shook his head.

"Hmm. Okay then. Well, how about a story with a genie?"

"Nah. That's for girls." Toku told her.

"Not that kind of genie, Toku. I'm talking about an Ifrit." She

explained.

"If what?" Henry asked with a raised brow.

"Genies made from smoke and fire."

"Oh. Well, do they give wishes?" Henry needed to know. The

wishes were important.

"They do."

"Okay. I'm ready then." Henry said, and folded his hands behind

his head.

"Will this story have monsters, mom?"

"And monsters, Toku. Listen here. It's called Jinn."

King Alec sat in his private suite and listened intently as the

sorcerer explained to him in detail how to use the potion that

would make his soldiers strong enough to prevail against the

Bracan army that threatened to invade his city. King Alec was

losing the battle. The king was desperate, and if he didn't think of

something soon, his city would be overrun by the barbarian army.

"Your Magnificence, it is simple." The sorcerer told him in a conspiratorial tone. "Boil this potion in a cauldron of water. Do not be startled when the mixture begins to foam, but immediately take it from the fire. Once it cools, give a drink to each soldier before they go out to the battlefield. I assure you that every man you send out will return alive, and they will leave behind them a field of bloody Bracans."

The king dismissed the sorcerer and examined the potion that he held in his hand. If the formula worked as the magician had promised, his dwindling army would defeat the fierce Bracan soldiers and drive them back. More Bracans would surely come, but Alec's army would fight with a new confidence.

He should have known that when he had refused the Bracan king's offer of his daughter as wife that there would be trouble. King Ichabold had taken Alec's refusal as an insult. The Bracan king had wanted the union to bind the two kingdoms – Braca and Galzon. Alec was not interested.

The Galzonic kingdom was rich and prosperous. The kingdom teemed with philosophers, teachers, doctors and blacksmiths. Their women were lovely and the apples that grew on their lands were sweet. The problem was his people weren't fighters – not like the

30

Bracans at least. These lands hadn't seen war since the days when his grandfather had been king. The Bracans were barbaric and destructive. *A dirty people*, Alec thought to himself. The Bracan king was a tyrannical madman as far as Alec was concerned and he wanted nothing to do with him. He had almost laughed in King Ichabold's face when he'd offered his daughter in marriage. The Bracan princess was homely and had bad breath. Alec decided that he would rather hang himself than enter her bed chambers at night. King Alec summoned Abasi, general of his army and best childhood friend, who was undoubtedly in the armory preparing the men for battle. Alec paced his chamber and waited.

"Sire?" Abasi said, coming into the chambers without knocking.

"Abasi." He solemnly greeted his friend. "How are the men?"

"Their morality – confidence is low, your Highness."

The king gestured for his guard to leave the room. Once they shut the door behind them, Alec approached Abasi and spoke to him in a whisper.

"Abasi, I have to talk to you."

"What is it?" He asked.

Alec showed Abasi the potion that he held in his hand. "I got this potion from the sorcerer that was in my chambers this morning. He says –"

"Really, Alec?" Abasi exclaimed. "Your men are dying and you're preparing potions?"

"Quiet, old friend. Hear me out." Alec filled Abasi in on what the sorcerer had told him. "We're desperate, Abasi. It's worth a shot." He handed the potion to Abasi who reluctantly nodded and left the room.

Alec stood on the turret of the castle and watched the men prepare to do battle. He knew that Abasi had given the men the potion and he observed them carefully, wondering if the concoction would work. The ground shook as the Bracan soldiers approached beating their swords against their shields. Some were running eagerly at the Galzonic infantry hollering savagely and wielding clubs and battle axes.

Alec wiped the sweat from his brow as he watched the battle from his high post. He saw King Ichabold on a bank in the distance sitting atop his horse, his army general at his side. Alec knew that

Ichabold planned to take his kingdom by force, but he refused to see his people become slaves under barbarian rule. The Bracans, who were no better than common mercenaries, would destroy their beautiful lands in no time with their destructive nature.

Alec watched the battle nervously. At first, his soldiers had seemed stronger, more agile as they fought against the ferocious Bracans, but as the battle wore on, Alec watched in horror as the men began to become ill. He cursed as vomit flew from some and onto the Bracans who were beginning to kill them off slowly but surely. Alec was relieved when Abasi called for retreat and the men fled to the city. Had it not been for the archers firing arrows from the castle walls, their small army would have been annihilated as the Bracans gave chase. He could see King Ichabold and his general laughing and pointing. It was one thing to lose a battle, but Alec's army had been humiliated.

"The men are ill." Abasi told Alec as he ran to meet him. "Everything was fine at first. The men were stronger, faster but then –"

"I know, Abasi. See to them and I will meet you in my rooms in an hour."

Alec cursed again. Word had come to him that the majority of his army were deathly ill. On top of that, the Bracans now had the city under siege. It was only a matter of time before King Ichabold stormed the gates. Ichabold knew that he had more of an advantage over the Galzons now that their army was ill. He would soon strike. Alec was deeply distressed. *What kind of king was he if he couldn't come up with a plan to protect his people?*

Abasi entered his chambers and sat down, exhausted. "We are almost defeated, Alec. What shall I do?"

"If we don't think of something soon we will be over ran." Alec told him.

Abasi dreaded what he was about to say. "Alec, what do you know of the Jinn?"

"The Jinn?" Alec said quietly, wondering what his friend was thinking. "I know that they are said to be malicious and insane."

"There are people that have been helped by the Jinn, Alec."

"Yes, Abasi, but at what cost?"

"Do you want your wives and children to become slaves? Is that what you want? Do you want your daughters to become concubines to savages? What about the people who you rule? They are counting on you as their king to keep them safe. What do you have to lose, Alec?"

"Weren't you the one to lecture me about that cursed potion? This is just as absurd." Alec chastened him.

Abasi ignored Alec's protest. "I know of a woman who lives in one of our villages – a hermit who has lived among us since your father was king. She once served a Jinn. He released her from servitude when she solved one of his riddles."

Alec shook his head. He couldn't believe that this was how far he had fallen.

"We can go now – tonight. You and I together. We will leave under cover of night so that no one sees us. We will wear beggars' cloaks." The king didn't respond so Abasi rose to his feet, satisfied that the matter was settled.

Alec didn't know what else he could say. He nodded his consent and Abasi quickly left the room to secure horses for their journey.

As Alec and Abasi slipped silently from the castle that night, the king continued to feel apprehensive about what they were going to do. He was having second thoughts. Abasi believed that they had no other choice and Alec knew that his old friend was afraid of losing his family in the war as well. They approached the shack of the old woman. He decided that he would not turn back. He had to save his people at any cost.

They could see a light burning in the window of the ramshackle home. Abasi and Alec first cautiously looked around and then approached the door and tapped softly. After a few seconds, the door cracked slightly and they faced an elderly woman who peered out at them.

"What do you want?" She asked.

"We are very sorry to bother you, old mother, but we seek guidance." Abasi said to her kindly.

Skeptical, she eyed them in their beggar clothing and then began to shut the door. Alec quickly stuck a booted foot out before she could slam the ragged door in their faces and held out a handful of coins. She eyed the coins, still suspicious of Alec, whose face was

36

partially hidden beneath his cloak. She hesitantly opened the door and gestured for them to enter.

"What guidance do you seek?" She asked them, not letting the coins out of her sight.

"We seek the Jinn." Abasi told her.

Her eyes widened with fear and she quickly walked to the thin door and threw it open so fast that Alec thought it would fly off its rusty hinges. She vehemently shook her head and tried to usher them out.

"I know nothing of the Jinn." She said. "Now leave."

"There is more gold where this came from." Alec told her. "A lot more."

"This is dangerous what you are asking. I won't have anything to do with it."

"Please, old mother." He pleaded. "All we want to know is where to find them."

"You must be very desperate." She said with a warning in her voice.

Alec and Abasi exchanged a glance. They would not explain to her why they sought the Jinn. She looked them up and down now, observing not just the gold that Alec held, but the newness of their boots and how well groomed they were despite the frayed cloaks that they wore. She was greedy. *If all they wanted was to simply find the Jinn then there was no harm in taking their money,* she thought to herself. Besides, she was an old woman and she needed new blankets and firewood for her stove.

"You cannot just find any Jinn and expect them to do your bidding." She told them, softly shutting the door.

"Then what shall we do?" Abasi asked.

"You have to request assistance from your own djinni." She told them.

"Our own?" Abasi asked confused. He had never known anyone who'd had their own personal Jinn.

"Yes," she responded, "your own djinni. Every breathing soul made of clay has its own djinni. A djinni can be good or evil, and though they are made from a smokeless fire, their spirit is the mirror reflection of their clay twin. If your heart is good, then the heart of your djinni is good; but if you are evil or manipulative then your djinni will be the same." She explained to them.

38

"So how does one find their djinni?" Alec asked her.

"If you are serious then I can help you." She told him. "For what you have promised, of course."

"Of course." Alec told her, handing over the gold in his hand and what remained on the person of himself and Abasi.

She gestured for him to have a seat and Alec was startled to see her approach him with a knife and a small bowl.

"Just a little blood." She told him.

He held his hand out to her and she sliced him across the palm, turning his hand over and squeezing it to get the required amount of blood that she needed in the bowl. She carried the bowl to the fire and after muttering a few words under her breath, threw the contents of the bowl into the fire. They waited. The blood sizzled and hissed as it hit the fire, and for a moment, Alec didn't see what the point was. All of a sudden, the air went still around them and a strong wind blew through the rickety house, blowing out the candle and stoking the fire. A smoky mist appeared before the old woman as she stood on her feet seemingly in a trance and rocked to and fro on the threadbare rug that lay on the floor in front of the fireplace.

To their dismay, she shrieked loudly and placed her hands over her ears before falling to the ground writhing in agony. Abasi ran to her and pulled her from the floor and laid her upon the cot that sat in one corner of the room. Alec relit the candle as the old woman started to murmur and shiver in the suddenly freezing room. Abasi pulled a thin blanket up to her chin and whispered to the old woman.

"What did you see, old mother?"

"An Ifrit." She said in a hoarse voice. "His eyes burned like lamps. His head reached the heavens and he carried a large sword in his hand. When I searched for him he found me immediately. He was looking right at me. On his shoulder there sat a vicious, black owl. I thought it would devour my eyes while they sat in their sockets. The Jinn is called Ali. He is thousands of years old. He has been banished from Jabal Alkuhuf, the ancient home of the Jinn. He roams the earth alone. The sound of his voice seemed to pierce my brain as he spoke. He said to tell you, King Alec, that he is waiting for you in the wastelands." She whispered fearfully.

"The wastelands." Alec repeated to Abasi.

40

"Then that is where we shall go." Abasi said, leaving the old woman and grabbing his cloak.

"The wastelands are treacherous travel. We need more men." Alec told him.

"No." The old woman said. "You must not. If there are others then he may not appear to you. It is best if the two of you travel together. Leave at dawn and you shall arrive by midday."

"Old mother, you must rest. We thank you very much for your help." Abasi told her as they approached the door.

"There is always a price with the Jinn, King." The old woman said to Alec. "It is not too late to turn back."

He bowed to the old woman and shut the door behind himself and Abasi. He understood what she was telling him. He would just speak with the djinni to see what was required of him.

Alec and Abasi slipped back into the castle and made plans to travel to the wastelands the following morning.

*   *   *

They traveled alone through the underground tunnels that sat beneath the castle. If all went well, they would return by night with a way to defeat the Bracan king. They were dressed in disguise and planned to buy horses and supplies once they reached the next town. They carefully exited the tunnel. Although this was a secret passage, they still had to keep their wits about them. It wouldn't do well for them to be murdered as they snuck away from the city. Besides, the Bracan king was crafty.

They ran the five miles until they came to the small town of Kerjwood. They had come to this village because the people were money hungry, but minded their own business. They would gladly take the money from Abasi and Alec's hands with their short, greedy fingers and no questions would be asked.

They conducted their business within the town without consequence and were soon on their way to the wastelands with horses and the necessary provisions. They were armed well for the journey. If danger approached them on the road they would be ready for it. That is until they reached Dalshun. No weapon would help them there. They dreaded passing through Dalshun. Had they not been pressed for time, they would have took the long way and avoided the dangerous village all together.

They moved swiftly through the day, pushing the horses until they arrived at Dalshun. The village sat on the outskirts of the

wastelands. Alec and Abasi held their breath as they moved

cautiously through Dalshun. The black eyes of the village's

inhabitants stared blindly about. Some stood still, motionless as if

in shock while others moved about aimlessly.

Though stupefied and blind, the Dalshunic people were evil and

strong. As quick as lightning, a Dalshun would be upon them in an

instant – would likely jump onto the back of their horse to sit

behind them and began its eerie, confusing babbling. Their eye was

in their hand but was asleep unless awoken by its host who used it

to search around them when in search of prey. If the wrong

Dalshun got curious about either of them while it was looking for

food, it would certainly delay their trip.

Though they were two strong men, they were no match for one

male Dalshun. If other Dalshun got curious about what their

relative was up to, then Alec and Abasi's death would be certain.

Alec looked around at the dark, barren trees and hostile land.

When they had entered Dalshunic territory, the sun had fled behind

dark clouds and a dark shadow had fallen over them. The horses' hooves softly tread the sloshy, muddy ground beneath them. They moved slowly past miserable looking mud and straw huts, past Dalshun females who blindly nursed slick, bald-headed babies. They breathed a sigh of relief as they exited Dalshun and approached the wastelands. They lit their torches as they entered the barren land, their senses drawn tight. The wind howled loudly, but Alec was still able to make out the sound of wings flapping in the distance.

"Do you hear that?" He whispered to Abasi.

"I do. Whatever it is, it's large." Abasi replied, holding his torch out and peering into the darkness. The horses began to fidget.

"Something is spooking the horses."

Whatever it was, it was now overhead. Abasi and Alec held their torches up, anxiously searching the sky but seeing nothing. It was midday, but the desolate land was so dark that they could only see as far as the torches' light. Suddenly something moved fast to their right. They pointed their torches in that direction and gasped with fright at the creature that stood before them. It wasn't an owl that the old woman had seen. This creature towered above them. Its cold, beady eyes assessing them as it spread its huge wings.

44

"A Rukh!" Abasi said in awe.

"An Ifrit!" Alec exclaimed, pointing to the beast that sat atop the huge bird.

The beast had its huge, muscular arms folded over its chest. Horns extended from its hideous head and the beast's eyes glowed as a flame of fire. Thick golden bands adorned each of its wrists. When Alec pointed at the beast it threw back its large head and laughed, exposing large pointed teeth.

"You seem surprised, King. Did you expect me to come flying in on a magic carpet?" It said in a voice that rumbled from deep within its chest.

Alec didn't like the look of him. Maybe they were better off on their own. "Let's go." He whispered to Abasi.

"Don't be fickle, King Alec. If you leave now, the Bracans will conquer your kingdom in the blink of an eye." The Jinn said to them.

Curious about the two men, he eyed them openly and leaned around the massive bird to peer down at them to Abasi's discomfort. The Jinn looked as if he considered eating them and his fiery eyes searched them out thoroughly.

His smile was sincere. "I am here to help you, King."

"And what do you require in return?" Alec asked, not trusting him.

"The biggest jewel that your kingdom possesses. That is all."

That is all, Alec thought flabbergasted. *Did the Ifrit know about the large, jade stone that sat in the king's treasury?* No, how could he? The jade had not been moved since his great-grandfather placed it in the treasury almost a century ago.

"Of course, Master Jinn. That is the least that I can do in return for your assistance. Of course." Alec said, bowing in deference to the beast.

What was Alec doing, Abasi wondered in shock. They were desperate but he never would have thought that Alec would sacrifice the jade. The king was that desperate to save his people. Abasi was proud of his friend.

"Then make your petition, King." The Jinn told him.

"I need an army, a strong army that will defeat the barbaric Bracans."

"Ah, a fierce people are the Bracans. Pray tell, King, what was your insult?" He asked Alec.

46

"I refused the Bracan king's offer to marry his daughter."

The Jinn threw back his large head and laughed. Abasi counted two rows of sharp teeth in his upper and lower jaws.

"You have a way about you, King. I'll wager it was the way in which you refused." The Jinn said.

Abasi nodded in agreement. He remembered that his friend's nose had turned up into his eyebrows when he had viewed King Ichabold's daughter in his presence.

"I will help you, King, and then you will deliver the jewel and we shall be done. Agreed?"

"Agreed." The king said, bowing once again. "The Bracans will attack us by morning."

"Don't worry, King. I will be there."

Abasi and Alec left then with the promise that the Jinn would come to their rescue by morning. They moved swiftly through the Dalshun village without incident and then sold their horses back once they reached Kerjwood for half of what they'd purchased them for.

"Crooks." Abasi muttered under his breath in disbelief.

They cautiously made their way to the secret passage that led to the tunnel underneath the castle and ran the rest of the way until they made it to the king's chambers.

"Do you think he will come, Alec?"

"He gave his word."

"Will you really hand over the gem to the Jinn? It is our most precious stone."

"I know, Abasi. We must do what we have to."

The following morning, Abasi prepared the few remaining men for battle. The soldiers who were not ill had no confidence that they would prevail. They knew that the Bracan king was preparing to storm the city gates and Abasi admonished the men to fight to the death. When the battering of the gates began and the Bracans began to chant their war song, Abasi lectured the men on strength and bravery.

King Alec was standing on the castle turret when he heard the Rukh's wings and loud shriek. The sky seemed to part as the huge bird came into view. The men who were fighting below ducked their heads as they searched the air for the cause of the loud noise

48

and then saw the bird. This day, the Jinn was not sitting upon the Rukh. The bird shrieked loudly as it swooped down and grabbed several Bracan soldiers in its huge talons and then flew high into the air with them and flung them to the ground below.

Alec stood horrified as the terrified Bracans fell through the air and hit the ground. The soldiers, Galzonic and Bracan, began to scatter in fear. The ground began to quake and the men looked frantically about. Alec peered into the distance. A cloud of black, fiery smoke came swiftly toward the battlefield. The quaking grew louder and Alec recognized the sound as soldiers marching into battle. The soldiers started to scream and run as thousands of masked shadows descended upon them.

Abasi shrunk in fear as he was snatched into the air by a strong arm. He looked down into blackness of empty eyesockets. It pulled the mask from its fiery face and grinned at Abasi.

"Hello, Galzon." It said to Abasi before throwing him to the ground and running into the midst of the battle.

The fiery shadows were everywhere murdering the Bracans. Abasi could hear the terrified screams of the soldiers as they were thrown

49

into the air and butchered by the swift ghosts who seemed to be afire. He ducked as severed limbs flew in his direction. The battlefield was red with the blood of Bracan soldiers. The Rukh continued to swoop down upon the battlefield and seize hardened men who screamed for their mothers as they were made helpless by the piercing, sharp talons that sunk into their bodies. The bird would shriek and carry men off to the sun to be dropped again to the ground thousands of feet below.

Alec stood on the turret and laughed as he watched King Ichabold and his general try to flee only to be swept down upon by the giant bird. He clapped and stomped his feet as the Galzon soldiers stood below and cheered in triumph.

"You are victorious, King."

Alec jumped in surprise as the Jinn spoke behind him. He turned and came eye to eye with the beast. He didn't seem as large as he had the day before when he sat upon the large bird, but he was still big compared to Alec.

"Yes, Master Jinn, with your help, of course."

"I am here to serve." The Jinn told him happily. "I have come to collect."

"Absolutely. Follow me." The king told him.

Together they walked through the castle and into the king's hall, which was empty. Everyone was outside watching the battle. Alec went to his throne and gestured to an item that was wrapped in cloth.

"There it is, Master Jinn. The best jewel in the king's treasury." The Jinn bowed to Alec and stepped onto the throne. He reached down and picked up the heavy jewel and parted the cloth to look inside.

"A ruby?" He said, turning to Alec in surprise.

"Yes." The king said smiling.

"This was not our agreement, King. The agreement was for the largest jewel in your kingdom. This jewel is by no means the largest or the best."

Alec swallowed nervously as the Jinn stepped down from the throne. His large, booted feet struck the ground heavily and the sound echoed through the large hall.

"No?" Alec asked. "Well, if you are not satisfied, Master Jinn, I will gladly give you diamonds in addition to the ruby."

"That was not our agreement, King." The Jinn's friendly expression turned into a sneer. Alec knew that he was becoming upset. His fiery eyes began to glow like lamps. "Do you think to deceive me after I have saved your pathetic kingdom from annihilation?"

"Not deception, Master Jinn, but a compromise."

"We had an agreement!" The Jinn screamed before striking Alec hard enough that he slid across the marble floor.

"Okay. Okay." Alec said, holding out a hand in defense as the Jinn angrily approached. "I will give you the jewel. You are right, Master Jinn. That was very wrong of me. I am sorry."

The Jinn stopped and suspiciously stared down at Alec. "You will make good on your word, King."

"I will." Alec agreed. "Please follow me." *Were all his men still outside?*

The Jinn followed Alec deep into the castle and then down a stone staircase that was alit with candles that led them into the bowels of the castle. Alec went to a wall on the south end of the room and pulled out a cornerstone. The fake, stone wall slid open for the king and Jinn to enter through, and Alec gestured for the Jinn to follow him inside. He led him to the middle of the floor of the bare room. Alec fell to his knees and cleared the dirt from a door that sat in the floor. He removed a gold chain from his neck. A silver key dangled from the end of the chain.

He opened the door open and said to the Jinn, "Down there, Master Jinn, is your jewel."

There was a room beneath and it was filled with treasure. The Jinn dropped to his knees and peered into the hole then cocked an ear as if listening. He looked up at Alec and smiled.

"I will not be angry with you, King. I will remove my jewel and leave your kingdom."

The king bowed to the Jinn and then watched as the beast dropped lithely into the hole. Alec hurriedly slammed the door shut and locked it, trapping the Jinn beneath.

"King Alec." He could hear the Jinn screaming. "Release me!"

"You, Master Jinn, will be my greatest treasure. You will do as I say." Alec screamed back at him.

He could hear the Jinn laughing hysterically beneath him. "You are a fool, King. Do you really think that you can control me? You can't even save your own kingdom. Had you been honorable and kept your word, I would have served you and your offspring for the rest of your days, but now you have tricked me twice. To you, I will be more vile than the Bracan king. Your people will watch their precious king bow before my feet at his own throne."

Alec stumbled up the stairs and rushed into his hall. The Jinn's words played through his brain. He bumped into Abasi who was out of breath.

His friend excitedly embraced him. "I have been searching for you all over, Alec. We have won the battle with the help of the Jinn army. We should have a celebration in his honor. Have you seen him?"

Alec was quiet and this gave Abasi pause. He could tell by the look on his friend's face that something was wrong.

"He's in the treasury." Alec said.

"Ah, grabbing the gem. Let's go assist him." Abasi said, moving away.

Alec grabbed Abasi's arm. "He's locked inside."

"What do you mean?"

"I trapped him inside."

54

"What would make you do such a thing, Alec?" Abasi asked, surprised. "This isn't how you treat a guest who has saved your life."

"I tried to give him the ruby that your father was gifted by the Peronians, but he wasn't satisfied." Alec said, running a hand through his hair.

"That wasn't the agreement." Abasi said quietly to his friend.

"I couldn't bear parting with the jade. I wasn't going to place the stone in that beast's hands. I really need you to be with me on this, Abasi."

"Are you mad, Alec? What were you thinking?" Abasi was outraged. "I'm going to set him free. Give me the key." He held his hand out to Alec.

"I am still king, Abasi." Alec warned his friend. "The ultimate decision is mine."

"Ah, I see." Abasi said, taking a step back. "And how long do you think the Jinn will allow you to hold him prisoner?"

"Calm down, Abasi."

"He wields a ghost army for crying out loud. They are made of smoke and fire. You weren't out there, Alec. You didn't see them slaughtering the Bracans. Set the Jinn free."

"I will not be ruled by a beast, Abasi. He will serve us."

Abasi paused. "My king, you have no honor." He bowed and walked away.

That night, once the kingdom was finally silent save for the loud beating of the Rukh's wings above the castle, Abasi discreetly snuck to the stone staircase and toward the secret room in the lower parts of the castle. He removed the brick that would open the room to him and stepped inside. He lowered himself to the ground and laid an ear upon the door.

"Master Jinn, can you hear me?" There was a long pause. "Master Jinn?"

"I hear you just fine, friend of the king. Have you come to beg for your life?"

Abasi swallowed. "Why do you allow yourself to be held captive?"

"I am admiring my stone, small man. It is beautiful. A speaking fire burns within it and mesmerizes me for hours with its thoughts."

56

"It is a magic stone?" Abasi asked.

"It is a wise stone, brave friend of the king. It shall be my companion."

"What will become of us, Master Jinn? Will you murder us all because of Alec's deceit?"

"So you have come to beg for your life then." The Jinn said.

"I have come to beseech you, Master Jinn, for the lives of the people in this kingdom who know nothing of you or the craftiness with which their king has dealt with you." Abasi waited for a reply.

"Master Jinn?"

He exhaled in disappointment. The Jinn was not responding. He got up to leave then quickly dropped to the ground again as he heard the Jinn begin to speak.

"Your king will touch the ground with his face before my feet in front of you all, small man. And then I will take my jewel and leave."

"Then it will be as you say, Master Jinn."

Relieved, Abasi got up from the floor and left the room. He believed that the Jinn would keep his word.

The following morning the people sat in the king's hall and offered him gifts in thanks for his success in defeating the Bracan army. The people did not know where the inhuman army had come from that aided in the victory, but the rumor circulating throughout the kingdom was that the king had employed a warlock, and that the battle had been won by benefit of witchcraft. The huge bird cast a shadow over the castle as it hovered above.

"For you, brave king." A nobleman was saying to Alec as he offered him a gift of honey. "From my own bees, sire."

Abasi shook his head in disgust. Alec was actually sitting there as if nothing was wrong – as if he wasn't holding a Jinn hostage in the bowels of the castle. This had been going on all morning and he wanted that damn bird gone. Its constant flapping of wings made him think that the castle was falling down upon itself. His thoughts paused as a hooded, robed man approached Alec's throne and stood quietly.

"Do you offer a gift?" Alec asked.

The figure was silent and held nothing in its hands.

"Remove your hood, sir." Alec said, sitting forward on his throne.
58

The Jinn removed his hood and glared at the king. The people gasped at the sight of the beast. His eyes gleamed with a wicked light and his horns extended from the back of his head.

"I shall depart now, King." The Jinn said. "But first you will bow before me."

"I will not." Alec said, still surprised that the Jinn had escaped. "Guard!"

The king's guard did not move. They were too petrified. Alec froze with fear as the Jinn stepped onto his throne and grabbed him by his throat with one hand. The Jinn snatched Alec to his feet and drug him from the throne. Some of the people screamed in fright. Abasi smiled to himself. Of course, Alec was his friend, but it seemed only right that he learn an important lesson.

The large Jinn's booted feet struck the floor loudly as he dragged Alec to the middle of the court. The people watched as the Jinn held their king out in front of them. Alec struggled but his feet were too high above the ground for him to get any leverage.

"Since you, King, behave like a weak man then you shall look like one." The Jinn sat Alec upon his feet and people shrieked and backed away in horror as he withered and became frail and feeble before their eyes. The old women began to faint. Alec fell to the ground and his forehead bounced off of the Jinn's boots. The Jinn looked down at him and smiled.

"Goodbye, King."

The people quickly parted to allow the Jinn to exit. His footsteps echoed through the court. Abasi ran to Alec's side and helped him to his feet.

"My king." He said.

He hadn't expected this at all. He'd thought that the worst that would happen was Alec would get a bop upside the head, but his friend was now decrepit.

"What have I done, Abasi?" Alec's thin shoulders quaked with grief. "What have I done?"

Abasi helped his friend to his chambers. He did not want the people to see their king sob.

"More blankets, Abasi. I'm freezing." The king said in a hoarse voice as Abasi helped him into bed. His leathery skin was thin and wrinkled.

Abasi sat across from his friend and stared at him in utter shock.

60

He could no longer hear the wings of the Rukh.

All those years sitting right under their nose had been a gemstone that burned with a fire that spoke and not one Galzon king had realized it.

What would happen if another kingdom decided to invade their city? That was inevitable. Soon word would spread that the Galzon king was infirmed and derelict; that he employed the use of witchcraft to win battles. Abasi sat and listened to Alec's labored breathing.

Why Alec had tried to trick the Jinn, Abasi would never understand. This was his thought as he made his way to the ramshackle home that housed the old woman. He wasn't wearing beggar's clothes on this night. He approached the new, wooden door and knocked. She opened the door slightly and peeked out as before.

"What do you want?"

"The Jinn." He told her directly.

She shook her head and opened the door. Abasi removed his cloak and rolled up his sleeve. She watched him quietly.

"The knife and bowl, go. Get them now." He told her.

"You didn't learn from the king's experience?" She asked him.

"The last time I was here you said to us 'if your heart is good, then the heart of your djinni is good; but if you are evil or manipulative, then your djinni will be the same'. Old woman, conjure up my Jinn." Abasi threw two small, cloth bags full of gold coins onto the table.

The old woman exhaled a nervous breath. She wanted the coins.

Abasi held his hand out to her. "Conjure my Jinn."

She went and retrieved the knife and bowl and then came back to Abasi. He held out his hand and she sliced him across the palm the same as she had once done Alec, turning his hand and squeezing to get the amount of blood that she wanted into the bowl. She carried the bowl to the fire and began chanting as before then threw the blood into the flames. The blood crackled as it hit the fire and Abasi waited. He tightly wound a cloth around his hand that he had brought with him specifically for this purpose.

The air around them went still again and a fragrant wind blew through the rickety shack, blowing out the candle and stoking the fire. A smoky mist appeared before the old woman who had been rocking to and fro as she stood on her feet seemingly in a trance. This time she didn't shriek and fall to the ground. She stood still and her gray haired head fell back. Her shawl dropped to the floor and she turned to Abasi.

"Your jinniyah is waiting for you in the wastelands. Her voice is as sweet and smooth as silk in my ears. Her fragrance is like the aroma of fresh, red roses. Her beautiful hair touches her bare, slender ankles and her eyes glow like the moon at night. She sends you a message. She requires your price up front. She says that you are to bring her a living, breathing infant Dalshun or don't come at all. She says, good luck to you, honorable friend of the king. If you complete such a dangerous task in order to make it to her then she will be very pleased and you will be greatly rewarded."

Abasi donned his cloak and left the old home. He would go to the Kerjwoods with a ransom of gold and diamonds for the first man who brought him two, healthy Dalshunic infants. The greedy Kerjwoods would burn the Dalshun village to the ground in order to get their hands on the babes and then the ransom.

When Abasi traveled to the wastelands, he would avoid the Dalshunic village and go the long way around to make it with the infants. He made his way to the castle to rob the king's treasure.

*   *   *

"That was stupid." Susan said to Paula and laughed.

"I liked it." Isaac said, taking a drink from his beer. "You try, Ms. Smartie."

"I will then." Susan told them as she sat up.

CATCH OF THE DAY

There was an old man who fished in the sea
He caught a catch that was as little as could be
The fish said, Oh my God, Oh my God,
What mayhem is this?
That this large headed creature catches me with a stick
Throw me back, throw me back
You huge headed beast!
I am way too small for your big, crooked teeth

The old man growled and said to the fish,
What have you to do with this stick?
I will throw you back
Once I close your little mouth
Won't have you carrying tales back to a trout
About an old man who sits on a brick
And catches little fish for bait with a stick

For bait? For bait?
Then the little fish understood
That he was now the worm
That sat in his stomach like wood
No, no,
No, no, he begged the old man
Let me go and I will find you a big fish that stands
And he will satisfy your behemoth frying pan

The old man thought and turnt it about
Then said, okay, I will throw you right out
True to his word, he tossed the fish in
And never saw the lying rascal again

THE HUMBLE

"Therefore to him that knoweth to do good, and doeth it not, to him it is sin." James 4:17

(Inspired by a true story)

My name is Hattie Mae Cline and I am eighty-three years old. I'se born in the year 1893 on a cotton plantation in Mississippi. My pa was a sharecropper on Mr. Joe Michaels' land. My ma and pa had nine chillun', three girls and six boys. I'se the eldest chile.

Well, my ma was a woman what had religion. She made sho' all us chillun' known 'bout the savior, bless His heart.

I was a chile who was wild, honey. I was young and beautiful, slender and big breasted, the color of warm honey with big, brown eyes and long legs. I like to go out to the juke joints and dance and holla, listen to jazz and drink that moonshine wit' a little reefer. I'd hang 'round wit' a different fella almost every night – white or black -- and they put in my hand whateva I asked for. So that's the way I went on for a while there.

I ain't forget none what my ma had told me. Always when I laid down at night the Lord would say to me, Hattie, what are you doing? I would always mean to do better but I was having fun, honey, and that likker had me.

66

Slowly but surely, He wore me down tho'. One time I remembers I went and got me some money from a man, right, and I tell you soon as I get home and lay on my bed to rest didn't the spirit jump right on me! I knows what it was cause I got this hard buzzing all through my body. Ain't another feeling like it. Did I do right after that? Nope. So the Lord got more rigorous. *What's your name*, He would say to me at night. *Hattie*, I'd tell'em. Did He forget me? He was forgetting who I was! *I'm Hattie Mae Cline, Lord*! I lay there and fell asleep worried, honey.

Once I was there in the darkest dark I had known and the Lord said, Hattie, do you want to die? I guess, I told Him. Well, I started to fall fast into the abyss – what's the word? Plummet. I began to plummet into the abyss so fast that my heart dropped. No, no, I screamed – and just like that I awoke and, chile, I knew where I had been on my way to. I hear a suffering voice say, Oh, Hattie, I can't take this for eternity. Hattie, I wish you could feel one drop. One drop of damnation! Lord, Lord! And it ain't no God in hell. No more talking to my Jesus? I can't live like that, I say. And so I began to follow the path as it's written here a little, there a little. It whatn't none easy neither. The Lord was mad at me, but he chastened me wit' love tho', chile. Now I'm gone leave some stuff out what's only 'tween me and the Lord, but He supported me and helped me put one foot in front of the otha'. And then I had to forgive myself as well. Ain't no excuse for living like a heathen on purpose.

Well, He lived wit' me after while and He neva left. We goes on like that still, me stumbling and the Lord grabbing me afore I fall. Same been true throughout history. When folks get to pointing they fingers I say, oh no, King David was a righteous man, but he killed a man for his wife and God forgive him; Paul murdered followers of Christ 'til the Good Lord showed him the way, but folks be just a pointin' and got filth in they closets piled up high. Now let's talk about the flip side. Just like there's God, there's also a devil and he is mean for sin, chile. My ma used to say he eat feces. Lucifer will attack anything God loves just to hurt Him. I remembers this one time I'se dozing in my bed and a demon jumped on me. This was 'round the time I'se just starting to try and get myself together. I opened my eyes 'cause sumthin' was on me heavy and I was a fightin' and a scratchin'. I throws it off me and I

68

was a hissin' like a she-cat and that thing fled. I surprised myself how I fought.

Another time I dreamt I'se in a room and there that devil was molesting a woman against the wall. Poor thing, I'll neva forget her. I'se scared to death. I looks to my right and I sees one them dolls what look like a raggedy ann – big tho', tall as me sitting in a rocking chair. It had big, black buttons for eyes and its mouth was stitched on and it was beckoning to me. My Lord! I hopped on His lap and we rocked there together and He says to me that if I eva' see the devil just look over and He gone be right there. Well, my word! I sho' appreciate it, Lord.

Well, I continued on the path. The Lord would say, Hattie, follow me. I'se obedient to the Lord 'cause He tells you the right way to go and who to deal wit'. It's your own choice if you don't listen. He tell you straight up too. Ain't no pussyfootin' around – ain't His way.

I prayed and prayed and I talked to the Lord all day everyday – when I was going here and going there, and doing this and doing that. I seek his counsel in everything, chile, and I swears He got the best advisin'.

Anyway, I had darn near stop screwin'. Jesus was working his magic and I ain't won't nobody touchin' me. I was still sippin' on that shine tho' 'cause I knew soon He was gone chase that off too. Sho' nuff, He says, Hattie, you gone stop that drinking for three months. Three months? Who was gone do that? Humph!

He got them three months out me tho' and didn't that devil try and tempt me in the last days and God send a believer to strengthen me? She said, naw, sista, we gone drink apple juice. Thank you, Lord. After them three months I was just fine, honey. But now I got to be rid of my tobacco. Cut me a break, Lord! Can't do nuthin' 'round here, I stumps off. Do that, go here, talk to this person, don't talk to that person – and He ain't gone leave me alone about my tobacco? What's next, I thought? Stop gossipin', Hattie, He comes back. My word!

Well, like always when you loves the Lord here come the devil. So I'se laying on the couch one night. It was cold outside and I'se all wrapped up warm to the neck in a blanket. I'se dozin' and I remembers feeling real cozy. All of a sudden I gets a hard yank on the foot! I hurry up and looks down and I don't see nuthin so I gets

70

comfortable again. Suddenly I feels two strong hands wrap

theyselves 'round my ankles and damn near drag me off the couch.

I grabs the back of the couch wit' my hands and gets myself into a

sittin' position and me and that devil fought like that wit' him

trying to drag me down into water. Yes, yes. My feet was in water

and he was trying to pull me down in it. I got to 'renched a leg

loose and got to kickin' him all in the head hard as I could. I was

furious! Then all of a sudden I'm in midair right there in the living

room.

The only time I had been threw in the air in my sleep was when the

Lord came in my dreams and toss me around sometimes. He

would throw me and toss me and I'd just relax 'cause wasn't much

I could do about it. He wanted me to trust Him that He wouldn't let

my head hit the wall. This thing here wasn't the Lord. This was a

huge serpent that was wrapped around my body and he was

squeezing me. He was trying to bind me. The rage I felt! I got to

kickin' and cussin' and then I heard one word – PRAY. Just that

simple. So I started, Our Father, who art in heaven, hallowed be

thine name…And that wicked dog dropped me. I got up and dusted myself off and then woke up sitting right there on the couch. My word!

I'll say one thing, I don't know why the Lord called me. I'm stubborn as all hell; will do anything to pick a fight with a bully; I cusses like a sailor; and I only love followers of our Lord. God wants us to spread His word but I agrees wit' Jonah. Humph! If we don't put forth an effort to have a relationship wit' our God, it's not His loss.

Woman gone tell me one time wit' spite that it ain't no God. See, this was one of them unbelievers that's used to a Christian that wants to convince them about the glory of the Lord. Not me. I told that woman I don't care what you believe. You betta get your wicked ass away from me.

Lord says to turn the otha' cheek cause vengeance belong to Him. I'ma turn my cheek awrite and that whole side of my body wit' it so when I swing that momentum from the turn gives my fist the right amount of power to knock they teeth out.

Many are called but few are chosen and the connection ain't for everybody. That's what I tells the Lord. I tells Him, Lord, folks wanna do what they wanna do and they don't want no holy structure 'cause then they gots to mend they ways. Some folks is

wicked to they heart. Lord, concentrate on the ones that love you.

That's how I sees it. People ain't been right to Him since the

beginning. He don't ask for much. It burns Him up to see folks

chasing after otha' gods and it burns me up that He care 'bout'em.

Jesus bled his precious blood for us and we still gotta chase them

suckas? Pssh. I can't chase somebody what done heard the same

stories I have. If you want to deny your Maker, fine wit' me. I ain't

no recruiter. To each his own is what I say. I know the Lord don't

like that, but I ain't perfect.

APARTMENT 318

That big ole toad
He said, you old
Naw, Naw, I said
That's just a lil' gray in my head

What he talking with that big old belly?
Up in the kitchen eating all the jelly…

The woman writing this poem
I think she trying to rhyme
She thinkin'
This don't make sense
But I guess I'll keep tryin'

My husband, Charlie
I think he dead
He slipped and fall and bust his head
I didn't do it!
I swear! I swear!
He in there sitting on that dining room chair

He been messing with that big girl downstairs
What was I supposed to do
Go pull out her hair?

He knew he wasn't right
All along
I seen him sniffing on that big ole pink thong

You's an old man now
Charlie, I said
Don't go getting no dumb notions
In your big ole thick head

I might be movin' on, woman
He had…
…the nerve…

… and said
When after forty years I've warmed his bed!

But I told him he wasn't going nowhere
Now he sitting up in there dead

Thought he was gone leave me all alone
Sitting there sniffin' on that girl huge thong
What kind of nerve has he
Didn't he know he's a reflection of me?
She only called 'round the first of the month
But I'm the one that has to deal with his junk?

He ain't know whose husband he was?
He better be glad that I bust his head
Instead of giving him the plug

That's all right 'cause I'm gone collect that check
Now tell me Charlie
What you think of that?

TRADING PLACES I

Tonya peered at her from the cubicle where she sat doing payroll. Pepper was rehanging dresses from the rush that they'd had earlier in the day. It was their seasonal sale and the boutique was getting rid of all of last season's items. *How many times have I told her not to hang the solids near the prints*, Tonya thought. *Why had Joan hired her?* Tonya watched as Pepper went around tidying the store and putting things in order for the afternoon. Tonya looked around to see if they were alone. Seeing no customers in the store, she lifted her tall, lanky frame from the cubicle and quietly approached Pepper whose back was turned to her.

"I told you before not to hang the solid dresses near the prints." Tonya said in a loud voice. As she walked past Pepper she bumped into her and snatched a dress from her hands. Pepper jumped, startled, and fell into a table that held bras and lingerie. Pepper grabbed ahold of the table to brace herself, and once she had regained her balance, she jabbed an accusing finger at Tonya.

"You did that on purpose. You almost knocked me down."

"I don't know what you're talking about." Tonya told her smirking." Maybe you should pay attention to what you're doing.

You've been here three months and you still can't seem to follow directions."

Pepper looked at Tonya and smiled. She knew exactly what was wrong with this *perra*. She crossed her arms over her chest and shook her head at the ugly girl. She hated working with Tonya. She liked the chubby girl better. Joan. She was pretty and confident. She was always friendly to Pepper. This one took every opportunity to be rude.

"You're trying to get me fired. I know what you're doing." Pepper told her.

"English please." Tonya whispered meanly as a customer entered the store.

Pepper knew that Tonya was being mean about her accent and she started to cuss the taller girl, but she bit her tongue and turned to greet the new customer. She refused to let this tall, sweaty girl ruin this great job for her. She loved the boutique with its old clothing and unique customers. She never knew who she was going to meet – a shy housewife would come in to try on a dress, and to Pepper's surprise, would be covered in tattoos all over her body. Or a woman, seventy-five, looking for a pair of red lace panties. Or a pretty girl, fifteen, buying her first pair of high heels. No, she loved this job. She even got an employee discount and Pepper loved fashion.

Tonya sat in the cubicle and watched as Pepper interacted with the customer. *She needs to stop wearing makeup to work. She looks like a slut.* Pepper and the customer walked past her to the register. They were laughing about a scarf that the customer was holding. Pepper's long brown hair was shoulder length and curly. She was petite and curvy with hazel eyes and long lashes. *Probably fake,* Tonya thought, chewing absentmindedly on a pencil.

She looked up as the bell over the door chimed and then sighed. *Leo.* She didn't know his last name, but he was Pepper's boyfriend. Tonya had loved him since she'd first set eyes on him three months ago. He was a trainer at a popular gym downtown. He was gorgeous. Tall, with dark hair and brown eyes and the sexiest smile that Tonya had ever seen. He walked up to Pepper and hugged her to him, bending slightly to accommodate her small body. Tonya swooned as the muscles rippled in his arms.

Ay papi, she could hear Pepper whisper to him. Tonya closed her

78

eyes and exhaled. She wanted to sling that little whore across the room. She watched Leo help Pepper into her coat.

"Hi, Leo." Tonya called out.

Leo looked up and smiled. "Hello, Tonya."

"See you later, Pepper." Tonya called out cheerfully, watching Leo's back side as they exited the boutique. She wanted to run her eager hands over the bulging muscles in his chest.

She got up to lock the door for lunch. Leo was helping Pepper into his car. Tonya sighed. Pepper's life was so perfect. She was beautiful, outgoing and had the perfect boyfriend. She could see how much Leo loved Pepper and that was one more nail in Tonya's heart. She laid her forehead against the cool glass and watched them drive away. She had tried to like Pepper but couldn't. She usually just ended up wanting to put Pepper's pretty head through a wall. Nobody was that sweet and perky. *Give me a break*, she thought. Tonya went back to her cubicle and daydreamed about Leo. *I'll bet he's insatiable in bed.*

The bell chimed and Tonya looked up, startled. She had locked the door. Maybe it was a draft, she thought and got up to check. She first noticed the young woman when she rounded the corner. She was standing against the far wall looking up at the antique dolls that sat on shelves near the ceiling. She was covered from head to foot.

"Excuse me. We're closed for an hour, ma'am."

The young woman turned and removed the scarf from her head and regarded Tonya coolly. She was as petite as Pepper, but her hair was stark black and plaited in four thick braids that were pinned to her head. Her slanted brown eyes were wide and attentive and reminded Tonya of the way a cat looks when they're about to pounce.

Pretty, Tonya thought, *but weird.*

"I want that doll there." The young woman pointed to a porcelain doll that was dressed in a red, velvet dress. "How much is it?"

"Didn't you hear me? I said we're closed for an hour." Tonya said again.

The woman held an arm out and a chain fell from her sleeve. There was a charm attached to the end of it and the young woman caught it in her palm and then took a step toward Tonya. The look in her eyes was threatening and Tonya was taken aback by the small

80

woman.

"I know what you covet." The black haired woman said to her

"What I what?" Tonya asked, astonished.

"Hi. I'm Selene." She said, now seeming bubbly. She extended a hand to Tonya. Her entire demeanor changed and her eyes became friendly.

"We're closed for the next hour." Tonya said again, speaking slowly as if the other woman were slow.

Selene walked away from Tonya and leisurely perused the store. She stopped at the lingerie table and fingered the silk bras and then looked up at Tonya. She walked over to the dress rack and chose a small, white summer dress.

"Leo wants to buy this dress for Pepper." She said, coming over to Tonya and handing her the dress.

"Leo?" Tonya asked. *Did this woman know Leo?*

"You want him. I can help you."

"How?"

"Pepper is very happy with her life. Are you happy with your life, Tonya?" Selene asked quietly. She walked over to the jewelry display and trailed her hand along the glass.

"Of course."

Selene turned to Tonya and looked her up and down. She laughed.
The girl was tall and skinny. Her limp, short, brown hair was
combed back from her broad forehead. Her large nose emphasized
her thin lips and greasy skin. If her looks weren't bad enough, the
misery that Selene felt coming off of her in waves was. "Really?"

"How do you know my name?" Tonya asked. She could feel
Selene silently judging her.

"It's on your name tag." Selene answered and shrugged her
shoulders as if she were guessing. *What does it matter, gump?*

"How do you know Pepper and Leo?"

"Pepper and Leo. A beautiful couple, don't you think?"

Tonya didn't reply.

"Pepper is almost perfect. I'll bet he makes love to her all the time.
What do you think?" Selene asked. She was enjoying Tonya's
discomfort.

"He only wants her because she flaunts her body." Tonya replied.

"Hmm. But what if you could have him? I mean, you're a lot
smarter than Pepper, right? Leo needs a real woman." Selene

82

enjoyed this part, the playing on their emotions. Her toes were tingling. This girl was so dumb. *What harm could she do? And grandmama needn't know.*

"He would never want me." Tonya looked down at her feet. "And anyway, he loves Pepper."

"Do you want Pepper's life, Tonya -- the beautiful body and face, the gorgeous boyfriend? I could help you." Selene gestured with a hand. Her eyes and voice conveyed sincerity.

"Who are you?" Tonya asked.

"I'm Selene, remember?"

"Uh huh. And how would you help, Selene?"

"A spell." Selene said nonchalantly.

Tonya laughed aloud. "A spell? Like magic? Really?"

"Really."

"Uh-huh. Okay. I'll bite. So how does this work?"

"It's simple. If you tell me right now that you want to be Pepper, I will do that for you."

"But why?" Tonya asked. "What's in it for you?"

"I just want to see you happy. And I'll even pay for the doll."

Selene winked at her. "But remember that once you switch, you can't go back. Pepper is happy with her life. That doesn't mean that you'll be happy with her life."

She has Leo. I'll be happy.

Just then Pepper and Leo returned from lunch. Selene watched Tonya and the way she drooled after Leo. The girl, Pepper, was vibrant and lovely. Leo wrapped his hands around her small waist and pulled her against him.

"See you later." He whispered, lovingly kissing Pepper in front of Selene and Tonya. He turned and left and Tonya watched Pepper coldly as she walked to the back of the store.

"What's the catch?" Tonya whispered harshly to Selene.

"Once you switch, you can't go back." Selene said pointedly. *Say yes, idiot.*

"Are you married?" Tonya asked Selene,

Selene was caught off guard. Married? No, she preferred cursing nasty people. When she wanted to mate, she did it on the full moon with other gypsies.

"No." She answered tightly.

"I'll do it." Tonya whispered.

84

Selene smiled and extended a hand to Tonya. The woman accepted Selene's outstretched hand and Selene cringed at the sweaty warmth of the woman's palm.

"Call her." She said to Tonya.

"Pepper." Tonya called out.

Pepper came into the store. There was a smile on her pretty face.

"Hello." She said to Selene.

"Hello. I'm Selene."

"I'm Pepper. Can I help you?"

"Yes. I'd like to buy that porcelain doll that's wearing the red dress."

"Sure. I'll get it down for you."

Tonya watched the two women interact. *What was the worst that could happen? It probably wouldn't work anyway. A magic spell. Geez.*

Selene purchased the doll and then handed it to Pepper. "This is for you." She told her.

"For me?" Pepper asked, surprised.

"Yes. It looks like you, don't you think?" Selene asked. She smiled when she heard Tonya's gasp of surprise. "Be sure to take it home with you."

"I can't accept this." Pepper told Selene.

"No, please." Selene said. "If you don't take it —"

"Take the doll, Pepper. Don't be rude." Tonya said. She didn't know what was going on, but she decided to play along.

"Well, then thank you." Pepper said to the woman appreciatively. She admired the old doll. Its curly brown hair and beautiful eyes intrigued her. *How nice*, she thought.

"Good day, ladies." Selene said, winking to Tonya again as she left the store.

Pepper smiled at Tonya as she walked to the back of the store.

"I'm going to put this with my things. I'll be right back."

Why did she buy her a doll, Tonya wondered as she absentmindedly chewed her pencil.

That evening as she prepared for bed she thought of the strange young woman, Selene. *How had she come to be at the boutique?* Tonya sat at the edge of her bed and daydreamed about Leo as she always did at night. Yes, a magic spell was a long shot. *What a crock.*

The following morning, Tonya stretched and yawned. She felt as if she had hardly slept. She lay there for a moment and then stretched across the bed. There was someone lying next to her. Startled, she cautiously lowered the blanket from over her head and looked to her left. *Leo?* Oh my – yes, it was Leo. Gorgeous Leo and he was lying next to her naked. Tonya jumped from the bed and ran to the bathroom.

She stared at her reflection in the mirror. Her hands flew to her face in surprise. She was beautiful. There were a few blemishes on her face – Pepper's face – that she could see, but that could be covered with a little makeup. She touched her body then ran to the full length mirror on the bathroom door. She was sexy! She turned and admired herself in the blue, lace nightgown that she was wearing. In a frenzy, she pulled the nightgown over her head. She wanted to see everything. She closed her eyes and turned to the mirror and then slowly opened them. Her breasts were perfect, small and plump with large nipples. Her stomach was flat and –

what the hell was going on? Tonya fell back into the bathtub. Her shapely arms and legs flailed about.

"Pepper! Are you okay?" Leo ran into the bathroom and pulled her from the tub. "Are you hurt?"

Tonya sat up stunned. She looked down at her body again in shock. She heard the words that Selene told her as clear as if the woman were standing there. *Once you switch, you can't go back.* She could hear Selene's laughter ringing in her ears.

"Are you okay, babe?" Leo asked again.

Tonya nodded. What could she say?

Leo pulled her to her feet and into his arms. She looked down at his naked body and then at her own.

"Come back to bed." He whispered, kissing her passionately on the mouth.

"Okay. I'll be right there." She said.

He left the bathroom and Tonya turned to the mirror again. She stared at her new body in utter shock. This wasn't what she had wanted at all. This wasn't how she thought it would be. She stared at the penis on her new body. Still not believing, she hesitantly poked at the small, flaccid member with her fingers. Pepper had
88

been a man. Tonya felt dizzy and grabbed ahold of the edge of the sink. For the first time she wondered what had happened to Pepper. Did Pepper have her body now? *Pepper is happy with her life. That doesn't mean that you'll be happy with her life.* She could still hear Selene's hysterical laughter ringing in her ears.

"Pepper, honey, I need you." Leo called to her from the bedroom. He looked over to the doll that Pepper had brought home from the boutique the night before. *Hmm, that's strange.* He threw the sheets back and got out of bed to go over to the doll. He bent and stared at it for a moment and then picked it up by its red, velveteen waist and brought the face eye level with his own. *Was it crying?*

THE PENNY

Don't lick that penny, Little Johnny, she says
That penny has been through too many hands
Hands are dirty, dirty things indeed
They also touch way too many things
They scratch itches
Dig ditches
And move things about
Some people even put their hands in their mouth

That penny you hold in your little hand
Was once played with by a lad
'Twas taller than you stand
He flipped that coin and tossed it about
After he'd scratched his bum
Before he'd picked his snout

He lost that little penny, you see
To another lad much older than he
This lad badly wanted that penny to match
To another that he'd had tucked in his hat

Both pennies, dear see
Were meant for his loafers
A pair of Penny's that he'd just gotten from his mother

He fit those pennies into his shoes
That on the bottom
Soon became covered in street goo
Spit, blood, gum and disease
The debris of which caused poor Lincoln to sneeze

When his loafers were all torn about
The careless lad just tossed them right out
These two pennies ended up in the trash
Where a hobo searched them out to add to his stash
Lucky me, lucky me, he thought to himself
Though he knew that the pennies belonged to that snot nosed

whelp
Who pushed and teased and mocked him about
So bad that he wanted to punch a child in the snout

It was his lucky day, he thought with glee
While he held his small ding-a-ling for a pee
He shook with one hand and wiped with the other
Tucked and zipped
Then rubbed the pennies against one another

One of those pennies, my love, Johnny dear
Was used in a magic trick that Ole Pap did with your ear
He twist and turned and flipped it about
And made you believe it had come from the round,
The roundest part of your lobe, do you see
And you yelled and jumped and you were so
Happy!
Never knowing that penny had been all about
In alleys, in shoes
Near bum dongs and boy snouts

TAKEN

Marley had to hurry and dress. She had had to stay late at the school to talk to the parents of one of her students, a blind teenager named Rachel. She hadn't wanted to wait until Monday morning and the father had been willing to come to the school and speak with her directly after his shift ended. Marley had decided to wait the couple hours for him to arrive, but the meeting had taken longer than she'd expected. She'd promised her best friend and roommate, Janice, that she would come watch her sing tonight at The Atlantis Club, a hot new spot in town that Janice had been booked at for the next month.

"Are you ready yet?" Janice screamed from the living room. Marley could hardly hear her with the loud music that Janice now had blaring from the stereo. She ignored her and went back to applying her makeup. Janice walked into the bathroom and placed her hands on her hips. She stared impatiently at Marley. She was taller than Marley and had a luminous olive complexion and dark curly hair that complemented her brown eyes and long, curly lashes. Janice was a bombshell. She was also outgoing and outspoken – brash, her mom had always called Janice. Men broke their necks to do her bidding.

"I'm ready." Marley said. "Wait, where are my glasses?"

"You are not wearing those ugly things." Janice replied, turning her nose up at Marley and walking away. "I'll give them back to you tomorrow. Now let's go."

Marley allowed Janice to drag her from the apartment and down the street. She had been determined to bring Marley with her to this new club. Janice's family was religious and didn't know how to handle Janice's free and overly sexy character. Marley loved her friend just the way she was. Janice couldn't live without Marley. They loved one another like sisters.

As they came up the street, Marley could hear the loud music vibrating through the air. When they approached the newly opened club, there was already a line around the corner; sharply dressed men and scantily clad women attempted to bribe the doormen into allowing them inside ahead of VIP. Janice and Marley went around back and were let in through a private entrance. As they entered the club area, Marley shaded her eyes with her hands as the disco lights cast an array of colors onto the crowded dance floor and the people who were swaying and dancing wildly to the loud music. Marley found an empty stool at the bar and sat down.

"What do you want to drink, Marley my love?" Janice asked with a mischievous gleam in her eye.

"A coke." Marley yelled exaggeratingly as if the music was unbearably loud.

"You are such a prude. Tonight we drink tequila." Janice said with a rock of her hips.

Marley shook her head but didn't argue. She was feeling slightly animated. This place played good music. She took the shot glass from Janice and gulped it down, unprepared for the sting of the liquor, and began to cough.

"Damn, girl," Janice said giving her a few good raps on the back, "you forgot the lemon."

Marley took Janice's shot and gulped it down and then took the lemon wedge and bit into it. Whew, she was feeling a lot better. Janice ordered two more shots and they drunk them together and then ordered another round. After that Marley was feeling no pain. She followed Janice back into the dressing room and danced by herself to the music in a tipsy state as she waited for Janice to

94

change clothes. When her friend appeared again she was wearing a red, silk dress which seductively clung to her voluptuous form. Her red peep toe stilettos accentuated her long, shapely legs. She had piled her curly, dark hair atop her head, letting a few ringlets escape to curl around her pretty face and neck. Her eyes were lined with black kohl eyeliner and her full lips were a red that matched her dress.

"Aww, baby, come and let me tell you something." Marley said in her best mock sugar daddy voice and then humped her hips at Janice in a raucous manner.

Janice pouted her lips and gave Marley her best come hither look and then flipped her the bird.

When Marley entered the club area again the lights had been turned down. Janice sashayed onto the stage and people clapped and whistled in appreciation as she belted out one sultry melody after another. Marley sat still in the dark, smoke filled room and sipped her tequila slowly. She watched her friend work her magic on the happy crowd and wished that she was more like Janice – just sexy without even trying. Maybe then she could find someone to love her. After Janice's performance, she came back out to Marley dressed in jeans and ready to dance. Marley allowed her to drag her out to the dance floor. She had to admit that she was having a lot of fun. She and Janice danced for hours only stopping for more tequila. By the end of the night, Marley had shed her inhibitions.

"See, didn't I tell you it would be fun?" Janice asked as they strolled leisurely down the street arm in arm.

"Yeah. I had a great time, Janice. Thanks for getting me out of the house."

"You still can't handle your liquor, girlfriend. Hey, do you remember when we were in college and we got drunk on Thanksgiving at my parents' and you fell down the stairs?" They both burst into drunken giggles.

"Do I remember?" Marley slurred, "I thought my mom was going to have a heart attack. She didn't speak to me for a month."

"I told you, you couldn't fly. And remember you had on those grandma pa-pa-panties?" They were laughing so hard that Janice could hardly talk. "Your nightgown flew up in the air and all I

96

could see were those huge drawers – parachutes, and you

blubbering, 'I can fly. I can fly'."

Marley's stomach was hurting from laughing so hysterically. She

thought she was going to bust a gut.

"I can fly." Janice bent at the waist smacking her leg.

When they finally got control of themselves they resumed their

walking.

"Have I ever told you I love you, Marley."

"I loves you too, sweet pea. Now how about some more tequila?

Where is the nearest buy some liquor place!" Marley said, taking

off running down the street with Janice following suit.

Before they rounded the corner a gunshot stopped them dead in

their tracks. Janice grabbed Marley by the arm and snatched her

into the shadow of a dark doorway. Janice looked over at Marley,

whose gray eyes were big as dinner plates. She slightly raised her

hand and pointed in the direction of the alleyway. Marley

followed the direction in which Janice's finger was pointing. She

squinted her eyes so that she could see what was going on in the

alley across from them. The street was only slightly illuminated by a nearby streetlamp. She could see two police officers standing with another giant man who was wearing plain clothes. They were standing over what appeared to be a person doubled over on the ground. The two police officers leaned over and picked the person up, half dragging him through the back door of a building adjoining the alley.

"Let's get out of here." Marley whispered when she knew they were out of earshot.

"Come on." Janice said, stepping out of the doorway. "I want to see what's going on."

"No." Marley said hysterically, snatching her back. Her tipsiness had fled. Her emotions were turned on high alert. "Are you crazy? I think they just shot that guy. Let's get the hell out of here before they come back out."

"Come on. Stop being a girl." Janice said nonchalantly, rolling her eyes. "They didn't see us. What could happen?"

"No. Screw that." Marley whispered feverishly. "Let's go now!"

"Well, just stay here. I'll be back."

Before Marley could get another word out, Janice snatched away from her and shot down the alley.

"Janice." Marley called in a loud whisper. "Janice – damn it!"

Marley stood in the doorway and watched her friend half creep,

half jog down the alley.

She was scared stiff. Why was Janice always getting her into

crap? Against her better judgment, Marley followed the path that

her friend took and silently eased up behind her. Janice was trying

to crawl atop a garbage can that she had turned upside down so

that she could see into a window that was above her head.

"Will you get down and come on!" Marley said in a panicked

whisper, beside herself with fear.

"Shhh." Janice held a finger to her lips and stared at Marley as if

she were the one that was crazy -- and she probably was because

she was seriously thinking of leaving Janice there, but damn it, she

was her best friend. Janice, eyes big, whistled quietly, peering

into the window from her perch on top of the can and said, "Whoa.

Look at all of that money."

Marley stood on her tiptoes beside Janice and looked into the

window of the abandoned looking building. She saw the money

but she also saw something else. There were two wooden kegs –

to Marley they looked like beer barrels – but there was one barrel which was overturned, and spilling a white powdery substance onto the floor. There was also a small box truck that was parked between a police squad car and a black sedan. The truck had an emblem on it that Marley recognized from an Irish bakery on the west side of Philly.

"And there's the powder." Janice whispered.

"How do you know that it's drugs?" Marley asked.

"I assure you it's not sugar, honey." Janice whispered back sarcastically.

Sonofagun, Marley thought, *look at all that dope.*

Her suspicions that the guy that they had seen on the ground had been shot were confirmed. He was sitting in a chair, rocking back and forth clenching his stomach. The front of his shirt was covered with blood. Marley could hear the big guy in the plain clothes screaming at him saying something to him about did he think he'd get away with...something – Marley couldn't hear well enough -- and he kept pointing to the drugs. To Marley's dismay, the two cops didn't appear to be concerned at all, and sat there watching, not at all attempting to help the man. The big guy backhanded the

100

wounded man with a massive blow that knocked him from his chair. The cops laughed as he hit the floor and said something to him – again Marley couldn't hear, but one of the cops called the large man Johnny. The man on the floor was furiously shaking his head back and forth and looked as if he were trying to explain something to Johnny who had a sneer on his face, and who didn't seem to want to hear anything he had to say anyway. Johnny took a step back and shot the man in the face.

Startled, Janice fell off the trash can, causing it to crash into the can next to it. Horrified, Marley looked backed into the window and saw one of the police officers staring directly at her. Oh no, they were starting for the door. Janice was on the ground holding her ankle.

"Get up. Run." Marley screamed.

Janice stumbled to her feet and they ran down the alley and across the street to duck into the same dark doorway that they'd hid in earlier. They heard the door crash open and the frightened women flattened themselves against the brick wall, wanting to become a part of it. Marley's heart was beating so fast that she thought it would come through her chest. She could see the two police officers looking up and down the street trying to see which way they had gone. The officers separated, each going in a different direction. Marley wished she'd insisted that Janice give her, her glasses. She squinted into the alley and searched for the man called Johnny who had the gun.

"They're gone." Janice whispered. "Let's go."

"No. What about the other one?" Marley whispered frantically. Janice was shaking badly and had started to cry. Marley hugged her friend to her chest and stroked her hair trying to give her comfort.

"Just two seconds, sweetie." She whispered to her.

They waited that way for a moment, with Janice and Marley clinging to each other for dear life. Marley stuck her head out partway just enough to look one way up the street and then the other to see if she could see the officers. Wrong move. The bullet hit the building right above her head and sent pieces of brick flying onto her face. She quickly jumped back. Having no other option, she grabbed Janice and they sprinted down the dark street as fast as they could. The gun went off again and Marley ducked to one side as she ran, not knowing where the shots were coming from, and accidentally bumped into Janice and knocked her down. Janice got up to run again but cried out in fear and surprise as another bullet hit the ground at her feet.

Marley grabbed her by the arm and they ran. Heavy footsteps pounded the pavement behind them, giving chase. She knew that if she screamed she would give away their location to the men chasing them. There were no other people outside and Marley knew that there was no way they would make it without help. The three men would catch them eventually if they didn't do something.

They rounded another corner and Marley yanked Janice down with her to crouch behind an SUV. A few seconds later, Marley watched as the behemoth Johnny rounded the corner and slowed to a walk, looking around for the women. He peered into the dark for them, not having any streetlights to aid him in his search. Marley was somewhat thankful that the street was almost pitch black. She could hear her heartbeat pounding in her ears. He peered around cars and into the dark doorways of storefronts trying to flush them out. Marley pulled Janice with her and they crawled underneath the SUV.

He continued his search and Marley closed her eyes in disappointment when she realized that he was starting to look under parked cars as he passed them. Somehow he knew that they hadn't gotten far. As he approached the SUV his cell phone went off and he stopped to answer it.

"Yeah." Marley heard him say. "No. No." Then a pause. "I'm on some street called, uh -- " He

seemed to be looking around. "Grove." Another pause. "Okay. No. I see you."

From under the car Marley could see another set of feet come up and then --

"You see'em?" A male voice said.

Marley and Janice stared at each other wide eyed. Marley assumed it was one of the cops. She heard someone say --

"I saw them come this way but I lost'em."

"Well, I don't know what to say." They could hear the frustrated voice say. "Dominic's back at the warehouse and he's pissed that the product was left like that."

104

"Damn." Someone spitted.

Marley thought she heard fear in his voice. *Who the hell was Dominic?* Marley watched as the men walked away. When she thought the coast was clear, Marley stuck her head out and peered down the street. She saw the man and the cop talking to another man on the corner. Johnny was pointing down the street from the way he had just come. Marley nudged Janice and they crept from underneath the truck and crawled towards the sidewalk. Marley looked over her shoulder and almost screamed when she saw the man running back towards where they were hiding. He seemed to be in a hurry now.

Janice tried to pull her back beneath the truck. Marley resisted and pointed towards another alley on the opposite side of the street. She could see some huge dumpsters and she thought their chances were better there. There was no way she was going to be cornered under that SUV, Marley thought to herself. She tried to pull Janice with her but she wouldn't budge and was frantically shaking her head at Marley. Marley looked up the street and saw the big man getting closer. She looked at Janice and jerked her head towards the alley. Janice shook her head back at her and pointed at the cement that she was lying on, signaling to Marley that she wasn't moving.

Marley half ran, half crawled across the street on her hands and knees and crouched in the shadows of a dark doorway where she still had a full view of the street. She saw him as he rounded the corner. She could feel her fear turn to sweat that trickled from her underarms to run down her sides.

He stopped and stood still for a moment as though thinking, then as if he had remembered something, he hurriedly approached Janice's hiding spot. He walked past the truck and Marley exhaled a relieved, strangled breath, but as he passed, Janice began to panic and he heard her whimpering. Marley knew that he had heard her by the way he stopped and looked at the SUV. She covered her mouth with her hands to keep from crying out. Janice turned in Marley's direction. Her friend knew that she had been found.

Run, Marley screamed to Janice in her mind. She could see that her friend was paralyzed with fear. The man bent and looked under the SUV and spotted Janice. He reached underneath the truck and pulled Janice out by her hair. She fought like a she-devil but was no match for the large man. Marley wanted to run out and help her friend but she was too petrified. Janice started to scream and the big man smacked her, rocking her head to the side.

"Where's that other one you were with?" He said, shaking Janice like a ragdoll.

Marley could see Janice defiantly shaking her head from side to side. Marley cupped her hands over her mouth tighter to keep from screaming. She watched as Janice was picked up off her feet and brought face-to-face with her assailant. She still made meager attempts to fight Johnny off even after he struck her again.

"Where is she, you nosy little --" He growled as Janice kicked him in the crotch and spat in his face.

After that everything for Marley went in slow motion. She watched as he lifted Janice up into the air as if she were no more than a sack of potatoes and slammed her to the ground. Marley heard a loud crack and placed her hands over her ears, not wanting to believe what she knew. Hot tears slid down her face. She watched as he stood over Janice and nudged her with his feet then nonchalantly shrugged his shoulders. Seeming satisfied that she wasn't going anywhere, he took one last look around and then walked away. When Marley could no longer hear his footsteps she fell against the wall and rested her head between her knees and sobbed. What was happening?

She had to find some help. Cautiously, she peered into the street. Seeing no one, she ran to her friend and fell to her hands and knees before her.

Janice lay there still, her beautiful brown eyes caught in a blank stare. Blood ran from her nose and mouth. Marley pulled Janice to her and cradled her in her arms. She checked her pulse even though she knew that she would find nothing. Marley buried her head in Janice's neck and inhaled her perfume. Her heart broke into a million pieces.

"What did he do, sweet pea? He broke you. What did he do?" Marley sobbed, beyond herself with grief. "Oh, no."

She sat there with Janice and rocked her in her arms. *Why didn't you help her*, Marley asked herself. She was a coward. Janice had died protecting her and she had done nothing to help her. Marley gently pulled Janice out of the street and laid her on the pavement then crossed her limp hands over her chest. She took one last look at her friend that she would never see smiling again and then stood up. She had to get help.

She backed away a step and then stopped cold. The street somehow seemed quieter than before. She felt the hairs on the back of her neck stand up. She quickly turned and squinted into the dark. *There*. The silhouette of a man standing in the street about thirty feet away. He wasn't big enough to be the man who had killed Janice, and no, it wasn't one of the policemen. Marley squinted into the darkness. This man was…different.

Her feet seemed to be glued to the ground. She couldn't breathe. He tilted his head to one side. She could feel the coldness of his eyes settle upon her. They stood there in the dark silence while he observed her. He began to pace slowly, taking three steps in one direction and then three steps back only to stop again and stare at her. Marley felt a dangerous chill run down her spine. She took a step back. He took two steps forward and then stopped. Marley backed away a few more steps and so he took double the steps forward and stopped again. *Run,* her brain screamed. Marley took off as fast as she could, looking over her shoulder to see him coming right behind her.

*   *   *

Dominic Kennedy awoke to his phone ringing. Yawning, he walked over to his jacket and pulled out his cell, checking the caller ID.

"Yeah, Carl." He answered, walking back to his chair.

"Wake the hell up." Carl sounded upset, his Irish accent almost a growl.

"What is it?"

"Something went wrong with the drop."

He had his brother's full attention now. "What do you mean, something went wrong?"

"I don't know. I just got a call from that idiot, Johnny. He said something about the guy not having the money."

"Where's Johnny now?" Dominic asked, quickly dressing.

"He says he's at the warehouse."

"I'm on my way." Dominic hung up the phone and grabbed his pistol as he ran out of the house.

He jumped into his car and sped across town steaming the whole way. The guy didn't have the money. He had specifically told

110

Vladimir to make sure that the guy had all of the money. He knew

Vladimir and didn't see him trying to screw him and he knew

Johnny and knew that he was a hothead. Why in the world did

Carl send that big, dumb shithead? If Johnny had messed this deal

up he was going to stump a mudhole in his ass.

Dominic felt his head starting to pound and he gritted his teeth. He

was going to tear somebody's head off if they messed with his

money. He pulled up to the warehouse and got out of the car. He

didn't see anyone around as he ran through the alley. He saw some

empty garbage cans toppled over in front of the entrance of the

warehouse and looked into the window. There was a dead man

lying on the ground and the dope was out for the world to see with

one barrel knocked over. He walked into the room and looked

around.

There was no one there and all three of the vehicles were empty.

He opened the door of the sedan and looked inside. The keys were

still in the ignition and the headlights were on. He popped the

trunk and walked around to the back of the vehicle. There were

two duffle bags inside. One of the bags was open and filled with cash. He checked the other bag and found the same thing -- filled with cash. *That dumb dog*, he thought to himself. Now he had to explain to Vladimir why his man was dead. He hated explaining himself. Just then one of the cops sauntered in, stopping dead in his tracks when he saw Dominic.

"What happened?" Dominic spat at him, gesturing to the dead man on the ground.

"He didn't have the money."

"What the fuck do you call this?" Dominic screamed, irate, pointing at the trunk of the sedan.

The cop's eyes opened wide when he saw the cash. "Shoot, man. All I know is Johnny said he didn't have the cash."

"Where is Johnny now, and why the hell did you idiots leave the shit here like this?" Dominic said, not believing the men Carl used.

"We were chasing these girls."

"What!" Dominic thundered in disbelief, almost pistol whipping the man.

"These two girls were looking in the window." He said with his hands up, trying to calm Dominic. He took a step back and pointed
112

towards the window. "They saw Johnny pop him. We went after'em but lost'em in the street. We were out looking for'em, but I thought I should come back here."

"Yeah, I'll just bet you did." Dominic said, reading his mind. "Go get Johnny and tell him to get his ass back here now."

The cop turned tail and ran to retrieve Johnny. Dominic turned around and zipped the bag. He carried the money out to his car and put the bags in the trunk. *Idiots!* When he got ahold of Johnny he was going to hand him his ass on a plate. He drove his car into the warehouse and picked the toppled over barrel up and pulled it back into the truck and rolled the door closed. A few minutes later Johnny and the cops came back. Johnny knew he was in trouble and only stepped partways into the room. Dominic leaned against the trunk of the sedan and glared at him.

"So, what you're telling me is that you left not only my money but the product and this guy here who has a bullet in him to go chase after some broads. Is that what you're telling me?" Dominic asked him.

"They saw everything that --"

Before he could finish his sentence, Dominic had made it across the room and punched him in the face, knocking him down. He squatted in front of Johnny. Dominic leaned back on his haunches and stared at him.

"Did you catch them?" He asked quietly, cocking his head to one side and staring at Johnny from his place on the ground.

"I caught one. I couldn't find the other one." Johnny said, struggling to sit up.

"And where is she?"

Johnny told Dominic what happened with the dead girl. Dominic listened and then stood up.

"Pick your big ass up off the floor." He said to Johnny. "I want you to take these other two idiots here", Dominic said pointing to the cops, "and take that truck and my car and drive them to Carl's. Pick your dead friend up too and take him with you. If something happens and you don't make it to Carl's, I'm going to go visit your mother. You understand what I'm saying?"

Johnny nodded. "Hey look, Dominic, I --"

"Shut up, Johnny, and just do what I told you."

Dominic watched as they hurriedly left and then called Carl and

114

told him to be expecting them. He then left the warehouse and ran up the street to where Johnny said he had left the girl. It was still late and if no one had found her, he might be able to find some ID on her. If he could find out where she lived he might be able to find her friend. As he rounded the corner he saw a woman in the dark street hunched over what he assumed was the dead girl. He stopped, thinking that someone had found her. No, he smiled. He could hardly believe his luck. This had to be the other woman. She was sobbing and holding the dead woman's head to her chest. He slowed to a creep and stopped in the middle of the street. He could hear her crying and saying something was broken. Her sobs were gut wrenching. *Geez, what a mess*, he thought. He was willing to bet money that she now wished that they hadn't been so nosy.

He watched her as she pulled the dead woman out of the street and onto the sidewalk and stood up. She must have sensed his presence because her head snapped up and she looked right at him. She staggered back a step, and Dominic took a step forward. He knew she was going to run before she took off. He didn't want to risk anyone hearing a gun, so he'd have to break her neck. He was surprised at how fast she could run and he had to chase her at full speed. He was almost on her when he saw a police car in the street about a block down. He slowed to a walk, not wanting to call attention to himself. She saw the squad car and started screaming and erratically waving her arms and jumping up and down. She was now about twenty feet away. He slowed more. He watched as the police car hit the corner not seeing her. *Dumb police couldn't even help a girl in trouble,* he thought to himself. Dominic broke into a full run again.

She looked behind her and saw him coming and started to run again then looked up the street and stopped. He could see a look of relief wash over her face. *Shit,* he thought. Dominic stopped running and slowed to a walk again thinking that maybe it was another squad car. She looked over her shoulder at Dominic and made a sudden left at the corner. He made it to the corner just in time to see her boarding a bus. He ran to the bus attempting to get on, but the driver closed the door before he could reach it and sped off. He could see her pointing at him and frantically talking to the driver. *Damn it,* Dominic thought, not wanting to lose her.

He ran back to the warehouse as fast as he could and jumped into the sedan and took off. He raced back to the street and after a while, found the bus as it traveled in the same direction down the road. She wouldn't have gotten off so soon. If she had, she couldn't have got far. He saw the bus going through a green light and sped up to it. He could see the woman sitting on the opposite side of the bus nervously looking out of the windows. He slowed down and followed the bus for several miles before it stopped and the doors opened. *Must be the last stop.* He parked on the opposite side of the street and waited. Three or four people exited the bus. It was still pretty dark, but Dominic saw her when got off. She looked scared shitless. *Pretty girl too. Too bad this is how it was,* he thought. *What is she a Latino or something,* he mused.

The driver stepped off of the bus and put an arm around her. As they stood on the sidewalk, he began pointing as if he were giving her directions. Dominic knew exactly what they were talking about. There was a precinct in this area and Dominic was sure that she was trying to make it there. The driver patted her on the back and she took off in a fast walk in the direction that the driver had pointed. Dominic waited until she was out of sight and then drove around the corner and cut her off between two buildings.

He quickly jumped out of the car to grab her. When she realized what was going on she turned to run but was too late – he was too close. She screamed as he grabbed her from behind and placed his hand over her mouth and half carried, half pulled her between two buildings and then threw her into one. Her body slammed hard against the brick. The air whooshed out of her and she slid down the building. After looking around, Dominic grabbed Marley and twisted his hand in a handful of her hair and pulled her up, looking around to see if anyone had heard them. He could hear her crying and looked down at her. He pulled her head up so he could look at her face. She had black smears on her cheeks from her mascara running.

"Please don't." Marley could hear herself saying over and over again. "Please."

Her legs felt like rubber and the only thing holding her up was his hand in her hair pulling so tightly that she thought he was trying to tear her scalp out. He let her go and she fell down against the building, her legs giving out from under her. He squatted down in

118

front of her and she shrunk back. Marley was shaking so badly

that she thought she would have a seizure. He was so much bigger

than her. She knew that she wouldn't make it if she tried to fight.

He just sat there calmly staring at her, so she tried to be as still as

she could, hesitantly returning his gaze. As she looked at him, the

first thing she noticed was the small scar that ran through his

eyebrow. He looked as if he hadn't shaved for days. He was

wearing a skull cap. He moved closer to her and she shrunk back

further against the wall. He grabbed her chin to look into her eyes

then let her face go and stared at the ground to his side, shaking his

head.

Dominic was having a hard time with this one. He laughed to

himself. He had never physically hurt a woman. He was feeling

wrong.

"What's your name?" Dominic knew it was a mistake to talk to

her. He should just break her neck and leave her there.

"Marley." She whispered, noting his accent.

"Okay, Marley. Here's the deal. Me and you, we're going to get

up and go to that car. If you scream or if you try to run I'm going to break your neck. You understand?"

Marley believed him so she nodded her head and carefully rose to her feet. He grabbed her by the arm and pushed her out in front of him. Even if Marley had wanted to scream there wasn't anybody out to hear her. She was worried because she didn't know where he was taking her. They approached a black sedan and he grabbed her by the arm, opening the driver side door. *No, this isn't right*, Marley thought. Though afraid, Marley resisted as he motioned for her to get into the car.

"No." Marley told him. "Do it now. Whatever you're going to do to me, do it now."

"What's that now?" He asked amused.

"If you're going to kill me, do it now. I'm not going who knows where with you so you can torture me or something." Marley said, scared as hell but still raising her chin in defiance.

Dominic laughed then grabbed her by the head and shoved her in the car, pushing her over to the passenger side seat and then climbed in himself. As he drove away from the curb he wondered what his problem was. For some reason he couldn't bring himself to hurt her. He looked over at her. She was a mess. Her clothes

120

were disheveled and her hair was all over her head.

"You thinking that maybe you and your friend peeked in the wrong window?" He asked her accusingly.

Tears welled up in Marley's eyes and she bowed her head and stared at her hands. Dominic sighed and rolled his eyes.

"She was my sister." Marley said, tears rolling down her face.

Oh, boy, Dominic thought to himself. The last thing he needed was a crying broad in the car with him. He was becoming disgusted with himself.

He took a better look at her. Gray eyes. He had never seen anyone that complexion before with gray eyes. Her eyes were surrounded by dark lashes. She was saying something and Dominic looked down at her mouth. Lush, full lips were speaking to him. His body responded against his will. *Had it been that long since he'd had a woman?*

Marley was scared and she couldn't stop shaking. Where was he taking her? He was going to change his mind and kill her. She just knew it. She wondered if anyone had found Janice's body. The sun was rising and surely people would be on the street soon. She thought of Janice and how she had died and started to sob. She was all alone out there.

He pulled into a dark parking garage and parked. Marley sat still and waited.

"Get out." He told her.

Marley opened the car door and got out of the car. He grabbed ahold of her and they walked together to an elevator that took them to his apartment which was on the top floor of the building. Dominic led Marley to a door where he stuck a key in the lock and then gently pushed her inside. He flicked on a light and Marley stood in the front room where everything appeared to be black – black plush carpet, black marble, even paintings and sculptures that were done in black. There was a balcony and a winding staircase in the huge apartment. He pointed upstairs.

"That's where I'm going. I'm tired. If you try to leave you'll only lock yourself between the apartment door and the elevator. The only phone is in my pocket. There's food in the fridge."

And then he left her standing there just like that. Exhausted, Marley balled her jacket up and used it as a pillow as she collapsed

122

onto the couch and cried herself to sleep.

She was there lying next to him. He started to ask her how she had gotten there, but she placed a finger to his lips. *Shhhh*, she said. She moved atop him, pushing away the sheet that separated them and spread her warm body over his. Dominic groaned with pleasure, feeling the heat that radiated from the juncture of her thighs. She lowered her mouth to his and began slowly sucking at his bottom lip, her soft tongue attempting to gain entrance to his mouth. Marley rotated her hips over Dominic's, sliding back and forth on him, letting him feel her body parting over him until he could feel the slick hotness of her caressing his swollen member. Dominic grabbed Marley's buttocks, desperately seeking entrance to her soft body. Marley sat up and straddled Dominic, her full breasts exposed to his hungry eyes as her hands rested on his muscular chest for support while she slowly worked the hot tightness of her body over him.

Dominic could think of nothing but how exquisite it felt inside her -- like soft, liquid heat. Once she had taken him comfortably,

Dominic raised his hips to meet her gentle thrusts and Marley moaned so sweetly that he became savage. He wanted her under him so that he could take what he wanted from her. Dominic flipped Marley over and held her hands above her head, greedily plunging into her. Marley lifted her hips to meet him, moaning, taking him deeper into her body. He grabbed her buttocks and plunged into her soft wetness while his tongue quarreled with a nipple that had been teasing him…

As Dominic was about to make his final thrusts to release, thrusts that seemed as if they would carry him into unspeakable bliss, his alarm clock buzzed loudly and awoke him from his dream and into reality, and he realized that what he was clutching so lustfully beneath him was a pillow that was cradling his frustrated member and he exhaled forcefully, his body still taut with desire. *Marley.*

Marley got up from the couch. She was glad for the short rest. She could hear him in the kitchen and she went in search for a bathroom. When she found one, she shut the door quietly behind her, and looked at herself in the mirror. Her hair was matted and her makeup had run all over her face. She looked terrible. Marley found a clean towel and cleaned up. Once she felt more presentable, she tip-toed to the kitchen and stopped in the doorway. His back was to her, and to Marley's surprise, he was cooking. He must have sensed her behind him because he turned and then stopped at the sight of her.

"You want some dinner?" He asked her.

Marley's stomach had already begun to growl at the smell of the food. She hadn't eaten since the day before. She nodded and he gestured toward a large table that sat in the dining room. There were two places set. She sat at one and he approached with a glass of red wine.

"Drink this." He said to her. "It'll make you feel better."

Marley sipped the wine and waited. He was right. Her nerves began to calm. They ate in silence. Dominic watched Marley unabashed.

"What do you think of me, Marley?" He asked her.

"The truth?" Marley asked. He nodded.

"Janice is dead because of you." Marley responded. Tears welled up in her eyes.

Dominic shook his head, disagreeing. "No. I'm sorry, honey, but Janice died because she wasn't minding her business."

Even though Marley knew what he said was somewhat true, it still upset her that he would say something so cruel. Dominic could see that he had made her angry.

"I know you're not going to let me go. I mean, why am I even here?" she asked.

"Marley." He whispered to her. "I think I want you."

You are such a nutjob, Marley thought to herself.

She really looked at him then. *It was too bad he was crazy*, she thought. He wasn't a bad looking man. He was taller than her, over six feet. She remembered how easily he had lifted her off her feet and the hardness of his body. His hair was coal black. His nose was a little crooked but it gave his face character. His eyes were the main point of interest on his face. *Like the color of a black sea*, she thought to herself. Marley looked at his mouth and blushed. *Not bad.* If it hadn't been for Janice…she looked up and he winked at her. He had caught her staring at him. He knew exactly what she was thinking. Marley's face started to burn. She wished the

126

floor would open up and swallow her whole.

"What is your name?" She asked.

"Dominic." He told her. *Ah*, Marley nodded. *Dominic.*

"Dominic, I'm not hungry anymore." She said to him. "I'm tired. I want to go home."

"No more home, Marley. If you want to lie down there's a spare bedroom upstairs." He got up and started to clear the dishes.

Forlorn, Marley climbed the steps to the spare bedroom and shut the door. She was glad to see that she had her own bathroom. After a couple of minutes, there was a knock on the door and to Marley's surprise, Dominic pushed the door open and stuck his head in.

"I brought you some bed clothes. Here are some extra blankets and these pajamas are too small for me." He handed everything to her and then stood there for a second as if he wanted to say something. He changed his mind and walked away.

Marley locked the door and then undressed before heading to the shower.

She was in Dominic's room. She was in his bathroom. Dominic

had just gotten out of the shower and he was staring at her. He watched her intently. He wanted her. She started to ask him how she had gotten there, but he placed a finger to her mouth. *Shhh*, he told her. He was naked. She wanted to run her fingers along the fine hair that covered his washboard stomach and trailed down to…Marley looked at the springy dark hair that surrounded his -- her face began to burn. He was so thick down…Marley's mouth went dry. He stood still, and as always, just watched her.

Before she knew what was happening, he had grabbed her by her upper arms and lifted her off of her bare feet, bringing them eye level. He was going to kiss her. She knew it before he tried and braced her hands against his chest feeling as if she were pushing against a steel wall. In spite of her efforts to free herself, he pulled her steadily closer.

"Keep squirming." He whispered to her.

Marley froze, feeling his erection burn against her thigh. Dominic wanted her to feel him. He wanted her so bad that his mouth was watering. He lowered her so her feet were touching the floor, but still held her to him. She was so soft. He couldn't bring himself to let her go. He laid his forehead upon hers and deeply inhaled her

128

scent. *Mmm, she smelled nice*. Dominic deeply inhaled her again. *Nice and clean.*

Marley took a deep breath as he gently grasped her chin and forced her to look at him, and against her will she began to slip into the deep, black sea. And just like that, it begins with a kiss…

For Marley, it was like being consumed by a hard, unyielding heat. She was overwhelmed by the persistent firmness of a demanding mouth, a hot tongue that sensuously coerced its way between her lips and then she was explored quickly at first and then more slowly – a massage of her tongue with another, the delicious suckling of her mouth combined with masculine growls and whispers of how she should be punished with a ravishing of her most private areas.

Dominic wanted access to her privacy. She tasted as sweet as he knew she would. Her sweet tongue darted in and out of his mouth so erotically that he…*hmm, how badly he wanted to put something in her mouth*. Dominic wound his hands into Marley's hair and held her head back to kiss her soft throat.

She knew he was going to be forceful and she could feel a moist, throbbing heat beginning to burn in her loins.

"You want me, don't you?" He asked her.

You shouldn't be here, Marley's brain screamed to her. But her mouth whispered...

"My body is aching for you."

Marley wrapped both of her soft hands around him and softly stroked and squeezed him as she kissed his mouth. Dominic groaned aloud and his eyes closed in pleasure but then flew open again as he felt her mouth suckling his fingers. Dominic clenched his eyes shut to control how his body was processing the pleasure that she gave him. *So soft.* He looked down to see Marley on her knees in front of him. She rubbed her face against his thighs and placed a soft kiss on the head of his penis, her tongue snaked out to wrap itself around him. Dominic felt his stomach spasm and he twined his hand in the back of her hair and tried to pull away.

He picked her up and held her away from him to take a better look at her. He took in the slim, shapely legs, the perfectly rounded hips and flat belly and his mouth watered once his eyes reached the full breasts where the nipples were hard and plump, beckoning to him. Marley teased him by seductively gyrating her hips against

130

him, inviting him to whatever he wanted.

Dominic picked her up and carried her to the bed. He turned her over onto her stomach and buried his head in her hair, attempting to regain control of himself. There he started, slowly licking the nape of her neck and then her slender shoulder blades, loving the silky smoothness of her skin. Marley moaned as his tongue touched the small of her back, circling gently before surprising her by sucking part of a buttock into his mouth and biting her softly. And then leaving a moist, hot trail down the back of her thighs and gently kissing the bend in her knees.

She could feel his tongue boldly searching her body and her nipples tightened and begin to ache. Marley smiled and stretched, glad that she had given Dominic access to her secrets. Her gray eyes darkened and she was exquisite as she reached for him, mesmerizing his mind with a seductive rotation of her hips. He remained still, loving the feeling of her trying to take him while he lay still atop her. He closed his eyes and savored the sensation of her tight body stretching to allow him entry and then gratefully slid into hot, plush velvet.

Marley looked into Dominic's unfocused eyes and relished his blank stare as his eyes glazed over with pleasure. She kissed him, sucking his tongue into her mouth to match the rhythm of their hips. This drove Dominic insane. It was like penetrating her in two places at the same time and he quickened his pace, holding her thighs apart as far as they would go.

Marley snapped awake. She jumped out of bed and looked frantically about. She was in the room alone. *The dream had been so real*, she thought. Marley ran to the door and threw it open. Dominic stood there, his hair still ruffled from sleep -- his hand raised in midair. He stood there staring at Marley with the same incredulous look on his face. *The dream had seemed so real,* he thought.

BACK WHEN

She separated them at birth. Penelope kept one child because it was beautiful, but rejected the other because it was not. Miranda secretly hated her daughter for giving the child away and did not speak to her for years. Jack, on the other hand, continued to love Penelope as he always had and would bring the other child home with him to visit its grandmother. Knowing that Miranda was bitter to Penelope in the deep recesses of her soul, he thought that the child would be a comfort to her and would ease her misery. It had been two years but she still refused to let it go.

"I asked her. I asked her, Jack! You know that." She said to him for the hundredth time in two years. She was still outraged.

"I know, dear."

"I asked that little conniving…I said, Penelope, if you don't want the child then I will raise it, and she just gave it away behind my back. She wouldn't even tell me where to look." Miranda sat at her vanity and rigorously rubbed night cream onto her face and neck.

"I should've throttled her." She said, almost in tears. "Why would she do that?"

Jack exhaled and looked at his wife. He did not know why.

"Penelope didn't want the reminder, dear. She couldn't handle it."

"She is a selfish, spoiled woman. She always has been. She is not welcome in my home, Jack. Don't you dare ever bring her here."

It hurt his heart to hear the contempt in Miranda's voice for their only child. Though he loved Penelope, he had to admit that what she had done was terribly wrong. Their small family was traumatized -- especially Miranda. As far as their daughter, Penelope, was concerned though, it was her own decision to make. In Jack's mind, Penelope had always been strong willed and intelligent. As far as Miranda was concerned, Penelope was selfish and manipulative. To him, she had been a perfect child. He and Miranda had tried to have children for so long and had all but given up when Penelope popped up by surprise. They were in their late thirties then and Jack had become very successful and owned several used car lots in their hometown of Wichita, Kansas.

As a baby, Jack had been intrigued by Penelope – by her almost hairless head and little toes and fingers and then later at how precocious and darling she was. She had been such a gorgeous child. Miranda had been proud of her once, he'd wanted to remind

134

her. Yes, he would get upset at Penelope sometimes when he thought about his lost grandchild who was somewhere in this world alone. He hoped that someone loved the child -- maybe someone whose heart was not as cold as its mother's. That was another reason their granddaughter visited them so much.

He did not dare tell Miranda that Penelope had begun to mistreat little Charla. The girl would be with her grandparents for weeks at a time before Penelope would bother to call and ask about her. Miranda noticed this and would mutter under her breath about mothers who didn't worry about their two year old babies.

Charla's father was a married man. He secretly gave Penelope money to keep her quiet, but he wanted nothing to do with her or the child.

"Another excuse for Mother to look down her nose at me." Penelope would say to him, her lips puckered into a pout. Those were the times when he wanted to shake some sense into her.

Miranda and Jack did not know where they had gone wrong with Penelope. Being an only child, she had been the center of their attention and they constantly showered her with love. *Jack indulged Penelope's every whim,* Miranda said, *and that was the problem.* And he would be the first to admit that he had. Penelope was a daddy's girl and he had seen no reason to deny her things that he could easily give her –a little red Fiat for her sixteenth birthday, a trip to Paris with her friends when she turned eighteen, a condo when she turned twenty-one. Miranda had wanted Penelope to stay home, to finish college, but instead Penelope sold her condo and ran off to Hollywood with a musician to pursue a career as an actress. How could Jack tell his baby girl no when she called and needed cash? Besides, he would tell Miranda, she's young. Let her live a little. And he felt that he was right. Penelope eventually came home at twenty-six, a little rougher around the edges, but street wise. She always joined her dad for his nightly routine of a cigar and a glass of bourbon. But history repeats itself and Miranda started in on Penelope about her "future" which led to Penelope leaving home again – this time for the arms of a married doctor who kept Penelope in the style that she said she was accustomed to. Miranda threatened Jack with divorce if she caught him giving Penelope one more dime and he didn't; not because he believed his wife's threat, but because he didn't like it at all that Penelope was making time with another woman's husband. No matter what, she hadn't been raised that way. They had tried to instill good morals into Penelope and provide her with a steady value system with which to make her decisions by and he would not stand for it.

"He's going to leave her, daddy. We're getting married." She would say happily.

"They never leave, Penelope." He tried to tell her.

"If you don't like my choices, daddy, then don't come back." She told him coolly.

She hurt him with that comment, but he never said another word about the doctor. He knew that sooner or later she would get her heart broken and he would be there to pick up the pieces for his little girl as always. It wasn't her fault that she had been seduced by a charming, older man. He knew that she was about to learn an important lesson about life. When she became pregnant though, he and Miranda were devastated. Penelope had the nerve to not even be embarrassed.

"How shameful! What about his wife?" Miranda had screamed at her.

"What about me, Mother! I'm supposed to be his wife." Penelope said.

"Where is he?" Miranda asked her sarcastically, knowing the answer. "Why isn't he with you?"

Penelope had been coming home more. Miranda thought it was to eat, but Jack thought she wanted to be closer to them because she was "at a vulnerable point in her life". *Bullshit,* Miranda said. *She's just broke.*

"He'll be by eventually. He's been putting in a lot of hours at the hospital." Penelope told her haughtily.

She didn't tell her mother that it was over; that he had told her that he didn't want any children outside of his marriage; that if she didn't abort the pregnancy then he wouldn't have anything else to do with her. She wouldn't allow him to use her and then throw her away like trash, she told him. *So much for him leaving that hag he called a wife.* She'd felt him beginning to pull away from her anyway and she'd had to think fast. The best idea she had come up with was to miss a birth control pill sometimes.

By the time she began drinking, Jack was already at his wits end.

138

First it started as a glass of wine and then she began drinking every

day. By the end of her second trimester, Jack and Miranda decided

that it would be best if Jack went to stay at her apartment full time

to keep her from drinking, but Penelope still would somehow

outsmart him and he would smell alcohol on her breath at times.

He would go home to visit his wife, but not before making

Penelope promise not to drink while he was away. She would

promise -- profusely, in fact. But as always, she lied, and Jack

would arrive the next day to find her passed out on the couch in a

state of exhausted inebriation with one leg stretched out onto the

coffee table and an empty pint of bourbon tucked beneath her big

belly.

He was there that day at the clinic when Penelope went to the

doctor for a prenatal care appointment. The doctor had begun to

speak to Penelope about a congenital complication, but she had

shushed him and asked Jack to leave the room. He did so,

hesitantly at first but then quickly. He wanted to talk to Miranda.

He did not trust his daughter.

"A complication?" Miranda said to him. He made the phone call from the clinic parking lot.

"Yes, a complication. She asked me to leave the room. I think she's hiding something." He told her worriedly.

On the ride home, Penelope seemed happy and relaxed and rested her hands on her pregnant belly as if nothing was amidst.

"Is everything all right?" He'd asked, nervously trying to keep his eyes on the road.

"Everything's fine, Daddy." She'd told him with a bright smile.

"And the babies?"

"Just fine, Dad."

Jack sighed. She was lying to him.

As sometimes happens though, life throws a curveball and plans get sidetracked. That happened when Miranda's mother passed. Towards the end of Penelope's pregnancy, Miranda and Jack flew out to Dallas to make funeral arrangements. Penelope went into labor during this time and Jack was caught off guard when the hospital called him while they were in El Paso.

"Mr. Smith?" A female voice asked.

"Yes, this is Jack Smith."

140

"Mr. Smith, this is Nurse Ford at Washington Memorial. I'm calling to let you know that your daughter has delivered. Are you able to come to the hospital? She's under a lot of stress and I don't think she's in the right state of mind to make this decision alone." The nurse said.

He could feel Miranda stirring beside him. "What is it, Jack?" She asked.

"I don't understand, Nurse. What decision?" He asked suddenly confused.

"Well, the adoption of course."

"Adoption!" Jack yelled out loud.

"What!" Miranda said behind him.

"Maybe you should speak with your daughter." The nurse said, sounding as if she felt that she had spoken out of turn. "I'll connect you."

There was a momentary pause and then another female voice came onto the line.

"Room 1211." It said.

"This is, uh, Jack Smith. I'd like to speak with my daughter,

Penelope, please."

"Sure." The voice said, sounding relieved.

There was a pause and then, "Daddy?" Penelope's hoarse voice came onto the line.

"Penelope, honey, how are you?"

"I'm okay, Dad."

"And how are the babies?" He asked.

There was a long pause and then she began to cry. Jack looked over to Miranda who had her hands out. She wanted the phone. *Oh boy*, Jack thought as he handed her the receiver.

"The nurse is talking about adoption, Penelope. Why?" Miranda asked her sternly.

There was another pause and then Miranda put a fist on one hip as she paced their hotel room. *Mm hmm*, she would say. Then, *I can't believe you, Penelope*. Then desperately, *don't do that* and *I'll take care of it.*

"Just wait for us, Penelope." Miranda said." We'll be home tomorrow."

Miranda hung up the phone then collapsed onto the bed and sobbed on Jack's shoulder.

"Now, now. Now, now." He told her soothingly as he gently rubbed her hair. He needed her to calm down. He was worried and anxious to know what was going on.

"She was going to give it up for adoption." Miranda said between sobs.

"One of the babies? What do you mean?" He asked as he handed her a Kleenex.

"She said that there's something wrong with one of them. I couldn't really understand with all her blubbering, but I think one is handicapped. She was actually going to give it away, Jack. Her own baby!" She cried into the napkin. "Well, I told her we'd raise the baby. It's my grandchild and I'll be damned if it goes to some foster home. To hell with her. How could she, Jack? How could she?"

Jack didn't know how she could. "I don't know, Miranda, but let's just get home, okay? Come back to bed, dear."

The following afternoon, they went to the hospital straight from the airport. By the time they made it though, it was too late.

143

Penelope had sent the child away the night before.

"What did you do?" Miranda screamed at her.

"It was my decision and I didn't want to look at the ugly thing!"

She screamed back at Miranda with a nasty sneer on her face.

"I'll kill you, you little bitch!" Miranda growled as she lunged at

Penelope with her fists balled.

Miranda was in such a fury to get to Penelope that Jack almost

didn't make it to her on time and damn near had to tackle her to the

ground. Jack thought she was going to kill the girl.

"You selfish bitch! What did you do!" Miranda screamed as Jack

pulled her from the room and down the hallway past shocked

patients and nurses and out of the hospital.

She cried herself to sleep that night. *His mother-in-law wasn't even*

cold in the ground yet and Penelope goes and pulls this crap. What

would possess her to give that poor child to a stranger instead of its

very own grandmother? *Plain old mean is what.*

The hospital called the next day for Jack because Penelope and the

baby needed a ride home. Penelope threatened to call the police if

Miranda returned to the hospital and Miranda said that Penelope would need the police, so Jack went alone. He held his granddaughter for the first time while her mother dressed.

"Hello, sweetie." He whispered to her, gently running a finger over her soft cheek. Tears came to his eyes as he thought about his missing grandchild.

"What was it?" He asked her on the ride home.

She exhaled an impatient breath. "What was what?" She asked without looking at him, knowing exactly what he meant.

"The baby, Penelope. Was it a girl too?"

"What does it matter, Dad?"

"What does it matter? Are you that cold? Your child, Penelope, was it missing a limb? Did it have two heads? What happened? Your mother is beside herself with grief. How could --"

"Mother, Mother, Mother! What about me?" She asked coldly.

"How are you, Penelope? Some guy knocked you up and left you alone. Are you okay?" She began to cry and Jack wanted to smack her.

He stayed with her and the baby for a week until he learned that she'd been to see the married father of her children at his office and had made a scene. Jack was home alone at her apartment with the baby when the phone rang.

"Yes, is Penelope in?" A male voice asked.

"No, she isn't. Who's calling?"

"This is Dr. Paul Morgan."

"From Washington Memorial?" Jack asked concerned,

"No. I'm an old friend of Penelope's. I was hoping to speak with her."

Jack knew instantly who he was. "You got my little girl pregnant, right?"

"I –" The doctor was speechless.

Just the person that Jack wanted to talk to. He sat down and had a man-to-man conversation with Dr. Paul Morgan.

After the phone call, Jack was fuming. Not even a week out of the delivery room and Penelope was pissy drunk and acting a fool in a cancer clinic. The doctor had told Jack some things that he did not want to hear. She was blackmailing him for money, he'd told Jack. Otherwise, she was going to tell his wife about the baby. She had

146

already embarrassed him in front of his colleagues. She'd

threatened to bring the baby to his home. No, he didn't want

anything to do with Charla and please tell Penelope that he would

give her the money. Son of a bitch, Jack had called him, taking

advantage of a young woman like that.

"I assure you, Mr. Smith, that your daughter is no angel." Dr.

Morgan told him before hanging up.

Two years later and Penelope was still collecting from the good

doctor. She had kept her word though and stayed away from Mrs.

Morgan. She'd become a full blown alcoholic and had begun to

hang around a biker gang. That's where she met Milt. Scruffy and

built like a tank, Milt always had a beer in one hand and a cigarette

dangling from his lips. Jack didn't like the look of him, and

Miranda and Jack kept Charla at their home most nights under the

guise that they wanted Penelope to have time for herself. They

knew she would use Charla against them if she thought she could

derive some benefit or even just to make Miranda miserable.

And so that's the way they lived. Miranda and Jack aged happily

with their only granddaughter growing up in the bedroom right down the hall. When Charla turned seventeen, Jack took her to the car lot and told her to pick whatever she wanted and she did to his surprise pick out an old black, Ford Bronco.

"Thank you, Gramps." She told him with an excited hug.

He was so proud of her -- his granddaughter, honor student, high school track star and soon to be college student. She had been accepted to Kansas State and Miranda was beside herself with joy. Charla would not be far away and they could visit her as much as they wanted.

Penelope, on the other hand, could care less about her daughter's educational endeavors. She wanted Charla to maintain her figure and not waste her time on what Penelope called "ugly people". At Charla's high school graduation, Miranda and Penelope sat apart. They only spoke when they had to and only if it had to do with Charla. The only thing they agreed on was that Charla needn't know that she was a twin. Penelope had lied to her years ago and told her that her father was dead – had died before she was born even, and no, she had no pictures of him.

So when Charla left for college she was a well-rounded young woman. She had been nurtured to adulthood by her grandparents, but taught how to take care of herself in the streets by Milt and her mother. She loved Milt. He let her sneak beers -- which even her mother didn't do -- and he'd purchased for her and taught her how to use a switchblade. Milt was her favorite guy after Gramps. *The kids she hung out with sometimes when she visited her mother on the weekends would give her Gram and Gramps a heart attack*, she thought to herself with a chuckle. They were kids that belonged to the biker gang. Their parents were like her mom and she got on well with them. She had been friends with some of them since she was a small girl.

She looked over to her best friend Jacqueline, who was fidgeting in the passenger seat.

"Nervous, Jackie?" Charla asked.

"Oh my God, I am so nervous. What if I don't fit in? What if –"

She stopped. "College!" She screamed in excitement.

"I know right?" Charla agreed.

Things moved quickly once they got on campus and Charla and Jackie separated, both going to their own dorm room to meet their new roommates.

"Hi, I'm Alison." Charla was welcomed to her room by a tall, slim, brown haired girl in bifocals.

"Hi. I'm Charla." Charla told her as she started to unpack.

"Wow. You're gorgeous." Alison said in awe as she sat cross-legged on her own bed and nervously hugged a Hello Kitty pillow to her chest.

"Thank you." Charla responded.

"Do you have a boyfriend?" Alison asked her shyly.

"No." Charla answered as she made her bed. "You?"

"Yes. We've been together since high school. He's a student here too."

"Well, that's good, right?" Charla asked, getting a nod from Alison. "Hey listen, me and my friend, Jackie, are going for pizza later. You wanna come?"

Charla thought her classes were going to be a breeze until she made it to her algebra class. No way was she going to pass this class without help. Jackie and Alison, both math geeks, tried to explain algebra to her again and again, but she couldn't get it through her skull. Math had always been a weak spot for her, and

150

by the fourth week she was feeling lost and discouraged. An academic advisor at the college recommended a tutor, and so Charla set about to find one knowing that if she didn't get help soon she would fail algebra, which was to her unacceptable. She refused to waste the money that her father had left for her education.

"I know someone." Alison told Charla with raised brow. "He's different though."

"What do you mean?"

"He's very smart though and nice." Alison said, avoiding Charla's question. "Here I'll give you his number. He doesn't charge much."

Charla took the number and used it. She needed help now.

"Hello." A friendly male voice answered.

"Hi. I'm looking for Anthony Mitchell."

"This is Anthony."

"My name is Charla Smith. I was given your number and told that you were an algebra tutor. I was hoping you could help me." She said.

151

"Failing algebra, huh?" He said in a joking tone.

"Yeah." Charla laughed and relaxed. "I really need help. What do you charge?"

"Let's not worry about that for now. Why don't we meet at the library and I'll see where you are first. Do you have any free time tomorrow?"

"Sure. I don't have any classes tomorrow after one o'clock. Are you free in the afternoon?"

"How about we meet in the college library around two?"

"Sounds good." She agreed.

That afternoon Charla met Anthony at the library and started her first tutoring session. To his relief, she never said a word about his condition or stared at him in a way that made him uncomfortable and their first tutoring session went on without a hitch. When Anthony showed Charla how he perceived algebra, understanding exploded in her brain and when she got back to her dorm room, she studied that night the way he had shown her. She was sure to go back over notes that she had taken during their session. They continued to meet and Charla got a B on her next quiz. She wanted

152

to celebrate with Anthony.

"Come on, let me buy you dinner." She'd pleaded with him after a tutoring session.

"Nah." He said as he struggled into his backpack. "But I'll see you next week, okay?"

She nodded and they parted, each going their separate way. She went by herself for a burger and chocolate milkshake then pulled out her cellphone while she ate and went to Google and browsed "hunchback". *Kyphosis* -- her lips moving silently as she read the definition -- *is the result of a curved spine that results in an abnormally rounded back. Well, Anthony must have a severe form,* she thought, *because his back is really rounded.*

So Anthony had kyphosis. So what. She had a crush on him. She bit into her burger. He was sweet and funny and his intelligent brown eyes made her want to kiss his face off. Sometimes the way he crinkled his nose even reminded her of her Gramps. She had never had a boyfriend before and she was determined to make him the first. Now she just had to find a way to tell him. She understood algebra well enough now. She didn't really need the tutoring as much anymore, but she acted dumbfounded sometimes just so that she could sit next to Anthony as he tried different ways to explain this problem and that problem in a way that her mind would grasp.

She would wait for him to be almost exasperated and then she would dramatically slap her forehead with her hand and exclaim, "Oh! Now I get it." She was not ashamed of her actions either. The morning of her next tutoring session, she stopped into a flower shop and bought one red rose and carried it to the library with her.

She saw Anthony as she entered the library. As usual, he had his face bent over a book and didn't hear her approach. She sat down across from him and laid the rose on top of the history book that he was reading.

"What's this?" He asked her, confused as he examined the rose. "Another thank you?"

"Will you go out with me, Anthony?" She asked him directly. Now he was really confused. "Like a date?" He asked.

Charla nodded. *To heck with every jock who had asked her out since she'd been here. She wanted Anthony.*

"I don't know what to say, Charla." He said smiling

He's flattered, she thought. "Why not?" She asked him softly, batting her eyelashes and using her "woman wiles" as her mother had taught her.

"You're not doing that right." He told her. "It's more like this." And he demonstrated to her the most perfect, flirtatious eyelash bat that she had ever seen.

They both laughed out loud and then Anthony made her day.

"I'll go out with you, Charla, but if we do that, I can't tutor you in algebra anymore." He said.

"Fine." Charla said, gathering her books and walking away.

"You're fired."

"You have a date?" Miranda asked her excited granddaughter.

"Yes, Gram. And he's cute and he's funny and –" Her grandfather came on the line.

"A date?" He asked.

"Yes, Gramps." She said. "His name's Anthony and he's going to be a doctor and he tutored me in algebra or I would've failed for sure."

"Sounds like a nice young man. Well, you be careful, honey, and have fun."

Anthony picked his outfit carefully. They were going bowling so he shouldn't be too dressy, but he didn't want to be too casual either. He didn't want to give Charla the wrong idea. *I wonder what she's wearing,* he thought. He fell to the ground and did some push-ups to get his blood flowing. He walked to the campus gym and got on a treadmill and began his daily workout. Charla Smith. Hmm. He could hear Old Davis as sure as if he were standing there -- *you done, good, Anthony, she's a turnip.* Indeed she was. Smart too. All that time faking him on the algebra. He'd wondered what was up with her. He had to be quicker. Girls had all kinds of trickery in mind to get a fella to do what they wanted. *What was she wanting with a farmboy anyhow?* Joe, his roommate, had asked him if he was nervous going out with such a pretty girl. Heck, no. He couldn't wait to see Charla.

When he got home, he hurriedly showered and dressed then raced over to the girls' dorms to pick up Charla. She was waiting outside

156

for him and he was early. She had a big silly grin on her face when she saw him and he started to grin as well. They both stood there grinning like fools for a while.

"Well, you wanna go?" He asked.

"Okay." She nodded.

They walked to Anthony's car and Charla grabbed Anthony's hand smiling up at him when he looked down at her. They went bowling that night. Anthony let Charla beat him because he got an excited hug every time she noticed that her score was higher than his own. Afterwards, they went for pizza and talked to one another about their young lives. Anthony told Charla about the dairy farm where he'd been raised by adoptive parents, Maria and Old Davis Mitchell.

"That's what you called him, Old Davis?" She asked Anthony laughing, to which he nodded.

"They were good to me -- he and the old girl. They'd had me since I was six years old. Maria couldn't have no kids and that's how they got me. I was the only young'un around and Old Davis taught me everything I know. Maria home schooled me.

Old Davis died on us though and then Maria went last year. Her sister watched over me and let me stay on in the house until I was eighteen. Old Davis and Maria had left the farm and everything else to me anyhow."

"I'm sorry, honey." Charla said, reaching out and laying a hand over his own. "You never knew your real parents then?"

"No."

"Did you ever try and find them?"

"I did. I asked Maria once but she told me that my mother had died and she didn't know about my dad. Old Davis, he only told me my mother's first name. I went through their paperwork after they died, but I didn't come up with nothing." He sighed.

"What about the foster home?"

"I had thought about it but I never got around to it. There's been so much going on."

"I could help if you want?" She asked him

"How about you bat them pretty eyelashes at me?" He asked. And that's what she did.

Six Months Later

Anthony and Charla were inseparable. They made being in love
158

look like magic. They sat there together on Rucker's Lane in the backseat of Anthony's car and kissed slowly, Anthony's hand gently caressed Charla's smooth thigh beneath her skirt.

"Come home with me for the holiday, Anthony?"

"I wish I could, honey. I gotta get to the farm and help my aunt out. I wanted to ask you to come back with me."

Charla was tempted but she knew that if she went home with Anthony without her grandfather having a chance to meet him that Jack would come looking for them. She mentioned this to Anthony.

"I understand." He told her. "Let's get going. You've got class in the morning."

Charla smiled and crawled into the front seat. When they pulled in front of her dorm, Anthony got out and walked her to the door. After one last kiss, he was gone.

When Charla closed the door to her room she sighed happily.

"Well, lookee, lookee. And where have you been?" Alison asked, cutting on a light.

"Out." Charla said slyly.

"You guys are getting serious." Alison said in a sing-song voice before cutting her light back out.

Jackie was quiet on the way home. Charla hadn't seen her much this school year and wondered what was going on.

"You happy to be going home, Jackie?"

"I'm in trouble, Charla." She said.

"What's wrong?"

"I don't think I'm going back to school next semester."

"Why not?" Charla asked, worried.

"I'm pregnant."

Charla gasped. *Oh boy*, she thought. Jackie's parents were so strict that Charla was worried for her friend.

"How did that happen?" She asked her.

"Are you serious?" Jackie asked her.

"Well, I mean not how, but how? What were you thinking?"

"What do you think?" She asked sarcastically.

"Is it Terry?" Charla asked.

Jackie nodded.

"Does he know?"

160

Jackie nodded again.

"Well, what did he say?" Charla asked, becoming impatient.

"He isn't answering my calls." Jackie said then began to cry, her thick shoulders shaking uncontrollably.

Hot damn, Charla thought to herself. This was one of the reasons that her and Anthony abstained from sex. She couldn't imagine having to have this conversation with her grandparents.

"What do you think your parents are going to do?" She asked Jackie sympathetically.

"Ki-ki-kill me." Jackie said through sobs.

Charla whistled and shook her head. *The shit was going to hit the fan as her Gramps would say.*

Charla pulled in front of her friend's house and helped her with her bags. Jackie's mother ran out smiling and grabbed her daughter for a hug.

"I missed you so much." She told Jackie. "Looks like you gained some weight, dear." She said happily.

"Hi, Mrs. Parsons." Charla said.

"Hi, Charla. Do you want to come in for a while?"

"No, ma'am. Thanks but I have to get home." Charla hugged her friend and then climbed back into her truck and drove away. Poor Jackie!

Her Gram and Gramps were there waiting for her when she got home. To her absolute joy, her Gram hadn't touched her room. "I didn't touch your room, honey. I wanted everything to be just like you left it. Come downstairs and have some dinner when you're ready." She told Charla, kissing her granddaughter on the cheek before she left the room.

Home sweet home. She missed Anthony, but was glad to be home. *Oh, mom*, she thought, *where are you?* She pulled out her cell and dialed her mother.

Miranda allowed Penelope over for dinner that night – Penelope and Milt. That's how happy of a mood that Miranda was in to have her granddaughter home from college. Milt looked as if he had never sat at a table before, so surprised he was that he had been invited. He started to put his elbows on the table then changed his mind and looked around to see if anyone had noticed him. His eyes met Charla's and they laughed together secretly.

162

"Daddy tells me you have a boyfriend, Charla." Penelope said,

lighting a cigarette though she knew that Miranda didn't allow

smoking in the house.

Miranda started to speak but was silenced with a look from Jack

who nodded in Charla's direction. Miranda sat back in her seat and

exhaled an irritated breath. Penelope smirked at her and then ashed

her cigarette on the coaster that held her glass. Charla shook her

head. She didn't know why her mother persisted in trying to annoy

her grandmother.

"I do, mom. His name's Anthony."

"Anthony." She repeated. Her red lips curved into a smile. "Jock?"

"No, mom."

"No. What then?" She asked as if being a jock was all there was to

college life.

"He's studying to be a doctor, mom."

"Humph." Penelope said. Then, "Does his family have money?"

"Oh, Penelope." Jack said, sipping his glass of bourbon. Miranda

rolled her eyes.

"He's adopted. He grew up on a farm. His adoptive parents died and left him enough where he'd be able to take care of himself. He's a good guy, mom."

"Is he a country bunkin'?" Penelope asked her daughter in a mock southern accent.

Charla could tell that her mother had her legs crossed beneath the table and that the top leg was swinging to and fro because her upper body swayed back and forth in a rhythm all its own. Charla could almost see the black stilettos and fishnet stockings her mother wore under her grandmother's table without even looking. Penelope wore her customary red lipstick and her waist length platinum blonde hair was perfectly layered.

"No, mom." Charla laughed at her mother and Penelope smiled.

"Is he cute or is he a booger?" Penelope asked in the same mock southern accent as she took a hit from her cigarette.

Milt laughed out loud and almost choked on a mouthful of green beans. Miranda exhaled again and rolled her eyes ceiling-ward.

"I like him, mom."

"She's in love." Penelope said to Milt, elbowing him in the side.

Humph, was his only reply.

"So when do we get to meet him?" Jack asked her.

164

"Soon I hope. He had to go home and help his aunt out with the land, but he'll come as soon as he can."

"Well, we can't wait to meet him." Miranda said then looked sharply at Penelope, who knew instinctively that it was time to put her cigarette out.

Charla drove back to school alone after break. Jackie's mother and father decided that it wasn't a good idea for her to return to college pregnant. Mrs. Parsons had decided that it was best for Jackie to stay home and have the baby and then attend classes at the community college so that she would be able to continue her education and take care of her child. Jackie was depressed that Terry still wasn't answering her calls and Charla had been unable to cheer her up.

When she returned to school the first thing she did was meet with Anthony. She ran to him when she got to the campus and saw him waiting in front of her dorm. He grabbed her and swung her around and hugged her tightly to him.

"I missed you." She said, kissing him on the chin.

"I missed you more." He said, staring down at her lovingly.

"How was everything at home? How's your aunt?"

"She's good. She wanted to talk to me about selling the farm."

"What are you going to do?" Charla asked wide eyed.

"I don't know. That's where I grew up. She says some folks been around asking after it. I remember when they were trying to get Old Davis to sell and he wouldn't. I don't think he would want me to. Besides, I'm not ready for that anyhow. Seems too soon, you know?"

"Yeah." She said nodding. "Do you need the money?"

"Nah. I'm good." He said, bending and stealing a kiss.

After spending some time with Charla, Anthony went back to his own room and got ready for bed. He thought about his visit with his aunt and his conversation with Charla. He hadn't told her what else he'd learned. Charla was like a dog with a bone when it came to certain things, and although her passion for life was one of the things he loved about her, he really didn't want her pressuring him to pursue things that maybe he wasn't ready for yet. His Aunt Jan had told him what Maria and Old Davis hadn't; that his birth mother was alive when she gave him away. She had signed the

166

papers with her own hand. He hadn't expected the hurt that gave his heart. That's why Maria hadn't told him the truth. Who wanted to know that their own mother didn't want them? He wondered if it was because of his condition. He'd heard that before – parents giving up kids because they were somehow handicapped. Why else would she give him away?

He vaguely recalled how the other children had teased him when he was in the orphanage. Old Davis and Maria had never made him feel like he was any different. When he was a boy, Old Davis told him that the hump on his back meant that he was stronger than everybody else, and therefore, could clean the horses' stalls with lightning speed and even lift full grown cows into the air – though he shouldn't even try it because cows wouldn't produce milk if you did that. Six year old Anthony couldn't abide that – cows being unable to produce milk. He loved milk and needed it to strengthen his hump – because of this, he never once tried to lift a cow into the air. He remembered these things with a smile. Too bad Maria and Old Davis hadn't been his real parents. He had loved them just as much.

He knew that his real mother's name was Penelope just like Charla's mother. He knew that much at least. Charla too had been an only child just like him. That's probably why they got along so well -- both never really having anyone to share things with. Plus, they were only a few months apart so that helped too, he thought. He was born at Washington Memorial. Or at least that's what his aunt thought she'd heard Old Davis say to Maria once when he'd been going through some records of Anthony's.

Anthony wished he knew where Old Davis had kept those records. He'd searched the house high and low and hadn't found anything in their bedroom or in Old Davis' safe, which was now his safe. Old Davis had even left a letter in there for him inside an envelope that had been stuffed with cash. Anthony laughed as he read it and then cried at the end where Old Davis had written, 'Love you, Son.'

Next break he planned on going home with Charla, and then when he got a chance, he would go over to Washington Memorial and see if he could find out anything.

SIX MONTHS LATER

Finally, Charla thought. Anthony was driving home with her for break. They would have gone sooner, but he had broken his leg in a car accident and couldn't go. It had been enough for him just to get around campus.

"Are you nervous?" She asked.

"Nah." He said, though he was but he knew how important this was to Charla.

Her grandmother had insisted that Anthony sleep in the guest room at their home and wouldn't take no for an answer. That pleased Charla tremendously knowing that she would have him all to herself – almost. Her grandfather and Milt would give him the third degree, but she was confident that he could hold his own. She was worried that her mother would embarrass her by asking Anthony about his kyphosis. In fact, she knew that she would. Hopefully, Charla would be around when it happened and she would jump in and simply explain to her mother that it was a condition that Anthony had, had since he was an infant; that he had been born with it, and she would leave it at that. She wouldn't allow her mother to make Anthony feel uncomfortable and she knew that her grandmother would back her up as well.

When they pulled into the driveway, Jack came out to the car and introduced himself, shaking Anthony's hand and helping them get their things into the house. Miranda came to Anthony and hugged him.

"So nice to finally meet you, young man." She told him.

"Welcome to our home."

"Thank you, ma'am." Anthony said, blushing as he nodded to Miranda.

Jack and Miranda liked the young man instantly. He was polite and respectful and they could tell that Charla absolutely adored him.

The three of them silently worried about Penelope though.

Speak of the devil, Miranda thought as the doorbell rang.

Charla answered the door and Anthony knew from the way that Charla had described her mother to him that this was Penelope.

"Chest is still flat as a board but look at the rump on you, sugar." Penelope said as she took her coat off. "I was wondering if you'd –

"

When Penelope saw Anthony all the blood drained from her face and she took a step backward in shock and laid a slender hand on her throat.

170

"Mom, this is Anthony. Remember I said I was bringing my boyfriend this time?" She said to her mother in a tight voice.

Stop looking at him like that, mother, she thought

"Oh!" Penelope said, regaining control of herself. "I thought – I just – I'm sorry." She said to Anthony and extended him a reluctant hand.

Anthony shook her hand, not wanting to be rude. He had observed her over the last minute and didn't like her. She was loud and had a sense of self-importance about herself that he found distasteful. Also, he didn't like the way she was dressed. There was no excuse for a woman that old to reveal so much cleavage. But Maria would tell him to give her a chance, so he told himself that he would. She was Charla's mother after all.

Over dinner, Anthony and Jack discussed baseball while Miranda grinned broadly. *What a nice young man.* She gushed over Anthony and made sure that he got the biggest slice of her famous pecan pie. Charla was elated that her grandparents liked Anthony. It was her mother that she was worried about. When she thought that no one was looking, Penelope would stare at him strangely.

She was absentmindedly twirling the pearls that she wore around her pale throat and Charla could see tell that, that leg was bouncing beneath the table again.

"Where did you grow up, Anthony?" She asked, interrupting Jack's conversation. "Here in Kansas, was it?"

"Yes, ma'am." He responded, not really wanting to talk to her but trying to be polite for the sake of the table.

"And you were adopted you say?" Penelope asked, concentrating on Anthony's reaction to her questions.

"Mother." Charla protested.

"It's fine, Charla." Anthony told her.

"When were you born?"

He told her.

"So you're only a couple months older than Charla then." She said.

"How observant of you, Penelope." Miranda said. "Would anybody like another slice of pie?"

Anthony and Penelope watched each other for a while and then Anthony said calmly, "Is there something you want to know, Ms. Smith?"

"How'd you come to get that hump in your back?" Penelope asked

172

him just as Charla knew she would.

"Mother!" Charla said to her mother. She was becoming agitated.

"Penelope, don't be rude." Miranda said, pointing a finger at Penelope.

"It's okay." Anthony said again. "I was born with a congenital defect. It's called kyphosis, ma'am. I've always been this way."

Hmm, is all Penelope said before she went back to absentmindedly fingering her pearl necklace.

Jack picked back up on the subject of baseball to try to put Anthony back at ease. Miranda asked Penelope to help her in the kitchen while Charla sat there at the table and fumed.

The next day Anthony awoke early. He wanted to go to Washington Memorial and see what he could find out. He was going to drop Charla at her friend Jackie's house and then borrow her truck to go to the hospital. He'd told Charla that he needed to pick up some things at the mall. He hated lying to her but he wanted to do this alone.

Once he had dropped her off, he rode to the hospital in deep thought. He didn't get his hopes up about finding anything out, but he would go to the hospital anyway just to tie up a loose end. What would he say without a name? *Hey, anybody delivered any hunchback babies in the last twenty years?*

He pulled into the parking lot and then entered the hospital.

Maybe I should go to where the babies are delivered, he thought. *Nah, maybe they have a records department.*

"Sure, we have a records department. " The receptionist told him as she gave him directions to the elevators.

The dust assaulted his nostrils as he exited the elevator and he sneezed wondering why in this new age of technology they still had all these file cabinets.

"Help you?" A voice asked from behind.

He turned to see a middle aged black man standing behind him. He was dressed in a security uniform.

"Yes, sir. I'm looking for the records department."

"Well, I know they're moving all the records to computers now. How far back you trying to go?" He asked Anthony, scratching his stubbly chin.

"About twenty years, sir."

174

"Well, hold on then. Let me grab Ethel." He told Anthony and shuffled off.

An elderly woman rounded the corner several seconds later. Her arms were filled with file folders.

She stared at him quietly for a moment then asked, "What you need, hon?"

"Yes. Uh, I know it's a long shot, but I was wondering if the hospital might have some information on my birth mother."

"When were you born?" She asked. Anthony told her.

The old lady sighed and shook her head. "I knew it was you when you walked in here." She told him, gesturing for him to follow her. Anthony's heart stopped. *Would she have some information about his mother?* She led him into a room that was filled with even more file cabinets and went to a desk and set the folders down that she held in her arms.

"What do you mean when you say that you knew it was me?" He asked, confused.

"Sit down, young man." She told him. She went to a file folder and after thumbing about, brought it to the table and sat across from him. "Do you know anything about your birth parents?" She asked him.

"All I know is that my mother's name was Penelope." He told her. She laid the file folder in front of him and left the room. She looked as if she wanted to cry. *What the hell*, Anthony thought. He opened the thin folder and began to read. After a few minutes he thought he was going to throw up. Penelope Smith…Baby Girl Charla…Baby Boy, deformed…twins.

He slammed the file shut and grabbed the desk tightly to steady himself. He was light headed. He would wager that Penelope had known exactly who he was and still she never said a word. *She was unbelievable.* She had given him away and the girl he loved was his sister. *Shit.*

Charla didn't know whether to be worried or pissed. Anthony hadn't come back to pick her up from Jackie's and he hadn't even bothered to come back to her grandparents' that night at all. He wasn't answering his cell. She didn't –

She ran to the front window and looked out. There he was. She ran to the front door and threw it open. Anthony looked disheveled and…was he drunk?

"Anthony, are you drunk?" She asked outraged.

"Yes I am, dear sister, my love. I don't know whether to kiss you or yank your ponytail." He said to her, drunkenly swaying back and forth as he stood on the porch.

What was he talking about? "Get your ass in this house and go lay down before my grandparents see you." She told him through gritted teeth.

She helped him up the stairs and into bed and then angrily slammed his bedroom door and stormed out of the house She could hear her grandmother calling her from the kitchen. She went to her truck and turned off the engine then pulled the keys from the ignition. She noticed the open folder on the passenger seat and hurriedly tucked the contents back inside and went into the house. She dropped the folder on the dining room table and then ran upstairs to check on Anthony. He was fast asleep. She pulled a blanket over him and left the room. She was going to give him a piece of her mind when he woke up. As she was coming back down the stairs, she heard her grandmother crying.

"What's wrong, Gram?" She said as she entered the living room.

"Where did you get this?" Jack asked her. He had been crying as well.

"It was in my truck. Anthony had it."

This made her grandmother begin to sob uncontrollably. Jack held Miranda to him. They both had shocked expressions on their faces. Charla grabbed the folder and looked inside. What she read, she couldn't believe. She had to sit down. This couldn't be right. Did this mean that Anthony was her brother? She had been a twin? Her mother and grandparents had lied to her.

"What the hell is going on?" She said angrily.

Penelope and her parents sat in the living room and stared at Charla and Anthony. Miranda was so happy to have her grandson home. She was convinced that this was nothing more than a momentary setback.

"Why did you lie to me?" Charla asked them. She was so hurt that she could hardly speak.

"We thought it was for the best, sweetheart." Miranda told her.

"And what about you, mother?" She asked Penelope.

178

"I have no regrets." Penelope said coldly, staring at Anthony as she said it.

That was enough for Miranda. She turned and slapped Penelope so hard that she fell from her chair. "You've had that coming for a long time." Miranda said to her.

"You knew who I was when I came here." Anthony said to Penelope. "You think I care that you don't want me around? News flash -- I can't stand you either." He said to Penelope's surprise. "That's right. You thought I was going to beg you to love me? Please, lady. Who's my father? I'd be surprised if you even knew." He asked her.

"He didn't want you either." Penelope spat at him hatefully.

"That's not true." Jack spoke up when he saw the pained expression on Anthony's face. "He didn't want either of you. He's still alive. His name's Paul Morgan. He's a doctor."

"Shut up, dad!" Penelope screamed.

"I'm tired of keeping your secrets, Penelope. All you do is hurt people. I'll give you the address." He told his grandchildren.

"Daddy, no!" Penelope screamed, trying to go after her father.

"You sit right there." Miranda said forcefully to Penelope. "And don't move."

Jack came back with the address and gave it to Anthony who jumped up and stormed out of the house. Charla went after him, grabbing her car keys.

"You drive." She told him, tossing him the keys.

They drove in silence together. Neither of them knew what to say. When they pulled in front of the Morgan residence, they just sat there.

"What will we say?" She whispered to Anthony.

"Hell if I know." He said shaking his head.

They got out of the truck and approached the house. A gray haired woman answered.

"Can I help you?"

"Yes." Charla told her. "We're looking for Dr. Paul Morgan. Is he in?"

"I'm Mrs. Morgan. Is Paul expecting you?" She asked them.

"No, ma'am." Anthony jumped in.

"Well, hold on then." She responded and closed the door. Seconds passed and then a tall, speckled man came to the door.

180

"Can I help you?" He asked.

"Paul Morgan?" Anthony asked him.

"Yes." He answered. Charla began to cry. Dr. Morgan came out onto the porch, shutting the door behind him. "What is going on?" He asked.

"We're your children, sir. That's what's going on." Anthony told him.

"What the hell are you talking about?" He asked Anthony. Anthony filled Dr. Morgan in on what had happened and the latter's shoulders slumped. He led the pair out onto the sidewalk. "I must be honest. I knew about you, Charla, from the beginning. I gave your mother money so that you would be taken care of. I even pay for your education. I knew that eventually you would show up here. I did not know about you Anthony. I did not. I don't know what to say." He removed his glasses and wiped his eyes with a handkerchief from his pocket.

"Why didn't you want me?" Charla asked him.

"I had a wife and a family already, Charla. I didn't want to lose my home over a woman that I'd had a fling with. All I can say is that

181

I'm sorry to you both."

"What about now?" Anthony asked him.

"Now maybe it's time I had a talk with my wife. The two of you need to meet your brother and sister." He told them. "Just give me a little time."

Charla and Anthony rode back to their grandparents' house in silence. *Their grandparents,* Charla thought. She still loved Anthony. Her feelings weren't just going to change overnight.

"I still love you, Anthony." She told him tearfully.

There was an awkward silence and then he said, "Charla, you were the best thing that ever happened to me, but you know that we can't do this. It isn't right. I mean, you're my sister."

"I don't care, Anthony. I know you as the man that I've been dating for two years. I love you like a woman loves a man. There's no reason why we can't still be together."

"Listen to yourself, Charla. What are we gonna do -- finish college and get married? Live happily ever after? Hell, if Penelope thinks I'm messed up wait until she sees our kids. I can't do it, Charla. I just can't. It isn't right." He told her.

He loved Charla but his feelings for her had absolutely changed.

182

Just the thought of some of the things that they had done in the backseat of his car…they'd never went past third base, but he was still embarrassed just thinking about the things that they had done. Charla, on the other hand, was heartbroken. They were over just like that. In the blink of an eye, her whole life had changed and Anthony had the nerve to treat her like she was some incest crazed nympho.

When they got back to the house, Miranda and Jack were waiting for them. Penelope had gone home. Charla went up to her room and started packing.

"What are you doing?" Miranda asked her.

"I'm going to Jackie's." Charla said sobbing.

Miranda shut the bedroom door and took her granddaughter's hands and pulled her down to sit beside her on the bed.

"What's wrong, honey?' Miranda asked Charla, smoothing her hair away from her face.

"I'm so hurt, Gram." She sobbed to her grandmother. "I'm in love with my own brother. What kind of sick feeling is that? And he's over it just like that. " Charla snapped her fingers.

"Oh, honey. I knew that this would be hard for you two. I'm so sorry, Charla." Miranda said to her granddaughter as she cried her eyes out. She watched as Charla packed a bag and left the house to go to her friend's.

"How is she?" Jack asked her.

"She's heartbroken, Jack."

"Yeah, so is he." Jack told her.

In spite of not wanting to be with Charla as a man is with a woman, Anthony still had to get over what the two of them had had together. She had been his first love and he would never forget her for that, but the dynamics of their relationship had changed and so should their behavior. Anthony sat at the dining room table with his head in his hands and cried.

They went back to school separately. Charla drove her truck back to college alone and Jack drove Anthony back. He loved his grandson already and was grateful to Maria and Old Davis Mitchell for loving him and giving him a good home. The boy had turned out well and he knew he had them to thank for it. He just wished that he'd had the opportunity to do it in person.

They saw each other around campus at times. They both were healing so they didn't speak. The awkwardness was still there and they didn't know how to bypass it. Months passed between them in silence, and during vacation time they would alternate visits to their grandparents. Anthony started to miss Charla and wanted to see her. He did not know that she felt the same. So one day to his surprise, as he was sitting in the library, his sister came and sat down beside him.

"I need help passing calculus." She said, not knowing how he would respond.

"Failing?" He asked her jokingly. He was so glad that she was there.

"Really bad." She said to him and smiled.

"Got your book?" He asked.

"Right here." She said, patting her book bag. *You will not cry.*

"I have some time if you do." He said to her and shrugged his shoulders.

And so they sat, Charla and Anthony together, and learned how to be brother and sister.

TRADING PLACES II

That day started like any other – almost. Judge William S. Thomas, III, sat in his chambers and enjoyed his morning coffee while he read the newspaper. *What a shame*. The local Philly gangs were murdering one another in record numbers. The police were conducting raids in the most dangerous parts of the city in an attempt to get the most notorious of these miscreants off the streets to prevent further instigation of the gang war.

A bunch of fiends, he thought to himself. He had nothing but contempt for these people who he thought to be common thugs. They were a drain on society – murdering and thieving from honest people who got up every day to earn an honest living. There was no excuse for an able-bodied person – man or woman for that matter – to not remain focused on their upward mobility. One's measure of success was defined by their accomplishments.

He couldn't understand what was wrong with today's generation. Young, single mothers collecting welfare checks as a way of life as they raced one another to the finish line to bring the next generation of lowlifes into the world; young men selling drugs and corrupting their neighborhoods. Well, he wouldn't stand for it. Not in his courtroom. He did not have a reputation for leniency. No, he would lock their useless asses up faster than their heads could spin. And their mothers! Oh, they would cry their hearts out for their "babies". They would sit there in his courtroom sobbing into tissues for their sons – ha. He would look the thug's mother in the eye seeming genuinely concerned, and then he would say to her, his tone dripping with sincerity, *I know you didn't mean for him to turn out like this, ma'am*. He should have been an actor. He chuckled to himself. What he really wanted to say is, *hey lady, as far as I'm concerned, your son's a deadbeat and lunch is at noon*. Innocent until proven guilty his ass. Everyone knew that was a crock of bull. He shook his head as he went over his cases for the morning. Same thing, different day.

Just as he was donning his robe there was a knock on the door. "Come in."

In walked George Miller, an old colleague and good friend of his. They'd once worked for the same law firm in Pittsburgh before George went into practice for himself and William decided to run for judge. George had been one of his strongest supporters. He now had a very lucrative law practice and defended wealthy criminals.

George had become portly over the years. His gray hair was starting to thin up top and he wore it in that ridiculous comb over that men tried to convince themselves covered their bald spot. William still had all of his hair and was proud of it – thick and black with strands of salt handsomely placed in his immaculately groomed beard and at the temples. He ate well and kept himself in good shape.

"William, old chum, how are you?" George asked, sitting across from the judge.

"I'm wonderful. Damn fine even. How's Maryann?"

"Just fine, her and the girls."

"Good. What brings you by?"

"A favor."

"Okay." William said, settling into the plush leather of his chair. "I'm curious."

"You know, Judge Mahon is out on a family emergency. His son is stationed in Malaysia – you know he's military?"

The judge nodded.

"Well, something happened to the judge's granddaughter – she got hurt or something – so he flew out to check on them. Well, just so happens, there's a guy here in lockup by the name of Marco Locke who's waiting to see Mahon. Over the weekend, Marco got pulled over on a routine traffic stop. He and the cop had some words, somehow Marco ends up outside of the car where he fights with the cop and is arrested for assault on a police officer and resisting. While he's in the back of the squad car, the cops search his vehicle, and what do they find, but an ounce of marijuana under the driver's seat. They take him in and he was scheduled to go before Judge Mahon again this morning."

"Does he have any priors?" The judge asked.

"He's on probation right now for joyriding."

"How old is he?"

"Twenty-two. Young punk." George said with disgust.

The judge raised an eyebrow and stared at his friend. "You seem to be taking this thing with this Marco kid personally. What's up, George?"

George leaned forward in his seat. "I'm going to level with you, Will. This punk knocked my Marissa up -- touched my little girl with his nasty, mongrel hands. He's trying to get her to run off with him. She thinks she's in love with him! I put too much money into that girl's education and I'll be damned if she becomes the breeder for some gypsy idiot."

"What about the baby?" William asked, sorry for his friend.

"I don't know." George said, looking exhausted. "I need to get this guy away from her or she's going to ruin her life."

"With the clients you have, George?" The judge said, alluding to the rich organized crime figures that George sometimes represented. "Why don't you get somebody to rough him up a little, you know?"

"You think I didn't think of that? She may be stupid for this guy but she's my child, Will – she's not an idiot. She knows who I am and she knows that I can't stand this punk. If that boy gets hurt Marissa is going to look right at me. She'll never speak to me again. I can't lose my little girl."

"What can I do, George?" The judge asked even though he could see where the conversation was going.

190

"Like I said, Judge Mahon's docket has been cancelled today but you know how he is. He's going to let that boy walk right out of here. He's violated probation, Will. Send him to Lewisburg for a while until I can figure out what to do about Marissa and the baby. She won't listen to me while he's around."

"Yeah, I don't know, George. This is Mahon's case. I get the feeling that I should sit this one out." William told him sympathetically.

"Help me out, Will. This kid was driving around with dope in his car."

"What does he say about the dope?"

"He said it isn't his. So what."

William smiled. "Was it really his dope, George? You didn't set that boy up, did you?"

"What does it matter, William?"

"So much for a routine traffic stop, eh?"

"You're in no position to preach about what's the moral thing to do. He's a criminal. He'll survive, trust me."

The judge didn't say anything so George added, "There's always something in it for you, Will."

William stood and adjusted his robe. "Take care, old friend." He said to George and extended a hand.

George nodded and after they shook, he grabbed his briefcase and exited the judge's chambers.

*   *   *

The clerk called the case and the judge watched as young Marco Locke was escorted by the courtroom guards to stand before the judge at the bench. In the back of the courtroom sat a heavily clothed woman. She looked to be in her mid-sixties. She had been staring intently at the judge all morning as he handled his docket, her dark eyes unblinking. William had saved Mr. Locke until last and they were alone in the courtroom except for the judge's staff, the district attorney, court appointed counsel, George and the old woman.

William glanced at the young man -- dark haired and muscular. Yes, poor gullible Marissa had wrapped her anxious, young legs right around this one.

"Judge, this case is actually on Judge Mahon's docket. I see that this is the only case of his that you have and I think there's been

some –"

The defense attorney was interrupted by the judge who held his

hand up to silence him.

"Mr. Donaldson, I am handling this case today until Judge Mahon

returns or other arrangements are made. I understand that your

client has pled not guilty to the charges of resisting and assaulting

a police officer as well as a plea of not guilty on the possession of

marijuana."

"Yes, Your Honor, but we ask that this case be held -- we are in

negotiations with the prosecution to dispose of Mr. Locke's case in

lieu of trial. There is new information that needs to be brought to

the judge's attention –"

George sat forward in his seat.

"Information? What information?" The judge asked.

"Well, Judge –"

The judge held his hand up again, impatient with Donaldson's

hesitation.

"What information?" He asked again, turning to the prosecuting attorney.

"I'm not sure, Judge." Michael Mills, the district attorney responded. "This information would be new to me as well."

"Well, since we don't know when Judge Mahon will return and we have no idea what this new information is," the judge said, watching a wary Mr. Donaldson over his glasses, "then I'll set bond at $100,000. If the family can post ten percent of the bond then Mr. Locke can await his court date with Judge Mahon at home." The judge told them. The woman seated in back began to cry into her scarf.

"Ten percent? Your Honor, the family can't afford that? Maybe --" Mr. Donaldson guffawed.

Marco Locke looked nervously back and forth between his attorney and the judge. "But it wasn't my drugs, sir. I swear! I fought that policeman, but I was defending myself, and I've been doing everything that Judge Mahon –"

The judge ignored the young man. "That's the bond, Mr. Donaldson."

"Your Honor, Judge Mahon –"

"Good day, Mr. Donaldson." The judge told him.

When the judge returned to his chambers, he removed his robe and stretched, yawning. He had done a good favor for his friend -- that's how he saw it. Now it was George's job to make sure that Marco waited for Judge Mahon in prison in Lewisburg. He rolled up his sleeves and checked the time on his Rolex. *Ah, time for lunch.*

*   *   *

Lewisburg, Pennsylvania

Gino Antonnaci reclined in his cell and stared curiously at his food wondering what manner of road kill they were slinging today. He cursed Andov for what had to have been the thousandth time. He had taken the beef for him on a gun charge and ended up here having to serve a little time. Already a felon, Gino had been sentenced to five years inside. His uncle Andov was a big guy in Philly and the cops were always sniffing around trying to pin something on him, and since they could never catch him doing anything substantial, they would take whatever they could get. Gino had felt that his uncle was too old to take the clip, so when the cops had pulled them over, Gino had taken the gun and put it in his belt. The gun was just a throw away and he knew that there weren't any bodies on it so he'd said fuck it. Of course, Andov never tried to stop him anyway, but Gino could handle it. He was in his element. The only thing he couldn't deal with was the fucking food.

Lock-up had gotten boring. Some of the other prisoners had tried him at first to make a rep for themselves, which he had welcomed. He'd needed the exercise. They needed to know that he wasn't taking shit way before they even knew that his homeboys were there on mafia row. He'd broken his fair share of bones in his two year stay. He liked to hear the crack. It was very satisfying to him. What was the word – soothing, yes. Now he lived in his cell alone. He worked out and read a lot but it still was dull at times and somewhat lonely. *Somewhat.* He would rather live alone than try and sleep with a psychotic perv in his cell. All his old cellies had ended up hurt and it wasn't his fault that some people didn't know how to get along with others. He lay down on his bed and yawned.

"Open cell eight."

196

Gino was interrupted from his doze by the guard yelling for his cell to be opened. *What the hell did he do now?* He jumped down off the top bunk where he had been reclining and watched as the bars to his cell slid back.

"Antonnaci, front and center."

Gino stepped out of his cell and came face to face with the guard who had been screaming on the tier.

"Convict, you got a new cellmate."

"You can kiss my ass in the crack, CO." Gino spat at him. "You put a motherfucker in there with me and I'll send his ass right back out to you all broke the fuck up."

"That's a real smart mouth you got there, ain't it? Too bad it's not your decision."

Gino glared at the CO as his new cellmate was being walked down the aisle by three officers, shackled hands and feet. He was about the same height as Gino but younger. He reminded him of himself the first time he had come to the joint.

Marco was also observing the man that he was to room with. He thought that this man was the most hideous looking person that he had ever seen. He was about ten years older than himself. He had thin, black hair that was slicked down on his head so tightly that it looked to Marco to be painted on. His skin was terribly scarred with acne and he hardly had any whites in his eyes. They were black as night. As the two men stood there staring at each other Marco thought to himself, *this sonofabitch ain't got no soul.*

"Marco Locke, meet Gino Antonacci. You two should get along real well." The CO said as he snickered with his cronies.

Marco looked to the guard and then back at Gino again. The other man stared back at him and raised both eyebrows simultaneously and then gave Marco a big, toothy grin. Marco shuddered involuntarily as he suddenly caught the willies. *Not a hello grin,* Marco thought, *but more like a hungry dog or something.* Gino stepped aside to allow Marco entrance into the cell. The guards followed to unchain the new prisoner and then left the two men in the cell alone, closing the bars behind them. The two stood there silently sizing each other up.

"You a faggot?" Gino asked him, crossing his muscular arms over his chest and rocking on the balls of his feet.

"Why? You like faggots?" Marco whispered, offended by Gino's

198

use of the word. He refused to be bitched by this hideous man. He mockingly licked his lips and gave Gino an appreciative look. The other man became instantly agitated as Marco knew he would. Gino could feel his head starting to pound behind his eyes. This guy was beginning to creep him out like no other. He stepped forward and got in the other man's face and pointed his finger at him.

"You're a fucking faggot, ain't you?"

"Not this month." Marco replied calmly, sensing Gino's discomfort. If the man wanted to behave like a dumb brute then he would treat him like one.

Gino knew that the younger man was purposely trying to put him on edge in an attempt to goad him into a fight. The tables had turned on Gino.

"Don't stress yourself. You ain't my type anyway."

"You try some faggot shit and I'll crack your fucking head wide open." Gino shouted into his face.

"Ooh, yeah. That's what I like. Give it to me, big daddy." Marco teased him.

The fight was on. Gino threw the first punch which Marco ducked, bringing his fist up and catching Gino square in the stomach. When he doubled over more in surprise than pain, Marco swiftly brought his knee up and caught Gino hard in the face.

Gino fell back against the bars in the small cell and Marco quickly ran toward him with a flying kick. Gino rolled to the side, avoiding Marco, and swept the boy's leg bringing Marco tumbling to the ground. He immediately jumped atop the younger man and began to rain blows upon him, slamming his fist repeatedly into Marco's face. For a while, Marco struggled beneath him, but then he finally succeeded in flipping the bulky man off of him. Gino grabbed Marco by the collar and hurled the young man across the tiny room where he fell hard against the toilet. Gino sprung upon him and grabbed him by the head and attempted to drown him in the toilet water.

Marco flailed about but the bigger man was leaning all his weight upon him and Marco couldn't break free. After several seconds of struggling, Marco finally went limp. Gino leaned over to try and get a look at his face and suddenly Marco came back to life and backed his buttocks into Gino's groin and gyrated his hips. The

older man leapt away from him as if he had been stung and fell
hard against the bunk. Groaning, Marco sat back against the toilet
and grinned at him as blood dripped from his face.

"That's all it took to get you off of me, huh, lover?"

They both stared at each other and then began to laugh
hysterically. When they both had gotten control of themselves,
Marco began cleaning the blood from his face.

"Look," he said to Gino, " I ain't no faggot but I ain't nobody's
bitch neither." He stared at Gino with a challenge in his eyes.
"We can do this every day if you want to, mister -- don't make me
no difference. Or, we can do our time in peace. I ain't got no
problems with you." He said. "Now how you wanna do this?"

"I guess I could use the company." Gino told him. The boy had
earned his respect.

"Shit, you're ugly." Marco said.

"Yeah?" Gino said, cocking his head toward a mirror that was
lying on the table. "You ain't no shining peach no more yourself.
Now which bunk you want?"

Selene Locke stood uncomfortably against a wall in the reception area of the prison. She hated her baby brother being in this repulsive place. Selene wrinkled her nose in disdain as she looked around at the other women who were there as well. She heard her name being called and got up to follow the guard into a room in the back of the jail. After going through the metal detector, she cooperated patiently as they checked in her shoes and inside her mouth for contraband and then jumped slightly as the female guard patted her down.

Once inside the visiting area, she quickly spotted Marco. His dark head was bent as he sat back in his seat. He seemed to be deep in thought. He looked up as she approached him and smiled and she ran and hugged him, almost crying when she saw how bruised his face was.

"What happened to you, Marco?' She asked.

"I got into a fight with my cell mate." He told her. "We get along like peas and carrots now."

"Are you telling me the truth, Marco?" She asked her brother, eying him suspiciously. "Did he take your –"

"No, no." Marco told her. "If that had happened I'd be in the

202

morgue. He would have had to kill me."

Selene exhaled a breath of relief. She knew that Marco would stand up for himself.

Marco eyed his sister lovingly. She had always been there for him. She and his grandmama had raised him all by themselves after their parents were killed when he was a boy. Unmarried and childless, his sister was a serious woman who rarely smiled. Though lovely, petite and dark haired, Selena remained alone, preferring instead to take care of Marco and their grandmother. They were from the Roma, a band of gypsies, but their grandmother had took the children and left the nomadic tribe to make a real home for Selene and Marco.

"I know this has something to do with that spoiled bitch, Marissa. You just can't stay away from her." Selene said angrily.

"I love her, Selene." And then, "She's pregnant."

"I can't believe you, Marco!" Selene exclaimed.

"Selene, I need your help. I have to get out of here or Marissa's father is going to make her get rid of the baby. I want you to talk to the judge."

Ah, now he wanted her to use magic when he had always been so against it. Selene didn't believe in abortion either no matter how much she disliked Marissa. Besides, that would be her niece or nephew.

"You're being a hypocrite, Marco." She told him with her arms folded. She couldn't let it go.

Marco paused, becoming impatient with his sister. Now wasn't the time to rub his face in things. "I'm asking you for your help as my sister."

Selene shook her head. "Grandmama told me about that wicked judge who sent you here. She thinks he's a devil. I wanted to do something anyway but you're always such a goody-goody. So what shall it be your Highness, flesh eating disease?" She asked him sarcastically.

"Only if he's unwilling to mend his ways." Marco told her.

He has such a good heart, Selene thought.

"What will you do?" He asked her.

Selene didn't want him to change his mind so she held his hands in her own and said, "Don't worry, Marco, I'll take care of it."

Judge Thomas stood in front of the vending machine and picked through the change in his pocket. After counting out the correct amount, he began to feed the coins into the vending machine one at a time. One lone dime continued to be rejected and fell out again and again as he fed it into the machine. *Damn it*, he didn't have another.

"Here, I have one." A female voice said behind him.

The judge turned to see a beautiful young woman standing behind him -- petite and dark haired with lovely hazel eyes. The judge looked down at her and smiled when he saw the dime she was holding out to him in her small left hand.

"Trade you." She said to him in a friendly tone as she smiled prettily up at him.

"Why thank you." He told her appreciatively as they exchanged dimes. The judge turned back to the vending machine and sure enough the dime worked on the first try.

He turned back to the young woman and she said, "You're a judge, right?"

"Why yes, I am." The judge responded, enjoying her attention.

"Do you have a case here this morning." *Aren't you a pretty little thing*, the judge thought to himself as he looked her over.

"No." She replied. "I was hoping to speak with you about my brother, Marco." She didn't elaborate. He knew damn well who she was speaking about.

The judge's demeanor changed and he stared coolly at the woman. "I believe that is a case that Judge Mahon is over. Correct?"

"True, but you sent my brother to prison. You set him up. I know you did." Selene told him directly.

The judge was taken aback by the accusing tone that the young woman was using.

"Young woman, be very careful about the next words that come out of your mouth." The judge told her. His eyes quickly scanned the empty hallway.

"No, you be careful." Selene told him as she took a step towards him. "My brother wants to give you a chance to mend your ways. If it was up to me, you would be crawling on your belly at Marco's feet right now."

Huh, the judge thought to himself.

"Are you threatening me?" He asked surprised. "Listen, get your
206

ass out of here before I have you locked up. Maybe you didn't know this, but you can't threaten judges." He whispered in a mean tone. "Your brother is exactly where he should be."

"So to you, so to me; so to mine, so to yours." Selene said to him as she rolled the dime between her fingers.

The young woman brought her pretty little hand to her mouth and blew the judge a kiss. He could feel the warmth of her breath slide across his lips as sure as if she had kissed him. Her brown eyes glittered dangerously.

"Did you just try to put a hex on me, you dumb little –"

The judge smiled and waved at his clerk as she left the courtroom and proceeded down the hall toward the elevators. When he turned again, the young woman had disappeared as if she'd somehow vanished into thin air. Uneasy and upset, the judge stormed off to his chambers and slammed the door.

"William, I'd like to have a word with you please."

It was a week later and Judge Thomas was just heading home for the evening. It was late and he hadn't been feeling well for days now. He just wasn't in the mood for chit chat. He turned to see Carl Mahon standing behind him. Carl had his hands in his pockets and a frown upon his brow.

"Carl, how are you? I didn't realize that you were back. How was your trip?" He asked him, wondering why the other man was always so uptight.

While they had always been respectful to each other they had never really hit it off. Neither man ever said more than he had to, to the other.

"Just fine." Carl said, dismissing the pleasantries with a wave of his hand. "I wanted to ask you about a case that you handled for me while I was away. A Marco Locke. "

"Okay." Judge Thomas said. He began to become nervous. He was tired of this boy.

"Okay? Why was that the only case you took? I was told that Donaldson informed you that there was confidential information that had surfaced concerning the case. Why did you send that young man to Lewisburg? He's not a hardened criminal, William."

"If he ended up in Lewisburg – I don't know what to tell you, Carl. The young man somehow ended up in my courtroom and so I

208

handled it for you. It's your case. You're here now and you're free

to do what you have to with it. Listen I have to go, Carl. See you

tomorrow." Judge Thomas said, turning to walk away.

"This wouldn't have anything to do with George Miller's daughter,

would it, William?"

Judge Thomas stopped dead in his tracks.

"I know that Miller was in your courtroom when you set Locke's

bond. He visited with you in chambers before you took the bench

that morning and then all of a sudden the guy who's making time

with his daughter ends up in your courtroom and then in a prison

that he's nowhere near ready for. What are you thinking,

William?" Carl said to him in disbelief.

William turned back to Carl and jabbed a finger into his chest.

"What are you accusing me of, Carl? Do you know how long I've

been on the bench? How dare you criticize any ruling –"

"You pompous, arrogant bastard!" Judge Mahon whispered to him

angrily through clenched teeth. "You and George set that boy up.

Don't you lie to me. You didn't follow my recommendation. You

didn't listen to a thing that Donaldson had to say –"

"What proof do you have of that? I'm a respected judge that's been on the bench for ten years. No one is going to believe that. Come now, Carl."

"George set that young man up. He paid that cop to plant that dope and Donaldson is going to prove it. The two of you are not going to ruin that boy's life because Miller's daughter can't keep her legs closed. You'd better watch your back, William." Carl said before walking away with his head down and hands in his pockets. Judge Thomas coughed into his hand and pulled the collar of his coat up around his neck as he left the courthouse. *Damn it*, he swore to himself.

On the drive home he tried to get in contact with George. He wanted to give him the heads up on what had just happened with Mahon. There was no answer when he called his cell, so he left a message and then tried him at his home. Maryann told him that George was running a little late but that she expected him soon and would have him call William as soon as he made it in. Was he all right, she had asked him. Sure, sure, he'd said, but please be sure to give George the message. After he'd hung up, he went into

210

another coughing spell. That damn gypsy cunt had given him a cold or something when she'd blew him the kiss.

As he drove along on that snowy, dark night he thought about what Carl had said to him. He wasn't trying to sabotage the young man's life at all. He had his whole life ahead of him anyway. With persistence, he would eventually make something of himself. Besides, now was a good time for him to learn when the right time was to stay in his place.

The judge squinted his eyes and peered into the night. Up ahead there looked as if an animal of some sort was standing in the road. He slowed down and turned on his brights. Realizing that it was nothing, the judge sped up again, wanting to get home out of the cold. He needed something for this cough.

Suddenly, out of nowhere something ran into the road right in the path of his vehicle. The judge turned the steering wheel to the right in an attempt to avoid hitting it and slid on the icy road, losing control of the car and colliding with a tree. He hit his head hard on the steering wheel and almost passed out.

When he looked up he thought he saw someone approaching his

car. *It's probably some dumb ass that stepped out in front of me,* he thought. His head was pounding and he was still dazed.

William tried to open the door but it was stuck, so he scooted himself over to the passenger side of the car and pushed the door open. That's when he saw her crawling around on the ground outside his car like an animal. This startled the judge so badly that he started to scream. His unheard shrieks bounced off the trees in the wooded area. The judge jumped away and threw himself against the driver's door. He was trapped. He watched her as she crept steadily towards him into the car on all fours, her dark hair long and disheveled. The judge was paralyzed with terror.

The last thing that the judge heard before he lost consciousness was her animal-like growl. "So to you, so to me."

When Judge Thomas regained consciousness, he was in the back of an ambulance. *Thank God*, he thought. Someone had found him. He tried to get up but found that he was handcuffed to a gurney. He closed his eyes and it all came back to him. That damn girl was crawling around outside his car. He must have been hysterical when the paramedics reached him.

212

The police had to be out there preparing to tow his car. He must have been fighting them after being so frightened by the sight of that she-devil. He couldn't believe that she had literally been crawling around out there on all fours as stealthily as any four legged creature. *Crazy bitch,* he thought. He was going to have her picked up for harassment. She was clearly obsessed.

"Mr. Thomas, how are you, sir? I'm Officer Stanley Gold."

"Officer, you have no idea how thankful I am that you found me. I could've froze to death. My car was undrivable I'm sure?" The judge queried.

The officer nodded to the judge. "So that is your vehicle?"

"Yes, yes. Now will you please release me from these dreaded handcuffs."

"I'm sorry, sir, but I can't do that. I'm afraid you're under arrest." The officer told him.

"What!" The judge exclaimed.

"Sir, we found a kilo of cocaine and an envelope with fifty grand in it in your briefcase." The cop told him.

"That's ridiculous. Uncuff me now!" He shouted at the officer.

"Do you know who I am?"

"I do, sir." The officer nodded. "With all due respect to you, Judge, I'm just doing my job. Once we get to the station you can call your lawyer."

Judge Thomas stood before the bench in shock. He could not believe his predicament.

"William Thomas III, how do you plead to the charge of possession of two ounces of cocaine?"

William looked up at Judge Carl Mahon and smirked. This asshole had made sure that he didn't get any special treatment.

"Judge, my client will plead not guilty." George Miller said to the judge. Sweat beaded on his forehead and he was hot beneath his expensive suit.

The Locke family sat in the courtroom and observed Judge Thomas' dilemma. George had been having nightmares about them ever since he and William had sent Marco to Lewisburg. In one dream, he was lying in bed alone and was covered with what seemed to be thousands of scorpions. He couldn't move and they would crawl all over him. He could even feel them crawling around inside him. They wouldn't sting; they would just crawl.

"A not guilty plea will be entered on behalf of your client, Mr. Miller." The judge was saying. "No bond will be given at this time. Mr. Thomas is believed to be a flight risk."

"Judge, I assure you that my client is not a flight risk. He has been a respected member of this community and –"

"No. Bond." The judge said, directed more to William than to his attorney. "Mr. Thomas will be remanded into custody until such time as a judge is appointed to handle his case."

"And when will that be?" William asked the judge with a sneer on his face.

The judge leaned forward and gave William a phony smile. "I'm sorry, Mr. Thomas. This is not my case. Guard, take the defendant please."

"Hey, man. Did you hear?"

It was that black guy Sonny. He had earned trustee status at the prison and was in good with some of the guards as well as the prisoners. Yeah, Sonny was okay. He kept Gino up on the latest --

kept him in the loop so to speak. No one talked to Gino because that's the way he wanted it, but Sonny was all right. He gave Sonny a look that said he wasn't really interested in what he had to say even though he was. The black man rolled his eyes and sat down in the seat across from him.

"Man, they shippin' that judge here. You know the one got caught with the dope. Did you hear?"

Sonny was so excited that he was almost bouncing up and down in his seat. Gino raised his eyebrows at him now with genuine interest. *Say what?*

Sonny rolled his eyes again. "Damn, man. Did you hear or not?" Dominic stared at Sonny impatiently and shrugged his shoulders. Sonny shook his head and rubbed a big, brown hand across his face.

"I know you ain't heard, man, 'cause you don't talk to nobody. You need to be nicer to people – affable and cordial – you know, an outgoing fellow like myself and maybe they'd tell yo' white ass something." He said this to Gino as if his life depended on it. Gino smiled against his will. Yeah, Sonny was all right. He never had to wonder where he was coming from.

216

"What's this here you wanna tell me, Sonny boy?" He asked him as he leaned back in his chair again.

"I ain't been nobody's boy for a long time, and I sure in hell ain't yours." Sonny quipped returning his smile. He liked this white boy. He didn't take no shit.

"So why send him here? I thought judges got special treatment or something." Gino said.

Sonny leaned forward and looked around as if he were giving out confidential information. "I don't know, but you know how many muthafuckas he done locked up in here, man?" He said with special emphasis on every word. " Pssh. They waiting on his ass."

"Who's this guy again?"

"Judge William Thomas, man. Damn don't you know nothing?" Sonny got up and walked away, eager to share his news with other inmates.

Gino leaned back in his chair again. *Maybe it might just get a little interesting around here after all,* he thought to himself.

The following day the prison was all in a buzz about the arrival of the newest inmate. Everybody wanted to have a look at him. Gino didn't see the difference between him and any other new inmate.

"Open cell eight."

Gino didn't leave his bunk this time. The CO solemnly escorted the judge into the cell and then left without a word. The judge seemed stunned.

"Hey." Gino said. "Which bunk you want?"

William sighed. *What did he care*, he thought, shrugging to the other man.

Gino watched the judge for a while then said, "My old cell mate took the top bunk. You know good cellies are hard to come by. My old cellie, Marco -- we got along real well."

Judge Thomas sat down and put his head in his hands. He would never be free of that boy. Gino leapt from the bunk and walked over to the judge, pushing up his sleeves. Gino yanked the judge up by his collar and threw him to the floor. When William tried to get up, Gino kicked him hard in the buttocks and laughed.

"Get up, fish."

A C E D I A

Lazy bones, Lazy bones
Clean up your house
Lazy bones, Lazy bones
I thought I saw a mouse

You been wearing them socks so long
They stand up on they own

Why you up here lying around?
Oh, I see
You got the drowns

Honey, you hurting bad?
I knew it that you was sad
Why did you wait so long?
You don't have to go through this alone

What's got you down so bad?
Oh, Mattie left you and now you mad
She left 'cause she said you what?
Wouldn't get up off your butt
Yea, honey, I understand
You just wasn't her kind of man

How long since you quit that job?

You know the one where you hauled for Bob

Oh, that work was just too hard

What about the one where you worked as a guard?

You quit that 'cause you what?

Had to get up off your butt

Yea, I understand

You just ain't that kind of man

To chase after thieving crooks

But now you got nothing to cook

And you expect poor Mattie to stand

And take care of a grown ass man

Man, you is something weak

Get your lazy butt on your feet

CIRCLES

Marilyn lay on the porch swing and swung lazily back and forth as she inhaled the fragrant smoke into her lungs. She closed her eyes as the marijuana started to take effect and relaxed as a tingling, warm sensation settled into her body. She had gotten this tree from Derek and it burned so good. She swung lazily back and forth on the swing. One leg dangled over the side, but her thick ankles and toes barely touched the concrete beneath.

She could feel the warm breeze tickling the fine hairs on her arms and legs. The heat that radiated from the Florida sun was warm and felt magnificently good on her body. The gentle, swaying motion of the swing lulled her off to sleep. She just wanted to doze off and sleep until -- but she couldn't just yet. Her eyes snapped open. She had to make this run for Derek. She had promised. He was going to give her an eighth of the same tree when she returned. She had a heavy marijuana habit that she couldn't afford to support, so she hustled a little here and there on the side. So when Derek had asked her to drop this package off she'd said no problem. *No problem, bro,* she said again to herself.

She lazily pulled her short, two hundred pound frame up and off the porch swing. She stretched then, her thick arms lifted high above her head and then she was off. In her marijuana induced state, she still made it to the address in good time. She'd only turned down one wrong street. Whenever she went the wrong way, she always blamed the GPS. She didn't want to admit to herself that she was too high and had probably zoned out when the robot lady voice said to turn right here or turn left there. *Screw her*, Marilyn thought as she put a cigarette in her mouth and pushed the car lighter in.

She pulled in front of the house and walked up the driveway and onto the porch. She could hear a T.V. on inside. Sam was chasing the bunny down the rabbit hole again. She beat on the steel, black screen door with the fleshy part of her fist and then waited.

Moments later, a bald-headed, tattooed guy came to the door.

"Yeah, what's up, girl?"

"Victor here?" She asked, ashing her cigarette over the rickety porch rail.

"Yo, I'm Victor. You Marilyn?"

Yeah." She said and nodded toward the car.

222

Victor followed her to the car and Marilyn got in behind the wheel and started the engine. She gestured towards the back seat for a dumbfounded Victor and waited. Once he reached in and took the package, Marilyn drove off and left him there standing in the middle of the street staring after her.

She went back to Derek's and laid down on the porch swing again. *Back in no time – easy peasy.* She relit her joint and leisurely puffed on it for a while before putting it out. She began to swing again as she stared out into the street. The kids were outside playing. Some of the children were riding bicycles while some little girls jumped rope at the corner. Ice cream trucks drove slowly through the neighborhood. *Trying to get them kids' dollars*, Marilyn thought to herself as she dozed there on the porch swing.

"Wake up, gal. Get up!" Somebody was yanking on her arm.

"Whatcha want, man?" Marilyn asked irritated. She opened one eye and stared into Derek's skinny face.

"You make that delivery?"

"Yeah, man." She answered.

"Well, come in the house then. Why you out here like that?"

Marilyn got up and went into the house with Derek. She sat down on the couch and Derek pulled a pair of rolling papers from his pocket and asked her, "You wanna blaze?"

"Yes, man. What you think?" Marilyn got up and went to the bathroom to clean herself up.

She stretched her body and yawned then sat down to pee. She had been sleeping good and easy on that porch swing. She needed one of those swings at her house. She washed her hands then went back out to smoke with Derek.

"Aye, baby gal. Thanks for handling that little business for me earlier." Derek said, passing her the joint. He went to the fireplace and grabbed a baggie of tree out of a canister on the mantle and handed it to her. "There's more where that came from."

"Man, this shit is so green." Marilyn said, lovingly opening the baggie. She deeply inhaled the strong aroma then rolled the baggie into a tight cylinder before folding it and placing it into her bra.

"That ain't no purse, girl. Chicks kill me doing that." Derek said to her laughing.

"Gotta keep that tree close to my heart, Dee." Marilyn told him.

224

"Seriously though, check this out." He said, leaning forward in his seat. "My homie owes me a favor on some money tip, right, but he ain't got that; he got somethin' else. You feel me?"

Marilyn nodded. "Why you not going then, Dee?" She asked as she passed the joint back.

"I need to be somewhere else. I mean, if you don't wanna do it –"

"How much?" She asked.

"I'll throw you an ounce and a hundred on top of that. What you think?"

Marilyn puffed the joint and thought about it. She had done this dozens of times – pick something up or drop it off. Simple. Plus, she knew Derek and he wouldn't put her in no shit and for a whole ounce of that fire…hell yeah.

"Straight. He gone be there 'bout ten o'clock. He say pull up and blink your headlights three times and he'll come to the car. After that you easy, baby. Just come on back, okay?"

"Cool." She answered as Derek handed her the address.

"Where you think you going?" She asked him smartly as he headed for the door.

"I'm 'bout to go get my freak on, gal. What you talkin' about?"
Marilyn laughed at Derek as he left. *You know your skinny ass ain't getting none,* she thought.

At 9:30 that evening, Marilyn had to drag herself from the couch. She drove the twenty minutes to the address that Derek had given her. She pulled up and parked then blinked her headlights three times and waited. Sure enough, Marilyn watched as a short, bearded man approached her car.

"You Marilyn?" He asked her.

"Yep."

"You know one of your headlights is out?"

"For real?" She asked irritated. "Naw, man. I didn't know, but thanks." She said as he handed her the brown paper bag through the open car window.

"Be careful." He told her and walked off.

Simple, Marilyn thought as she pulled her car out of the lot. She turned her music up and lit a joint. Oh, this was her song. Marilyn rocked and danced to the loud music that reverberated through her car. *These speakers are banging,* she thought happily. She noticed

226

the police car behind her just as she was about to get on the highway. *Oh, shit*, she thought. She turned the radio off and rolled all the windows down in the car. *Shit, shit, shit*, she thought to herself. Through the rearview mirror, she kept an eye on the cop car and slowly tried to lean over and open her glove compartment. The tips of her fingers would barely reach the handle of the compartment.

She scooted over in her seat, being careful not to let the car swerve and tried again to reach forward. *Damn it. She didn't want to look like she was reaching for shit*. She got the glove compartment open as she merged onto the highway. The squad car stayed directly behind her. She reached inside and grabbed the perfume then threw the heavy paper bag inside the compartment and closed it. *Breathe*, she told herself. She looked into the rearview mirror again as she sprayed the perfume around the car and noticed that the cop had moved a lane over and was several feet behind her. She mentally patted herself on the back for not panicking and slowly exhaled a pent up breath of relief and then *boom*! She rear ended the car in front of her. *Damn it*, she screamed at herself in the car.

The cop turned on his overhead lights and Marilyn and the other car were forced to pull over to the side of the road. The man in the front car jumped out and started screaming furiously. The cop walked over and tried to calm him down. Marilyn sat there for a moment. *Fine mess you done went and got yourself into.* She rolled up the windows and got out to see what the damage was. She couldn't believe this guy! There was hardly any damage to either car.

"You hit my car!" He screamed at her from behind the officer.

"Sir, I asked you to remain by your vehicle." The policeman told him, pointing towards his car. Reluctantly, the man backed away. Marilyn noticed that the cop was holding paperwork in his hand. *The guy's info probably. Kiss my ass,* she thought. She would have to go into the glove compartment for her registration and the cop would surely be watching her. He walked over to Marilyn. *Calm down*, she told herself.

"Ma'am, can you tell me what happened?"

"I think he hit his brakes too suddenly or something." Marilyn lied. The cop stared at her. His nose wrinkled. "Ma'am, have you been smoking marijuana?"

228

"I'm sorry what?" Marilyn asked.

"There's a very heavy odor of marijuana coming from you. Have you been smoking, ma'am?" He asked her.

"No." Marilyn lied again.

"Ma'am, why don't you walk over to my car with me." Marilyn followed him.

The officer got into his squad car and spoke on the radio then got back out and walked over to Marilyn.

"What's your name, ma'am?" He asked her. She told him then he asked her, "Ma'am, do you have any drugs in the car or on your person?"

"No." Marilyn lied.

Two more squad cars pulled up and a policeman exited one and a policewoman the other.

"Wait here, ma'am." He told her.

She watched as he walked over to the cops and spoke with them. Now she was shitting bricks. She looked over to the man who she'd rear ended and he smirked at her. He knew she was in trouble. The two male officers walked back towards the man and her car and the female officer approached her.

"Ma'am? Ma'am?" She heard the female officer say.

Marilyn's eyes were riveted on the two male cops. The newer one was shining a flashlight into her car and saying something to his partner. One of them approached and the female policewoman went over to speak with him. She came back to Marilyn.

"Ma'am, put your hands on the car please."

"What's going on?"

She placed her hands on the car as the female officer searched her -- the pockets of her shorts, inside her waist band, over her abdomen and under and over her breasts. *Shit.* The policewoman shook her head as a baggie of Derek's finest tree was pulled from her bra and placed on the trunk of the squad car.

"You're under arrest, ma'am, for the possession of marijuana. Place your hands behind your back please."

Marilyn watched in horror as one of the policemen opened her car door and got inside. Agonizing moments passed and then he got out. The paper bag that had been in the glove compartment was now tucked underneath his arm. As he approached she could see he was holding the joint that she'd carelessly thrown into the ashtray.

230

Marilyn allowed herself to be placed into the backseat of the squad car. She watched in disbelief as her car was towed away. The man that she had rear ended waved at her and got into his car and drove off. She knew what was in the aluminum foil inside the paper bag. *No, she didn't want to talk to no police.* That's what she told them. "I don't have nothin' to say."

It started to rain heavily. Fat drops of water hit the car as she rode behind the officer in the car. Her handcuffs were too tight. Twenty-three year old Marilyn began to cry.

WRATH

"You are so worthless." Anthony, Sr. was in one of his drunken rages again.

The three boys sat in the kitchen listening to their father berate their mother again. Anthony, Jr. sat at the table and bounced his head off the wall that he was leaning on. He just wanted to block out the sound of his mother upstairs screaming. John could see the veins bulging on the side of his brother's neck. He looked over at Michael, who stood at the window with a blank expression on his young face. It had been a long time since anyone in the house had took a beating. The boys were all but grown men now and bigger than their father.

Anthony, Sr. avoided John like the plague, sensing his son's hatred of him. Michael was hardly home, working as much as he could to stay away from the house. Anthony, Sr. was afraid of his sons and was careful not to hit Sonia when the boys were home. The last time that he had hit her in front of them, Anthony, Jr. had beat him so bad that he was laid up for a week. Their mother, Sonia, was a ghost in the house. She rarely left her room and hardly interacted with her sons.

Anthony, Sr. was drunk tonight and did not hear his sons enter the house. *No wonder Sonia wasn't right in the head*, John thought. Enough was enough. A person could only get their head cracked so many times before they started going coo coo.

He looked at his brothers and shook his head in disgust. Their mother didn't want them to get involved, but she had to understand that they weren't little boys anymore.

He was so done with this. John stood up from the table and rolled his sleeves up. Anthony looked up from the table at him and John nodded towards the upstairs and raised his eyebrows at him. They had talked about it for years but had never made a move. Anthony sat back in his chair and returned his brother's nod. John quietly gestured towards Michael, who had his back to them.

Understanding what John wanted, seventeen year old Anthony, Jr. got up from the table and asked his brother, Michael, to go outside with him to grab wood for a fire. The other two boys knew that Michael would try to stop them if he knew what they were thinking. Michael wouldn't talk about it and didn't want to hear

about it, thinking it the most terrible crime to harm one's parent.
Michael and Anthony put on their jackets and stepped outside.
Anthony, Jr. closed the door slowly, grinning mischievously at his
brother as he went. Once they were gone, John calmly walked up
the stairs to his room and picked up a three foot steel rod he had
found on his way home from school. Somehow he had known he
would find a use for it. He tossed it from hand to hand, testing its
weight, and then walked down the hallway and stood in the
doorway of his parent's bedroom. The door was ajar and he could
see Anthony, Sr. on top of his mother with one hand around her
throat. He was punching her in the face with his right hand. *Your
good hand, huh, Pops,* John thought to himself.

He pushed the door open all the way and crept into the room and
stopped directly behind his father. Sonia was on the floor on her
back under her husband trying to remove his hand from her throat.
When she saw her youngest son she froze and her eyes widened
when she saw the pipe that he was holding. Anthony, Sr., his fist in
midair preparing to strike, must have seen the surprise in her face.
He paused and turned around.

John raised the pipe like a baseball bat and put everything he had into the first swing. Anthony, Sr., caught off guard, tried to shield

his face by holding his hands out in front of him. John could hear

the crack as the first blow caught Anthony, Sr. across the face and

blood flew in an arc and splattered against the wall. He fell off of

Sonia, knocked out cold. John could hear his mother screaming

his name. He could hear the downstairs door slamming against the

kitchen counter and footsteps running up the stairs. He stepped

over his father and swung the pipe again.

Michael ran into the room and then fell back against the wall in

shock at the sight of his father lying still and bloody on the floor.

Anthony, Jr. sauntered leisurely into the room and leaned against

the door jamb, a huge smile on his face. John dropped the pipe and

stared at the bloody mess that had been his father. Chest heaving

from exertion, he squatted and inspected his work. Satisfied, he

got up and walked past his brothers and out of the room. With

unsteady legs, Sonia stood up and walked over to her husband,

spitting on him before going downstairs to comfort her son.

Bewildered, Michael looked over at his brother, Anthony, knowing

that he had tricked him into going outside with him. Anthony met his stare head on, challenging him to say anything. When he didn't, Anthony shrugged and left the room, whistling as he descended the stairs.

Michael sat with his head in his hands. He stood up and walked over to his father and stared down at him in disbelief. Anger surged through him to the point that he thought he'd explode. He looked at the steel pipe that his brother had dropped and then back at his father again. He clenched his fists and repeatedly punched the wood floor beneath him until his knuckles bled -- until he was exhausted. He was so furious. Grief stricken, he fell to his knees in front of his father and laid his head on his chest and sobbed.

When Geoffrey got the news, he wasn't angry or sorry for his brother, Anthony. Sr. In his mind this time was long overdue. He rushed to Chicago to see about John, who was his main concern. Even though his brothers had corroborated his story of self-defense, John, who was only sixteen, was still being held by the authorities, but Geoffrey knew that he could call in some favors. His plan was to take John back to Atlanta with him.

When he arrived at his brother's home his nephew, Michael, met

236

him at the door, embraced his uncle and asked about his trip.

Geoffrey felt bad for his nephew. Michael, who was only five

years older than John, was now expected to be the man of the

house. Young Michael's eyes were red and swollen and he looked

as if he hadn't slept.

"Where's your brother?" Geoffrey asked him, resting a hand on his

nephew's shoulder.

"He went to see John." Was his only reply.

"And your mother?"

Michael nodded toward the stairs as he took his uncle's coat.

Geoffrey ascended the stairs and stood in front of the closed door

preparing to knock, his fist paused midair. He lowered his hand to

the knob and turned it, pushing the door inward. Sonia stood at the

window and turned when she heard the door open.

He closed the door and walked over to her, standing beside her.

He was taken aback. Sonia was still to him so lovely. He

wondered if she was relieved to be rid of Anthony. He thought she

was still as beautiful as the first time he had laid eyes on her. It

had always been his regret that he had not met her first. He remembered the first time he had seen her after she had married his brother. She had been so happy and so full of life. Whenever he had come to visit, he had looked on her with longing. She had known of Geoffrey's feelings for her, but had made it clear that she intended to remain faithful to her husband. When his brother started to drink heavily, Geoffrey knew it would only be a matter of time before things started to fall apart, and when he saw his chance he took it, taking advantage of Sonia on one of his visits when she was most vulnerable.

Anthony had been so drunk much of the time that he could barely work to provide for Sonia and their two small children, and so Sonia bargained with Geoffrey to save her home. He had wanted her to come back to Atlanta with him but she refused, committed to staying with her husband, a brother that Geoffrey thought to be weak. He despised Anthony, Sr. for having what Geoffrey wanted the most, his Sonia. Over the years, his brother had slowly sucked her dry of all joy, and now she was void of the liveliness that she had once been so filled with.

"I've come to take him home with me, Sonia. You know that you're welcome as well." He said, standing behind her.

She behaved as if she hadn't heard him but he knew that she had. Sonia continued to stare out the window but smiled. *Geoffrey had always loved her and she had always loved Anthony,* she thought. In fact, she still loved him even though he had been such a terrible husband. She would probably always love him, but she would never forgive herself for what she had allowed him to do to her children and he had been a constant reminder of that. Things had happened exactly as they should have.

When she had realized that she was a failure she had stopped caring, retreating into her own world. She sometimes regretted not going with Geoffrey all those years ago. Her life certainly would have been very different. It was too late now. She was a damaged woman. She had made too many mistakes and she could never forgive herself. She turned and wrapped her arms around Geoffrey's neck.

He had never believed it when people said she was crazy. He returned her hug and then reluctantly let her go again for what seemed like the hundredth time.

She said, "Thank you, Geoffrey, for letting me keep him all this time. It's good that you've come for him now. Boys need their fathers."

They did not know that Michael was sobbing on the other side of the door.

N V

Valerie pulled up to the pump at the gas station and turned off the ignition. She looked over to her best friend, Tracy, and smiled. She was dozing in the passenger seat and she had drooled on her sweater. Valerie quietly snuck her cell phone from her purse and snapped two pictures of Tracy sleeping. These were going up on social media at midnight. Tracy was going to be so pissed at her tomorrow morning. She owed her one anyway for throwing that ice cold water on her while she was in the shower last week. She laughed to herself, smacking her hand against her thigh in elation then got out of the car to get gas.

Tracy awoke while Valerie was gone and yawned as she stretched her petite body in the small car. *Damn it, Valerie, you could've asked if I wanted a soda or something.* Valerie came out of the station holding two sodas and two bags of potato chips.

"You woke, sleepy head?" Valerie asked her.

"Girl, yes." Tracy replied, taking a soda from Valerie. "Those extra hours at Happy Burger are going to kill me, but I gotta get my money." She told Valerie, popping the cap on her soda can with a

241

perfectly manicured fingernail.

Valerie shook her head and smiled as she thought about her best friend. They'd met in kindergarten – one a shy, sweet butterscotch child and the other an outgoing, pretty chocolate one. They had grown up the same – Tracy dark and sassy and Valerie bookish and shy.

"Why are you so materialistic?" Valerie asked teasingly.

"Girl, I'm a Taurus." Tracy said, snapping her finger and shaking her perfectly wrapped bob. "I'm not materialistic. I just like my stuff right. I'm in college now and I need a new ride. Besides, I'm tired of riding around in your daddy's old station wagon." She told Valerie smartly.

"It is not a station wagon." Valerie said, cracking up. "It's a Volvo." She was crying. Tracy was so funny.

"Uh-huh. It's a station wagon." Tracy said, re-entering the car and leaving Valerie to put the pump back into its slot and fasten the gas cap.

By the time they made it to Byron's house everyone was already there and Tracy leapt from the car to go in search of Darren, her newest boyfriend. Valerie started to tick them off on her fingers as

242

she walked into the house. Well, let's just do sophomore year

college – Ricky, Joey, Tyrone, Michael, another Joe, Daniel…is

that it? Oh yeah, Darren. To say that Tracy liked the guys was an

understatement. She, herself, had had the same boyfriend since she

was sixteen – Byron Winston, the love of her life. How she had

gotten the most popular guy in high school to fall in love with her,

she did not know. He liked to tease her and say that the only reason

why he'd went out with her was because she gave him her

homework to copy, which she did sometimes. But sometimes his

homework was cutting into her time so…

"There she is." Byron said coming up behind her and kissing the

nape of her neck.

She turned and wrapped her arms around him and returned his kiss.

She relaxed as his hands kneaded her back and then traveled to her

behind and squeezed. She deepened their kiss, pressing her body

against his until he moaned her name.

"Okay, okay. Break it up." Tracy interrupted them loudly.

"We're having trouble in here Brandon. Can you pull yourself

away for a moment to help us out?" She said to Byron, gesturing over her shoulder with a freshly painted red thumb nail.

"It's Byron, Tracy." Byron said to her. He and Valerie were both laughing.

"Yes, I know, Bob. Let's go. You're stealing all of her oxygen." They followed Tracy into the living room where everyone else was sitting in front of the large television. It was fight night and they were waiting for the main event to begin. Byron adjusted some cables on the television and then sat down, pulling a happy Valerie into his lap.

Tracy lay in bed that night thinking about Valerie and Byron kissing in the hallway. She had seen how he'd touched Valerie. She wished he would kiss her like that. *No, no, you don't*, she corrected herself. She turned onto her side and traced the pattern of the bedspread with a fingernail. Byron was so sexy. She'd only been crushing on him for like ever. Valerie had just gotten to him before she'd seen him. When Tracy had first laid eyes on all six feet of that gorgeous caramel and those big, brown eyes…baby. What was she supposed to say? *Hey, Valerie, can I screw your man? You can have him back after that, girl.* Byron had been

244

captain of the swim team, popular, and most importantly, his family had money.

Yes, she was materialistic. Byron was always trying to buy Valerie expensive things, but she was too dumb – *no, you're wrong right now, Tracy. Valerie is your best friend.* She turned over onto her back and pulled her nightgown up to her neck. She raised her legs and placed her hands on her knees and slowly caressed her dark, satiny thighs, arching her back as her hands traveled over her hips and across her flat belly then up to her warm, plump breasts. She pulled at her nipples and thought of Byron's tongue lazily circling its way down her body.

Suddenly an image of Valerie came to mind and she exhaled in frustration. She pulled her nightgown back down and held her thighs tightly together to stifle the throbbing that was beginning between her legs. She pressed the heel of her hand into her groin and moaned, arching her hips forward as little sparks of pleasure exploded in her brain. Yea, Byron was real sexy. Her last thought as she trailed off to sleep was, *Valerie better watch him or somebody might take him.*

Valerie sat outside Tracy's house the next morning and waited for her friend. They were going to be late again. She tapped her foot on the gas pedal. *Two more minutes, Tracy, and I'm going to start blowing this horn like a crazy woman.* A minute later, Tracy emerged wrapped up tight in a pink coat and matching scarf and gloves. She was carrying a coffee mug.

"Hey, girl." She said as she got in the car and threw her bag into the backseat.

"Hey, Trace." Valerie said, her irritation quickly dissipating. "So guess what."

"What?" Tracy asked. Valerie looked excited. She was grinning from ear to ear. "What's up, girl? Tell me."

"Two things. Number one, I think I might get that job as the executive secretary at that pharmaceutical company. They called me back for a second interview." Valerie gushed. "Only thing is, I have to drive to Memphis this time to interview with one of the partners, which is no big deal. And then…" She removed her glove and showed Tracy the ring.

"Oh my God." Tracy said, taking Valerie's hand and examining
246

the ring. She was shocked. *Look at that rock!* She couldn't believe it. She faked happiness for her friend.

"Did you say yes?" She asked Valerie, who nodded. "I'm so happy for you, sweetie." Tracy told Valerie as she hugged her. *What the...*

"I want you to be my maid of honor." Valerie told Tracy, grabbing her hand.

"Of course I will." Tracy sat back in her seat and pretended to listen as Valerie went on and on about some silly wedding arrangements. *Whatever,* she thought. *You can marry him, Valerie, but not before I get a taste.*

Valerie looked around her bedroom and double checked to make sure that she hadn't forgotten anything. She mentally checked off in her mind everything that she needed for her trip and whether it was in the bag. Satisfied, she locked her apartment door and walked to her car. Her phone rung as she was fastening her seat belt and she had to rummage through her purse to find it.

"Hello." She answered.

"Hi, baby." Byron's deep voice responded.

"Hi, love. How are you?" Valerie said softly.

"I'm gonna miss you. I wish you'd change your mind and let me come with you."

"No, babe. You have to work and I don't need any distraction from you and those lips." She said, sensuously whispering the last part.

"Okay. I love you."

"I love you too. Be back soon." Valerie smiled as she hung up the phone. She loved her big, brown baby.

Tracy ended her phone call with Valerie and sat naked on the edge of her bed. She was reminding herself of all the reasons why she shouldn't do what she was thinking of doing. *You can't do this to your best friend, but how else are you going to get Byron out of your system.* She thought about what Valerie had told her about Byron and what a considerate lover he was. Her body screamed. She wanted him so bad. Tracy wound her fingers through her hair and pulled until her roots burned. As a last straw, a draft blew through a cracked window in her bedroom and fanned across her outstretched breasts and over her already aroused nipples. She got

248

up and went to her closet.

Tracy dressed carefully. She made sure that every hair was in place. Lace bustier and panties were hidden under a black, full length maxi coat. She slipped into high heels and sexy garter belts that held her stockings in place. She made sure not to get any perfume on the spots where she was sure to be kissed – and licked for that matter -- and then applied her trademark deep brown lipstick. Valerie was well on her way to Memphis by now and Tracy was going to visit Byron. She called a cab and waited impatiently. When she heard its horn blow, she ran out of her apartment.

Valerie's phone rung when she was thirty minutes outside of Memphis. "Hello."

"Hello. May I speak with Valerie Sutton."

"This is Valerie." She replied.

"Valerie, this is Donald Hubbard from AX Pharmaceuticals."

"Mr. Hubbard, hello." Valerie said, surprised that he was calling.

"Ms. Sutton, I know that we have an interview tomorrow morning, but I've ran into an emergency and, unfortunately, I'm going to have to cancel. I was hoping that we could do this over the phone. Do you have a moment?"

"Why, yes. Sure." Valerie said as she turned around on the highway and headed home.

Fifteen minutes later, the cab pulled in front of Byron's house and Tracy walked to the door and rang the bell. Byron came to the door looking as if he had just gotten out of bed.

"Hey, Tracy. What's up?" He asked, wondering why she was at his door this late.

Tracy walked past him and into the house.

Stupefied, Byron shut the door. "Why don't you come on in then." He said to her jokingly.

"Oh, Byron. I don't know what I'm going to do." She said in a forlorn tone.

"What's wrong, Trace?" He asked her.

"I need to talk to somebody. You know, like another guy. Do you mind?" She asked, sitting on his couch.

Did he mind? *Yes, I do*, he thought to himself. But what

could he say. "Okay. Want some coffee or something?"

"How about a beer?"

A beer. Okay. Byron went to the kitchen and grabbed a beer for

Tracy and a bottle of water for himself. He came back and sat

down on the couch and placed their drinks on the table in front of

them.

"What's going on?"

Tracy scooted closer to him. "It's just that I'm having some

feelings for someone and I don't know how to express it."

"You? Yeah, right, Tracy. What's really up?"

"Can you keep a secret, Byron?"

Byron looked at Tracy. She openly stared into his eyes and

moistened her lips with a pretty, pink tongue then bit her bottom

lip and scooted closer to him still.

Oh. Surprised, Byron scooted a little further away on the couch.

"Listen, Tracy. I love Valerie."

"I do too, Byron, and after tonight we don't ever have to talk about

it again."

She stood up and unbuttoned her coat and let it drop to the floor.

She turned around so that Byron could see how nice her butt looked in her sheer panties and then turned to face him so that he was eye to eye with the front of her crotch. She placed a high heeled foot on the cushion beside him so that she was open to his gaze. Byron looked down at Tracy in those panties and got an instant erection. He could see everything that she was trying to show him. He closed his eyes and Tracy leaned in and planted a warm kiss on his lips.

"No, Tracy." Byron said and started to get up but Tracy was smaller and quicker.

She hopped into his lap and straddled him, loving the feel of his erection between her thighs. She rotated her hips over him and he groaned. He tried again to stand up. *He actually thinks he's going to get me off of him without a fight.* Tracy laughed to herself. She grabbed ahold of his hard penis and started to expertly stroke him through his pants. Unable to fight her any longer, he succumbed to temptation and grabbed ahold of Tracy and kissed her to her absolute delight. His mouth moved passionately over hers and Tracy teased him by softly sucking his tongue into her mouth. She could feel his hands moving over her body and groaned as his full

252

mouth found a nipple and sucked at her so sweetly that she wanted to return the favor.

Tracy got on her knees in front of Byron and first licked him through a thin pair of lounging pants that he was wearing. Almost out of his mind with lust, Byron reached inside his pants and exposed himself to Tracy's hungry eyes. She took him into her mouth fully and Byron's hips bucked with pleasure. He groaned as she swallowed him whole again and again. Byron wound his hands into her hair and thrust into her mouth.

They were both so enraptured with one another that they never noticed Valerie watching them from the window. Tears streamed down her face. *What was happening?* She watched Byron turn Tracy over onto her hands and knees and stand behind her. *And he likes it,* she thought to herself. She choked back a sob and ran to her car then stopped. *You will not run away with your tail tucked in between your legs.*

She walked to the porch and sat down and waited there for them until the front door opened. They were surprised to see her.

"Hey, girl." Tracy said. Valerie could tell that Tracy was trying to think of a way to explain why she was at Byron's house.

Valerie folded her arms over her chest. "How long were you going to screw my man behind my back, Tracy?"

Tracy knew she was caught. She just smiled and shrugged.

"I don't want him, Valerie." She said with a laugh.

"And you have the nerve to stand there and laugh?" Valerie asked her angrily.

"Wait, Valerie. Wait, baby. It was a mistake." Byron said reaching for her.

"Don't touch me, Byron. You'll never touch me again." She told him bitterly.

"Valerie –" Byron started.

"Shut up, Byron!" Valerie screamed.

Tracy shrugged again. "It is what it is, Val."

Valerie balled up her fist and punched Tracy square in the mouth as hard as she could. Tracy fell back into the door in shock. She touched her mouth and became enraged when she saw the blood on her fingers. *She busted her lip!* Tracy ran at Valerie with her arms swinging and fists balled.

"Hey!" Byron said, grabbing Tracy by the collar with one hand and

254

steered her struggling body off the porch. "Get your ass outta here." He said, roughly shoving her onto the sidewalk.

"Byron." She pleaded.

"Come on, Trace, you know what this is." He told her coldly. He couldn't stand the sight of her anymore.

They both turned as Valerie started her car and sped away from the curb.

"Valerie! Valerie!" Byron screamed as he tried to run behind her car. Valerie hit the gas and Byron stopped in the middle of the street. He watched as she paused for a stop sign then turned the corner. He walked back to his house, shoulders slumped and heavy hearted.

Tracy ran toward him with her arms outstretched. "Byron, we can —"

"Get away from me, Tracy." Byron said, walking past her and into his house. Without another word, he slammed the door behind him and left her standing there on the sidewalk.

Valerie's phone rung for weeks -- first Byron then Tracy. *Message after message of their lying bullshit.* She thought about how Tracy had always been in her and Byron's business. *What a fool I am. How could I have missed it?*

She decided then that she needed a change. Mr. Hubbard had offered her a job in Memphis if she wanted to relocate. She decided that she would. She sold the engagement ring that Byron gave her and used the money to help her start over.

She had had to stop herself from calling Byron so many times. *Were they still seeing each other?* He had sworn in one of his many voice mails that it had been only the one time. She broke down some days thinking of Byron and Tracy together, but she knew that she had to be done with them both.

Yes, she was done with him. How do you ask a woman to marry you and then two days later go and stick your cock in another woman's mouth?

No, thank you, she thought. *I deserve better.*

C U P I D I T A S

Thirty-three year old Robert Sullivan nodded to the father and son as they entered. It had been some time since he had seen them face to face. They had been his very first clients when he had started buying and selling property ten years before when he was just a poor, rookie cop. Dante, Jr. had aged. His hair was now peppered with gray around the temples and his grin was not as boyish. He had always had a malevolent look about him. He'd once told Robert that his mother had always told him that his beauty was on the inside; but his father, Dante, Sr., had told him that he had fallen out of an ugly tree and hit every branch on the way down. He was a tall, slender man and towered a good three or four inches over Robert's six foot frame.

"Thank you for coming on such short notice. I won't take up much of your time." Robert said, as he got up to shake their hands.

That's how it started. With him buying a twenty unit apartment building that needed only a small amount of renovation. That apartment building is where he lost his mind.

Mei looked over the front cover photo of herself on *Mania!* magazine and smiled -- the eyes, the legs, the face. *I am so beautiful*, she thought to herself. Her agent, Ozzy, had better step his game up or she was going to replace him. A face like hers deserved to be on film. Mei padded to the bathroom to shower. She stood in the mirror and looked herself over. *What a beautiful body she had.* Other models she knew were either bulimic or simply starved themselves until their ribs poked out. Not her. Her slim figure was all natural. She ran a hand through her silky, waist length black hair and then turned slowly in a circle, her beautiful slanted brown eyes attentively inspecting her body as she moved. There were no dimples in the back of her thighs or her perfect derriere. If she ever saw anything resembling cellulite on her body she would simply die. Her small, perky breasts sat upon her chest without a sag in sight. She laughed to herself as she thought about her parents, who were back home in Beijing with her younger sister. Her mother always lectured her on the importance of virtue. Yes, yes, mama, I understand, she would respond. What she wanted to say was, mama, how could I allow someone the gift – no, the privilege of touching this silky, heavenly body? How,

258

mama?

He'd have to be a billionaire – an old codger that had one foot in the grave and the other on a banana peel. *I mean, look at me.* She only dated rich men. Why would she bother with some poor sap working a nine to five? She leaned forward and admired her face in the mirror. Her skin was flawless; her small, straight teeth were stark white. Men wanted her. They needed her. She saw the way that they watched her. *How could they not desire her?* She had to be careful how she behaved when she spoke to them. Even though her beauty wasn't her fault, it was still her responsibility to not drive every man that came into contact with her to the point of insanity with her perfection. She stepped into the shower and languidly soaped and cleaned herself.

After dressing, she went to the kitchen and stood at the sink and forced herself to drink her first sixteen ounces of water for the morning. She would continue this process throughout the day until she had consumed a total of sixty-four ounces. This was a habit that she repeated daily and a very important part of her beauty routine. She strictly drank nothing but water and the homemade fruit juices that she made for herself at home. On special occasions, she would partake in a glass of wine. She didn't smoke, didn't do drugs, never ate meat, and cleansed her colon regularly. Instead of running or aerobics to stay fit, Mei preferred bicycling or rollerblading. She was also careful about the amount of weights that she lifted during exercise, wanting to be strong and physically tone but still maintain a fragile, delicate appearance.

As she left her house that morning, Mei stopped once again to check her reflection in the vintage full length mirror that she'd purchased to mount on the wall beside her front door. She'd wanted to be able to see herself one last time before she left the house every day. Satisfied with what she saw, Mei left her apartment. She exited the building and climbed into the brand new Jeep that her ex-boyfriend, Frank, had purchased for her before she'd broken up with him. She donned her Cartier shades and pulled away from the curb. It was a beautiful day.

It would be wrong to say that he didn't stalk her. He liked to think of it as "he watched her closely". She looked just like Anna. He couldn't believe the resemblance. At first he followed her to photo

260

shoots or on shopping trips. Then he began lingering around the building – only watching at first, but after a while he became anxious and his compulsion took over. Once that happened, he began to enter her apartment while she was away. He hoped that no one noticed him hanging about.

He would sit in the chair beside her bed and bury his face in her pillows. She didn't smell like Anna, but he would remedy that. Maybe she would be more grateful than Anna had been and not just run off on him. *Why hadn't she loved him?* He twisted the pillow in his hands. *And her head popped off.*

He never would have known how to talk to his new Anna. He searched through her apartment and then her laptop and found out that she was on eLuv, a popular online dating site where wealthy men tried to attract young, good looking women. That night while he sat at home in front of his own computer, he signed up and shot her a message. It took a week but she answered. To Robert, Mei's behavior was shy, innocent. He thought her to be intelligent and funny – a woman that had no idea just how special she was.

They had planned to meet at the bar of a local restaurant. She told him that she would be wearing a red sweater.

"Robert?" A female voice had asked from behind him.

He turned and took a quiet assessment of this Anna look alike. Her hair was longer than Anna's had been and hung to her waist in thick, lustrous waves. She was petite and small breasted and her slanted brown eyes allured him with their shyness. He liked the way her off the shoulder sweater revealed her delicate shoulders.

"I'm Mei." She said smiling, attempting to break the ice.

Mei observed Robert as well. He was tall and lean, athletic build, brown hair and eyes. *He is gorgeous. What a change from the norm. Play this right, Mei.* She took note of the way his eyes quietly judged her. For a moment, she thought he was going to turn and walk away

"Robert." He said, pulling a seat out for her at the bar.

You are not a school girl, she kept telling herself. She was feeling giddy. She noticed him watching her and smiled.

To her utter surprise, Mei enjoyed herself with Robert. He gladly listened to her as she talked about work and complained about Ozzy. He put her totally at ease, and slowly but surely, Mei relaxed and enjoyed the attentions of a kind, handsome man who made her

262

laugh until her belly hurt.

"So you were also a police officer?" She asked.

"That was a long time ago. One day I woke up and decided that I didn't want to worry about getting my ass shot off, so I took some of my savings and bought a house, fixed it up and sold it. After houses, I moved on to commercial buildings and so on and so forth. Now I just sit back and enjoy the fruits of my labor."

He's rich, Mei thought happily. She sipped her wine as Robert told her amusing stories from his childhood about his father, a hardened Scottish butcher who was afraid of his mother; tales from his own days as a rookie cop -- some details which she was sure he exaggerated to her delight, and other details he omitted so as to not ruin the humorous mood. Their date ended with plans to meet again.

Mei quickly showered and dressed then ran out the door to meet Robert. He watched her as she exited her building. He admired the shape of her legs in the black leggings and high heeled boots that she was wearing. *Oh, he loved her,* he thought. He had stopped going into her apartment since he had free access to her now.

Mei got in and smiled at him and he smiled back. His heart skipped a beat.

"Ready?" He asked her.

She happily nodded her head and fastened her seat belt. *Men love when women play the innocent role.*

Robert looked very handsome in a white button up and brown woolen jacket. He drove the car with his left hand and rested his right hand on Mei's hands which were sitting demurely in her small lap. He caressed her fingers with his own. When they came to rest at a stop light, Robert leaned over and kissed Mei behind her ear and told her how much he wanted her. She turned to him and told him how lucky she was to have him. *I love how you shower me with gifts.* He wanted her to move in with him. She wasn't ready for that. She knew that he was in love her and she was enjoying his attention, but she also knew that sooner or later she would tire of him.

The diamond tennis bracelet on her wrist glittered and made her consider keeping him around just a little longer. The car behind them blew its horn and Robert began to drive, still massaging

264

Mei's hand with his own. He took her to dinner and a movie and
Mei smiled and made Robert believe that she was enjoying herself.
Robert liked to be in control so Mei never said anything when he
chose where they went. *Dinner and a movie again. Don't get super
boring, Rob.*

When they returned to her apartment, Robert walked Mei into the
building. Once they reached her door, she turned to Robert and
smiled. He was standing so closely behind her that she almost
bumped into him as she turned.

"Just one kiss." He said, pulling her to him. He had almost said
"please".

Mei leaned forward and allowed Robert kiss her. He held her in his
arms so securely that Mei almost melted against him. She caressed
his tongue with her own, teasing him by gently nipping at his
bottom lip with her teeth and moaning softly.

"It's late." Mei said, pulling away from him after one last kiss. "I
have to get up early. Thanks for dinner."

She stepped inside and closed the door, listening as his footsteps descended down the hallway. She leaned against the door and hugged herself tightly as she kissed her bracelet. *She'd have a new wardrobe in no time.*

"I want to see you." He told her on the phone the next evening. "No, I think I'll stay in tonight, Robert. I'm tired." She lied. She would keep him wanting her. She liked Robert but she didn't have the same feelings that he had, and she was no man's fool. He would see her when she allowed it. She found him very attractive but too clingy. He was very attentive but he sometimes smothered her. Whenever she tried to broach the subject with him he would become agitated. She kept telling herself that she should cut things off before he became too serious, but there were some things that she wanted him to do for her first.

"Come with me tomorrow night then."

He couldn't seem to stay away from her. He wanted to be with her every day. Finally, after making him beg for a while, Mei agreed.

Mei opened the box that had been delivered to her door that morning. She sat it on her bed and slowly opened it, knowing that

266

it was from Robert. She reached inside and lifted the dress out of the box. *Oh my*, she thought, caressing the black crushed velvet between her fingertips. She held it up to admire the bodice of the dress and how it would show off her shoulders and a modest portion of cleavage. The dress gathered at the waist and Mei smiled happily at the beauty of the velvet. The dress would flow gracefully on her small frame. The slit in the dress would show just a hint of leg as she walked. He always sent her the best gifts. She held the velvet to her nose and inhaled, truly loving the dress, then went to shower.

Mei blow dried her hair until it layered and framed her pretty face. She never wore much makeup, but tonight she applied mascara and some daring red lip stick. She slowly pulled black, silk stockings over her legs followed by black lace panties and bra and then stepped into the dress, loving the sensual caress of the velvet on her skin as she worked it up her body. She tied the bodice in place and admired the swell of her breasts, full and round under the dress. The final touch was a spritz of her favorite perfume and black slippers. Mei blew a kiss at herself as she looked into her favorite full length mirror and turned to and fro. *You're lovely.*

She was surprised by a knock on the door and was caught off guard to find Robert standing there. *Had the manager let him into the building?* No, he replied. He had caught the door as another tenant was leaving out, he told her.

He was dressed handsomely in a tuxedo. His diamond cufflinks glittered expensively. *He is not this sexy*, Mei thought. *Almost as sexy as me.*

After a drive, Mei laughed aloud when she realized where he had taken her. The casino! To be more specific, a yacht that had a casino on it! Robert grinned, thrilled that she was happy.

As they approached the yacht and parked, she could hear music coming from the boat. They exited the limo and Robert offered her an arm. Together they boarded the boat. Security parted at the door to allow them entrance and Mei looked excitedly about. There were people everywhere gambling and she wanted to try her luck.

"I want you to enjoy yourself tonight, Mei." Robert told her, staring at her adoringly as he offered her a glass of champagne.

Mei eyed the tables. Robert followed her gaze and then took her hand and led her past blackjack and poker tables where men sat staring intently at their cards with looks of determination, their minds set on beating the dealer, and onward to a table where dice were being thrown in a frenzy of mirth.

"Ever play craps?" Robert asked Mei. His eyes moved tenderly over her face.

She took a deep breath and nodded. They got chips and began to play – well, Mei played anyway. Robert teased Mei, telling her that he was only there as eye candy. He made her laugh as he blew prettily on the dice. Mei played just as she had seen the men at the card tables, eyes feverishly intent on the dice as they landed in her favor again and again. She yelled out in spite of herself and threw her arms in the air as the dealer cried out, "Seven."

Robert watched Mei jump up and down with excitement. She was having too much fun to notice him watching her. He loved how the dress fit her luscious little body and he stiffened in response as he thought about running his hands up under her dress and caressing her thighs -- the softness of the velvet competing with the silkiness of her legs. Robert had no plans of taking her home tonight. She was going home with him. It was time for her to learn her place.

Mei walked away from the craps table loaded with chips. She was grinning from ear to ear.

"Look." She told him proudly as she showed him the chips.

How innocent she is, he thought to himself.

"I see." He said to her wondering what she was wearing under all that velvet.

*   *   *

Mei was giddy from the champagne. She stood on the deck of the boat and smiled as she thought about her casino winnings. She had, had so much fun. Robert had been charming and indulgent as he showed her around the yacht, which he told her belonged to a friend of his.

"Thank you, Robert, for inviting me. I really enjoyed myself." She said to him.

Why does he have to look at me like that, Mei thought to herself.

I've kept you around for too long. Her toes began to tingle against her will. Robert came to her and cupped her chin in his hand and caressed her bottom lip with his thumb. An unexpected pleasurous

270

burn lit her body as his eyes traveled leisurely over her mouth.

Mei backed away from him and modestly lowered her head, but he came after her with a look in his eyes that made Mei feel as if she didn't know how much longer she could fight him. He pulled her into his arms and she smiled and tried to pull away, but he was stronger and easily pulled her back to him.

"Kiss me, Mei." He whispered to her.

She didn't want to. He was being too aggressive.

"Let me go, Robert." She told him. He was kissing her and trying to put his tongue in her mouth even though she was struggling.

"Stop it! Stop it, Robert." She told him, stumping on his foot to get away from him.

"Owww." He hollered. "What the hell is wrong with you?"

"I said no, Robert." Mei told him as she adjusted her dress. *Calm down. Think about the vacation to Hawaii.*

"You ungrateful little –" He stopped himself.

"Ungrateful!" Mei said in instant outrage. She couldn't pretend for him any longer. "I don't owe you anything!"

"I see. It's all fine and dandy when I'm buying you things and taking you places, but when I touch you, you don't want anything to do with me. You're just like her!" He said before he realized it.

"Just like who?" Mei asked. She was no longer tipsy.

"It doesn't matter." He said, shaking his head as he approached her again.

"Are you crazy? Who am I just like? Who?" Mei backed away. "You stay away from me, Robert. I mean it."

And her head popped off. Robert had to catch himself before he snapped her little neck. *You're not going to play with my heart, Mei,* he thought to himself.

Robert held his hands out to her. "I love you, Mei. I can't live without you and you won't live without me."

Mei stared at him wide eyed and in disbelief. *Look at how he's looking at me,* she thought. *Crazy mother – get out of here.* She left the boat in a hurry. Luckily, there were cabs sitting outside the yacht and she ran to one and made her way home. She nervously looked over her shoulder to see if she was being followed.

For a week he called every day, several times a day. When he would leave messages, it would be just the sound of him breathing

272

on the recording. The next week he didn't call at all but still sent flowers every other day. *Too bad he's a psycho*, she thought. Another week passed with no event. *Maybe he gave up.* Once a month had passed, she had just about forgotten about Robert. She had even recently begun to see someone else.

The fifth week rolled around and Mei was busy with *InSports*. She was going to be on the cover of the swimsuit edition and had been putting in some long hours at the studio. This particular day, she ran some errands after work and then went to the market to do some shopping. She drove home in silence that night and once inside her apartment, dropped her bags in the middle of the floor and ran to the bathroom to relieve herself, leaving the door slightly ajar. As she was washing her hands she heard the hallway light switch click and she turned around to see that the light was now out. In her hurry to get to the bathroom, she had turned on no other lights in the apartment. It was almost dark. Mei listened in fear to the silence that seemed to her to be so loud. She broke into an instant cold sweat and her heart began to pound. *Something was wrong.* The fine hairs stood up on the back of her arms.

Her legs began to tremble and she grabbed ahold of the sink to steady herself. She closed her eyes and told herself that she was overreacting and that the light bulb had simply died; that her mind was playing tricks on her and that she hadn't heard the light being turned off; and lastly, that she was alone in her apartment and that the footsteps she could hear coming down the hall were a figment of her imagination.

She stood there frozen. She looked around the small, dark bathroom for something to use as a weapon. The footsteps slowed then stopped. Whoever it was, they were standing right outside the bathroom door. The floor creaked and then the stranger stepped into the doorway. Mei's mouth went dry. She had hoped that she would never see him again. He stood there and watched her for a moment before stepping into the bathroom. She backed into the wall, wanting to jump out of her skin. She looked at his hands to see if he was holding anything. He must have read her mind because he held them up to show her that he didn't have anything and then smiled at her.

Robert took another step towards her and Mei squeezed her eyes shut as if not having the sight of him in front of her would make

274

him disappear. She had never been so afraid in her life. Against her will, he picked her up and carried her into the living room. He sat her on the couch and then removed his coat and sat down beside her. He could tell that she was afraid. Her spine was rigid and she was trembling.

"I missed you." He told her. He didn't like the way she was behaving.

"What are you doing, Robert?" She asked him.

"You didn't miss me, Anna -- Mei?" *She's seeing someone else just like Anna did.*

You're a psycho. She wasn't going to be bullied by him. "You can't just walk into my home whenever you want. Get out, Robert!" She said, standing up and pointing to the door.

Before she knew what was happening he was on her. She could feel his hands roaming her body and she began to fight him. He wrestled her onto the floor and held her down with his muscular body. Mei fought beneath him in an effort to free herself then kneed him in the groin. He grunted with pain and rolled off of her as he cupped his genitals. She tried to run around him to the door, but he grabbed her ankle and she fell again. He began to drag her back beneath him, but she kicked at him again and landed a sneakered foot into his jaw. She tried again to get away from him, but he was on her again. *He's too strong.* He rose to his feet, pulling her with him and then collared her. The toes of her sneakers barely touched the floor.

I want her to love me. Why is she acting like this? He closed his eyes tightly and fought the urge to take her from her home

"I know you're afraid of me, but I don't want that, Mei." He told her as he smoothed her hair away from her face and planted a kiss on her cheek. "You just make me so crazy sometimes. I know that we can work this out together. Don't you want that?"

"No, we won't, Robert." Mei tried to pull away from him. "I can't stand you. You make my skin crawl. Now get off of me." She told him, repulsed that his mouth was so near her own.

And her head popped off. Robert wrapped his strong hands around Mei's slim throat and began to squeeze the life out of her. *I can't believe I let you inside my body. I can't stand you,* Anna had screamed in his face. She had rejected his love just as Mei was doing now. They took so much and gave nothing in return. He
276

squeezed even harder as she fought as hard as she could to no

avail. Robert watched as her eyes bulged while she suffocated.

His rage overtook him and he screamed ferociously into her face as

he broke her neck, "Where's your smart mouth now?"

After her neck snapped, Mei went still and Robert snarled as he

threw her limp body onto the couch in frustration. He wished that

he could kill her again. He decided then to search for Anna again --

his lovely Anna who had beautiful, brown eyes. He quietly shut the

door behind him as he left Mei's apartment. *When he found Anna*

he was going to take her head off.

MALICE

"These six things doth the Lord hate; yea, seven are an abomination to him: A proud look, a lying tongue, and hands that shed innocent blood, a heart that devises wicked imaginations, feet that be swift in running to mischief, a false witness that speaketh lies, and he that soweth discord among brethren." – Proverbs 6:16-19

September 23, 8:55 p.m.

When Detective Justin Young walked into the A-1 Bar that night he was feeling relaxed and carefree. He was meeting a couple guys from his old crew for some drinks and he could hardly wait to see them. He saw Rich and Mike sitting at the bar and he walked over and clapped Mike on the back and then took a good punch in the side from Rich.

"What's going on, Mr. Homicide?" Rich said teasingly to Justin. He laughed and his smooth brown skin crinkled around the eyes. He gestured for the bartender and Justin ordered a beer.

"You know me", Justin said, sitting down on a bar stool between them, "I have the ability to solve crimes wherever I go."

Mike laughed and a deep rumbling issued from his barrel chest.

"We miss you out there is all Rich is saying."

"Awww." Justin said jokingly, ruffling Mike's red hair.

"How are they treating you over there at Homicide?" Mike asked, batting Justin's hand away.

"Not bad." Justin said. "It's a change."

"Yes?" Rich said. "I heard you got that floater, the Russian guy who turned up in the river?"

"Uh huh. It took a while to ID him. Never really got the whole story of what he was doing in the States." Justin guzzled his beer.

"Hmm." Mike said, running a hand through his beard. "We wanted to ask you about that. You know, word on the street is that the Russians are supplying the Irish mafia right here in Philly."

"What?" Justin said, surprised. "Mac Kennedy?"

Mike nodded to him.

"I don't think so. That guy is old school." Justin wasn't buying it. "Doubt it."

"No, no." Mike said, turning to Justin. "From the information we have, Mac Kennedy is being pushed out by his nephew, Dominic. Dominic knows that Mac's connects aren't going to deal with him while Mac's alive, and even though Dominic's a murdering bastard he's not gonna kill his uncle. He went direct to the Russians – not

279

Philly Russians, but Russia Russians." Mike looked at Justin to make sure he was following him.

"No." Justin said, still not convinced. "Mac is old school and so are the guys that he deals with. They'd get rid of this Dominic guy if he stepped out of line no matter who his uncle was."

"Not if somebody started to get rid of them first. You know Renaldo Shaughnessy in Chicago? Dead." Rich informed him.

"Alexander Quinn, still haven't found that guy."

"The old guy in Vegas?" Justin asked surprised.

Mike nodded. "We've got a CI that says the control of power has shifted. He says there's this guy in Russia by the name of Vladimir Arsov. Vladimir worked for a long time as a bodyguard for this Russian dude, Ivan Byko. Ivan was found murdered in his home about six months ago shot execution style. This dude was the main man in Russia, but in the end they found him in his boxers, on his hands and knees dead on his own living room floor. Now Vladimir has taken his place at the table, but people don't trust him because of what happened to Byko. Now if this Vladimir could get someone with enough cash to buy from him, someone as mean as he is, well, then he knows soon others will follow suit.

280

That's all we know for now," Mike said, "but from what we can tell, this Dominic has people afraid."

"And you're telling me that none of the Irish bosses are going to do anything about him?" Justin asked in disbelief.

"Well," Mike said, "not everyone is unhappy with the change if you catch my drift."

"What do you know about Dominic Kennedy?" Justin asked.

Rich signaled for the bartender to bring three more beers. "That he's a murdering bastard but he's smart. If we can get something on him we may be able to get to Mac Kennedy. Right now we're going after this guy Joey Boyle. The Black Hand has a contract out on this guy for popping some gangster's brother in a robbery. Thing is, Boyle used to work for the Kennedy family and if my gut is right – and it usually is – he's gonna have something on the Kennedys that we can use to get to Mac."

"What makes you think he'll talk to you?" Justin asked.

"Because he knows that the longer he stays on the street, the sooner the Hand will get to him and they're an unsavory bunch." He said, sharing a laugh with Mike. "We'll be the only thing standing between him and a bullet in his ass. I know you're

working homicide now, Justin, but we could use you on our side

with this. Maybe you'll find out what happened with your floater.

Captain says he can pull a few strings with Homicide to get you in

with us. What do you say?"

Justin didn't even have to think about it. "I'm in." He said.

September 25th, 4:23 a.m.

One. Two. Three. Justin counted silently to himself as he tried to

still his breathing. He closed his eyes and took a deep breath. He

waited as his ears tuned themselves to their surroundings -- until

the sound of the wind whistling through the bare, leafless trees was

as crisp as the cold air he was breathing deeply through his lungs.

He could feel the tension in the men around him. It was the wee

hours of the morning and all was quiet on the city block. He

nodded as Mike pointed two fingers at him, motioning to him that

he was to be second through the door and then, *boom*, the Enforcer

hit the door and they were in.

"Police! Hands up! On the ground now!" The squad quickly

entered the house, methodically spreading out to cover the upper

and lower floors.

282

With his experienced eye, Justin quickly took in the situation, noting the dimness of the room and the three men who were standing in the main dining area as they made entry. When they had approached the dilapidated house, Justin had noticed then that the windows were covered with what appeared to be blankets. Their fugitive, Joey Boyle, was a small, Irish, heavily bearded man who was rumored to have a paranoid, rather nervous disposition. He had been involved in an armor truck robbery three months prior, and in addition, was also wanted for the murder of one of the men who assisted in the robbery.

From what Mike had told him, the man Boyle had killed had secreted away to Philly with the intention of doing this robbery with Joey just to make some extra money on the side. He got himself murdered by Joey and another man in their attempt to rob him of his share of the money. Unfortunately and unbeknownst to Joey, the man that they robbed and murdered just so happened to be the brother of a member of the Black Hand, a Jamaican crime family out of New York. The police were hoping to get to Joey before the Black Hand did and offer him a deal and protection in exchange for information on organized crime in Philadelphia,

specifically, the Kennedy family. They had an anonymous tip that

Boyle was hiding out in this home.

Suddenly a gunshot rang out and Justin raced to the back of the

house through the kitchen and out the back door to see his

comrades wrestling a man to the ground. The struggling man was

average height, mid-forties, slim and wiry, heavily bearded and

strong as a man three times his size. Once they had him under

control and handcuffed, Justin kneeled down in front of him

"Joey Boyle?" He asked.

"No, Donald Duck, man. What the fuck's going on?"

"Mr. Boyle, I'm Detective Justin Young. We have a warrant for

your arrest. Here let me help you up." Justin said politely, as he

bent and lifted Joey off the ground.

Joey stared hard at the young detective and tried to gauge whether

or not he was soft. Though the detective was friendly and polite,

Joey could see the steely look in his eyes and decided that he

wouldn't do well if he tried to fight again.

"Yeah, well I don't know a Joe Boyle." Joey said, squaring his

shoulders and returning the detective's stare.

"Look, Joey," Justin said, "I can still arrest you for assaulting a police officer. You and I both know that when your prints come back the tag is gonna say Joey Boyle. Do you want to go down for murder and robbery?"

Joey stared at Justin and shrugged his shoulders.

Justin tried a different tactic. "When you go to the county to await trial, Joey, I can almost promise you that you're going into general population where the Jamaicans can reach you. All I want to do is talk, Joe. Maybe we can help each other out."

Joey exhaled and shook his head in disbelief. If it hadn't been for the contract on his head he would have refused. Either way, he was screwed and he was tired of looking over his shoulder. He nodded and bowed his head as Justin escorted him to the squad car.

Johnson Monaham sat on the porch in his usual spot and watched the residence that sat directly opposite his own house. It was four in the afternoon, and that pervert Larry Gordon would be leaving for work soon. Johnson sat at this very window every day at this very same time and watched Larry leave the house where he lived with his indulgent mother and venture off to work in a rusty, gray minivan. *Who would give a pervert a job?* Johnson did not know. Like clockwork, the short, peevish looking man exited the ranch style home dressed in his usual blue work uniform. Johnson leaned forward in his wheelchair, his eyes widened under his bushy, gray eyebrows, and peered at Larry the same as he did every day – as if he'd missed something about the man that he hadn't seen before; that if he studied him hard enough, he would discover that new flaw in what he already deemed to be a freak of nature. *Same flabby body, same receding hairline, same dark glasses.* Larry climbed into the van and drove away.

Johnson sighed and sat back in his seat. He had lived in this house for forty years and that Gordon woman had been in her house just as long. He remembered when she had moved in that house with her husband. Gary Gordon had taken the easy way out and blown his head off in the Gordon bathtub to escape having to live his life. Young Larry had been about ten then, but a peculiar child as far as Johnson had been concerned. While he had never had any children of his own, he had been around enough of them, and Johnson had never known a child – a boy child for that matter – that didn't go

286

out to play with other kids his age, ride a bicycle, climb trees –

something.

That boy didn't do diddly-squat. He'd sit on the porch sometimes

with a vacant expression on his face and watch the other children

play. When the boy reached his teenage years, he became even

odder. Mrs. Gordon didn't send the boy to the public school with

the rest of the children, but preferred instead to send him to a

private school for boys where he was gone most of the year. He

would come home from breaks solemn and reserved, but attentive,

and Johnson didn't like the way he watched the other children.

Johnson had known something was wrong with him and his

suspicions were confirmed when an adolescent boy from a few

blocks over accused Larry of sodomizing him in the Gordon

garage. Larry had lured the boy into the backyard with the promise

of toys. At seventeen years old, Larry Gordon was hauled off to the

penitentiary for raping an eleven year old boy.

Mrs. Gordon didn't move away as Johnson had hoped she would.

No, she held her ground though her house was egged and

vandalized with spray paint that spelled out the ways in which she and her son would burn in hell; she stayed through two vehicles whose gas tanks had been clogged with sugar.

When the notices came out in the mail that a sex offender was moving back into the area the neighborhood was outraged. Ten years later and Larry Gordon was coming home to his mother. Johnson didn't like it at all and a year later he continued to keep an eye on the Gordon home. Wheelchair or no wheelchair, if that son of a bitch touched another kid in this neighborhood he'd be eating one of Johnson's shotgun shells.

He was interrupted from his reverie by the sound of a car horn blowing. He leaned forward in his seat to peer down the street and then smiled. He heard the screen door slam against the house at the corner as little Lisa Young ran out to meet her uncle. Her blonde, seven year old pig tails flew behind her as she leapt into the man's arms. *There's his girl*, Johnson thought, smiling. Johnson and Lisa had made fast friends. She was allowed to ride her bike from one end of the corner to another, and on one of their many chats, she'd proudly told Johnson that her uncle was a detective.

Johnson had never met him, but he was glad that she and her mother had someone to look out for them. Lisa had once told him that her dad had died in a war – Johnson assumed the Middle East – and that her uncle, Justin, took care of them. Johnson chatted with the little girl almost daily and he looked forward to seeing her child grin – a grin that was missing two front teeth of which she assured him would grow back in no time. This led them to the discussion of Johnson having lost his teeth long ago which required him to have these nifty teeth that the dentist gave him which he could remove at any time -- he'd demonstrate to Lisa to her utmost *ewww* delight. He watched as the pair entered the house and then wheeled himself to the kitchen for a cup of coffee.

"Justin, what are you doing here?" Rachael asked her brother from her seat on the couch.

She was exhausted and hot. She'd done a ten hour shift at the factory and had just made it home with Lisa. Had Justin walked in five minutes later he would have caught his little sister sprawled on the couch under the fan in her undies.

"Just wanted to stop by and check on you guys." He answered.

Lisa was jumping all over him so he grabbed her by her ankles and hung her upside down while poking at her ribs.

"Stop, Justin, or she'll throw up." Rachael told him.

Lisa squirmed and laughed aloud. Her little glasses fell to the carpet beneath her head. Justin stood Lisa upon her feet and then rushed for Rachael who leapt from the couch. She was too slow and he caught her arms and subdued her then screamed to Lisa, "Get her!"

He and Lisa pounced upon Rachael and tickled her -- Justin attacking her rib bones as Lisa went after the soles of her mother's bare feet. She fought them feverishly at first, but eventually, they wore her down and together Lisa and Justin tickled Rachael until tears came to her eyes. She shrieked and her head thrashed from side to side as she tried to free herself. Soon the three of them were laughing hysterically. They showed her no mercy and the torture continued until she pleaded with them to release her. Justin was so glad to see his sister laughing. She was always so serious and it made him happy to see her smiling. He loved his sister and was proud of her for taking such good care of his niece all on her own. He reached down and helped her off of the floor.

Lisa jumped upon his back and they headed for the kitchen.

290

"What's for dinner?" He asked.

"Cereal." Rachael said, climbing back onto the couch. *She didn't have to watch out for Lisa while she played outside since Justin was here.* She closed her eyes and caught a few winks.

Justin stood in the hot shower with his head bent under the spray and his hands flat on the tile in front of him. He closed his eyes tightly and exhaled, letting the hot water run down his back and buttocks until it started to cool. He turned the knobs and stopped the spray before sliding the glass doors of the shower back and sighed as he thought of Rachael. She had left for the factory an hour ago. He'd gotten up and took Lisa to school so that his sister would be able to sleep a little longer before going to work. He'd stayed the night with them as he did sometimes and kept extra clothes at his sister's house for that purpose.

As he shaved, he thought about the interrogation that he was going to have this morning with Joey Boyle. Twelve years of being in law enforcement had introduced Justin to some hardened criminals and he prided himself on being able to hold his own, but Boyle was hard as nails. Joey had refused an attorney, wanting instead to make his own deal. He was smart and he knew he had a lot to lose by cooperating with Justin. He was now in protective custody and about to transfer to a federal prison under a false name while he awaited trial on the armor truck robbery. The Drug Enforcement Unit continued to gather information on Mac Kennedy with his assistance.

If he continued to cooperate with the police, he would do his time under an anonymous name. If he didn't cooperate, then he knew that he would be tossed into general population with no deal. Joey was content for now that the Black Hand couldn't get to him, but he knew that they weren't the type of people that depended on the police to dole out justice. He also knew that he was better off in the hands of law enforcement because eventually the Black Hand would catch up with him. There was a good price on his head and he couldn't run forever. Joey made his choice. He wanted to talk about the Kennedys anyway – particularly Dominic Kennedy. Justin dressed and grabbed a cup of coffee as he headed out the door.

LAS VEGAS

Joey Boyle sat in the passenger side seat of the van chewing his fingernails. Dominic had always given him the creeps. It'll be simple, his uncle had told him. Drive up to Vegas with Dominic and murk Alexander. Afterwards, they were supposed to throw him in the river. They wanted him found but not too fast. Dominic had awakened Alexander by shooting him in the leg while he lay in bed, and they were now riding around with him tucked in the large, aluminum storage bin that sat beneath the backseat of the van. Out of the corner of his eye, Joey looked over at Dominic who was calmly driving along like he didn't even hear the guy in the back crying. *What if the cops pulled them over?* Why couldn't they have just popped the guy right there in his bed? Alexander was scratching at the aluminum box and the sound was driving Joey insane.

"Shut up afore I come put another bullet in ya sorry ass!" Joey screamed towards the back of the van.

"You panicking?" Dominic asked Joey calmly.

"No. I just want him to shut up."

"Do you think, Joe, that maybe his leg is hurting? I mean, I'm sure it's pretty uncomfortable back there. Have a little compassion, why don't you." Dominic said, shaking his head in disbelief. Joey stared at Dominic wide eyed. *This guy was nuts! Compassion*! Dominic rolled the toothpick he had in his mouth around under his tongue. He seemed to be enjoying Joey's discomfort. He asked Joe if he put in his own work or if he was the type to send another guy. Joey responded that he did his own killing and Dominic snickered.

Kill him while he's asleep, Joey had said to him. Dominic didn't want to do that. What if a family member or something came by the next morning and found him. It would scare the hell out of them, Dominic had said to him. Besides, he'd said, he preferred to do it at the river. No one would be around this time of night. At times throughout the ride though, Joey felt that Dominic might have wanted to stuff him into the storage space with Alexander. He had to admit he was nervous. He had never killed a boss.

When they got to the river, Dominic pulled into an isolated area and he and Joey exited the van. Joey pulled his gun while Dominic opened the double doors at the back of the van.

294

Dominic stopped and glared at Joey. "Put that thing away. You trying to scare the guy or what?"

Joey reholstered his weapon. *This frickin' guy*, he thought to himself. He was confused. They were going to kill the dude anyway. What did it matter when he pulled his piece? Dominic reached into the storage space and grabbed Alexander who was so scared he had wet himself. Joey was so disgusted that he almost clipped the guy right then.

Dominic clapped Alexander on the back and smiled at him. "Hey, now. What you crying for?"

"Listen, Dominic --" Alexander started.

Dominic put his hand up to stop him. "Don't beg, Alex. It doesn't look good on a man of your status."

Alexander stopped then and stared Dominic square in the eyes. "How long do you think that everyone is going to sit by while you and your brother make –" Alexander grunted as Dominic kneed him in the gut.

Alexander caught his breath and then laughed as he lay there on the ground coughing and sputtering. "That's why we have rules,

Dominic. You know that and Mac knows that. How long do you think that they're going to let him keep breathing?"

"Who? Mac?" Dominic asked, laughing and shaking his head. "Let me be the first to inform you that Mac has been retired, Alex."

"That's not what people are saying." Alex said in a sing-song voice. "Do you really think that everyone believes that Mac isn't in on this with you? His betrayal is worse than yours. Please, Dominic. You can't protect him."

Dominic gestured at Joey to start walking Alex down to the river. He had to mostly drag him since the old guy could hardly use his legs from being kneed so hard. Dominic walked behind Joey and Alex.

"Do you really think, Dominic, that you're going to cut people out of your profits; that you're going to make all that money and no one is going to come after you?" Alexander was becoming hysterical.

"Is there a hit on Mac?" Dominic asked him.

"All I'm saying, Dominic, is that the people who you think have your best interest at heart don't." Alex put emphasis on the last word.

Joey threw Alex to the ground and began to kick him, telling him to shut up, then pulled his gun again.

Dominic snapped at him, "If I tell you one more time to put that thing away." He was beginning to become impatient with Joey. They watched as Alex tried to crawl away. Still seemingly deep in thought, Dominic grabbed Alex around the neck from behind and held him in a headlock. He choked the old man until he stopped flailing about.

"Get up and grab his legs. Help me get him in the water." Dominic barked at Joey.

Together, Dominic and Joey threw Alexander into the water then walked back to the van.

*   *   *

Justin sat opposite Joey Boyle who regarded the detective with a steely gaze. He wondered what else he wanted from him.

"And that's what happened, man. I'm telling you the truth." He said in his clipped Irish accent, gesturing with his slim, handcuffed wrists. "Only reason I'm telling you that is because I can't stand that bastard. He gives me the creeps. Now I heard what you said about Nevada offering the deal if I testify, but what I'm going to need is some serious protection." Joey said, sitting back and searching the face of the detective who sat across from him.

Johnson sat in his wheelchair in front of his picture window and glared at Larry Gordon with a scowl on his wrinkled face. He had known that it would only be a matter of time before the pervert reverted back to his old ways. Johnson watched him with a steady gaze. He was sitting there on the porch watching two little boys as they played in the street. With his very own eyes, Johnson watched as Larry slowly stroked a thumb over his groin, his gaze intent on the street. Johnson leaned forward in his wheelchair, his nose wrinkled in disgust. The two boys were small, probably eight or nine years old.

One of the boys threw his head back and laughed aloud and Johnson watched in disbelief as Larry grabbed his groin with both hands and gave his crotch a squeeze. He stopped and removed his hand as he looked around then nervously placed a finger in his mouth and began biting at a fingernail before directing his gaze

298

back to the street. Johnson grimaced in anger as he watched Larry's expression go weak and slack jawed as he leered at the boys. *Motherfucker*, Johnson thought as he watched Larry, *you are done.*

September 28th, 6:08 p.m.

The smell of death hit Justin as soon as he stepped foot onto the stairs. He closed his eyes and bit his tongue and fought back the rush of nausea that rushed over him. He pushed the door open and stepped inside. The stench was almost overpowering. He bent his head and looked around as he slowly entered the dim room and went to stand just outside the drying blood that had pooled on the floor. Slowly, he raised his eyes and took in the feet and legs, and then the severed head that rested in the bloody lap. Mac Kennedy had been wearing one of his expensive, tailor made suits and his hands rested on the sides of the white haired head that sat perfectly atop the expensive wool. Rigor mortis had already begun to set in and blood had dried and caked around the silver ring that Mac always wore on his left ring finger. It had a lion's head on it and the ruby eyes of the beast stared back at Justin blankly.

He closed his eyes and fought another wave of nausea. *If you faint in the middle of a crime scene, they'll never let you live it down.* He slipped on the latex gloves that he held in his hands and looked around the room searching for some sign of what had happened. There was an empty glass lying on the floor beside Mac's chair. Blood sprayed the walls and dresser, otherwise, the room seemed untouched. The bed was still made – the peppermints were still on the pillows. *What was Mac Kennedy doing in a motel room alone,* Justin wondered. He had obviously been caught unawares. Justin whistled under his breath. Dominic Kennedy was going to have a hissy fit.

Justin looked down at Mac's hands and saw the cuts on his bloody fingers. He bent and searched for wounds on Mac Kennedy's face as it sat in his lap. Justin stood up and nodded -- he had tried to fight. Whoever did this had either caught Mac off guard as he was coming in the room or was someone that Mac trusted. Rich was probably downstairs right now checking the security cameras. As far as Justin could see though, there had been minimal struggling so his guess was two or more guys. They had killed him on one side of the room and then propped him up in this chair so he'd be

300

facing the door. Mac was an old guy but tough, and he had still been strong. Justin would have been surprised if Mac hadn't fought.

He heard Mike come into the room behind him. "Someone from the inside did this." He said to Justin.

Justin nodded in agreement. "What about his bodyguard?"

"Dead in a service elevator on the fifth floor." Mike said.

"I'll bet –" Justin was interrupted by his cell ringing. It was Rachael.

"Hey, Rachael." He answered. "Let me call you back. I'm in the middle –"

"Justin, Lisa is missing." Rachael said in a panic.

"Calm down, Rachael. What happened?"

She was hysterical. "I don't know what happened to her. One minute she was there riding her bike and then the next minute she was gone. I looked everywhere. I don't know where she is."

"I'm on my way." Justin told her as he ended the call.

"What's up?" Mike asked, concerned at the worried look on Justin's face.

"Rachael says Lisa is missing. I gotta go, Mike." Justin told him, heading for the door.

"Yeah, man, go. Get outta here." He told him. "Let me know if I can help."

Justin ran from the motel and raced over to Rachael's.

When he arrived, Rachael was sitting in the living room with the police. The haunted expression in her eyes spoke volumes to Justin.

"I fell asleep, Justin. Oh my God." Rachael grabbed at Justin desperately. "My baby, Justin, she's gone."

"What's happening?" He said to a cop in the room and flashed his badge.

"We've got units searching the area for her, sir. Hopefully, she didn't get too far. We're talking to the neighbors but so far nothing."

"How long has she been missing?" Justin asked, looking from the officer to Rachael who was sagging against the wall in shock. Justin pulled her to a recliner that sat in the corner.

"She went missing around 5:30 this evening, so about an hour far as we can tell." The officer discreetly beckoned to Justin to follow him out onto the porch.

"What is it?" Justin asked, his heart was skipping beats. He had known that something wasn't right when Rachael called him at the motel. *Lisa.*

"We found her bike down the street there. Follow me." He said, walking around to the side of the house. "We haven't said anything to Ms. Young, but some kids in the neighborhood say it belongs to her." He pointed at the bike.

Justin nodded. "Where was it?"

They walked back out to the sidewalk. "Down the street there where you see the squad car. House belongs to Larry Gordon. They're talking to him now."

Larry Gordon. Justin gritted his teeth. Larry Gordon had been so quiet that Justin had forgotten about him. He was another one of the reasons why he'd told Rachael to keep an eye on Lisa while she was outside. Though their houses were on the same side of the street, Rachael's house sat at one corner of the short block and Larry's sat at the other. Larry Gordon was the reason why Justin had told Lisa to cross the street and ride her bike on the other side of the block. He didn't want her meeting Larry Gordon on the sidewalk. He'd pointed Gordon out to her and told her not to speak to him under any circumstances – to run screaming if he even came near her. *Why was her bike on this side of the street?* His eyes were beginning to burn in anger.

"I want to talk to him." Justin said.

"No can do, sir. Chief already called and said you're not to go anywhere near Gordon. He said that's an order." The officer said apologetically.

"Thanks, Officer." Justin said.

He glared at Larry Gordon's house as the officer walked away. *What were they doing down there?* He turned and went into the house. Rachael was still in the corner sobbing.

"What'd they say, Justin?" Rachael asked desperately, her eyes intent on his face. "Tell me."

He turned and looked down at her. *Damn it*, Justin thought, *how could you fall asleep, Rachael?* He thought that in fear and frustration. He would never say it aloud.

"Come here." He said, pulling her into his arms.

304

While he held Rachael to him, his cop's brain recalled bad things

that he'd seen and heard in the streets and he almost fainted. *Lisa.*

Larry Gordon sat on his living room couch opposite the detective.

His mother, Shirley, was about to have a fit and paced the cracked,

linoleum kitchen floor in her old house shoes. She was wearing her

flowered house dress that had the cigarette burns in the lap. The

lace around the sleeves had long ago begun to yellow at the wrists.

She stopped to lean against her kitchen sink and glare angrily at the

detective who sat across from her boy. She took a drag off of a

menthol and began flicking ashes onto her own floor. *I'm so*

pissed. She was fuming. She knew that the detective didn't believe

Larry. She could tell by the way that he was talking to him. *How*

dare they come into her house and treat her son like he was some

lusty child rapist that preyed on the oh so precious children that

lived in this fucking neighborhood?

"I usually work from 4:30 to midnight every day." Larry was

telling the detective.

Stop pausing and stammering like you're thinking 'bout your words, Shirley screamed to Larry in her mind. She knew that was

his way of speaking, but this no good pig didn't know how

sensitive and thoughtful her boy was.

"So tell me again why you're home today." The detective asked,

sitting forward in his seat, his gaze resting upon Larry.

He's a biggun, Larry thought to himself calmly. *So that pretty little*

girl with the blonde ponytails had gone missing. Hmm. Oh, yes,

and I'm the neighborhood pedophile. That's why he was here. He

wanted to tell the detective that he preferred little boys. That

probably wasn't a good idea though.

"I took the day off because I wasn't feeling well." He said instead.

"Just a coincidence I'm sure." The detective replied sarcastically.

Detective Jones didn't like him. He watched Larry Gordon's dark

tongue slither across his dark, chapped lips and inwardly shivered

with revulsion -- the total lack of muscle tone, his odd demeanor,

his mother. This guy wasn't right.

"So you don't mind coming down to the station and answering a

few questions then, right?" The detective said.

Are you asking me or telling me, Larry thought. "Sure, Detective."

306

Rachael Young sat on the edge of her daughter's bed and wept. It was after midnight and the police still hadn't found Lisa. It was her own fault. She thought about Lisa out there all alone and cried out. *Was somebody hurting her baby? Where else could she have gone?* When she had realized that Lisa was missing, she had frantically ran throughout the neighborhood looking for her. She hadn't been at the park and none of the other children had seen her. She was just gone. *Somebody had her baby.* If something happened to Lisa she would die. *Please don't hurt my baby.*

She remembered once hearing on a television show that when strangers kidnapped children, the child was usually murdered within three hours of the abduction. She had cuddled her own child in her arms. The thought had never occurred to her that Lisa would one day be one of those children. She cried as she thought about the lack of attention that she'd given to posters of missing children – somehow looking but not seeing.

Someone would overlook her baby's picture just as she had looked but barely imprinted in her memory the faces of missing children on posters and milk cartons that she had seen over the years. She had had no concept of how emotionally corrosive it was to have a child go missing. Rachael wanted to talk to Justin about her fears but he blamed her. He didn't have to say it. She knew it was true. He could hardly look at her. Pain exploded in Rachael's chest and she fell to her knees as she thought about her little Lisa. She told herself to breathe. *Breathe, Rachael.* She got up and ran to the bathroom to vomit.

Sept 30th, 2:23 pm.

Johnson welcomed the detective into his home. "Can I get you something? Coffee?"

"No." Justin said.

"Please sit down." Johnson told him, gesturing toward a chair. "I was so sorry to hear about Lisa. Me and that little girl made fast friends."

"You knew her?" Justin asked, snapping to attention.

He was tired and he could hardly concentrate. He hadn't slept in days. He had tried to sleep at Rachael's house the first night, but had to go home for fear that he would walk down the street and kick Gordon's door in. Now he just sat up and wondered where Lisa was and what was happening to her.

308

"Yes. She would ride her bike this way and sometimes we would chat."

"I see." Justin asked. "I know the police talked to you. You said you hadn't seen her that day, right?"

"Right. I wasn't out that day. I wish I had been. That's for sure."

Justin looked the man over. "Can I ask how you got in the chair?"

"Oh, I can get around well enough without this old chair. I got into a brawl at a bar some ten years ago or more and some guy went at me with a sledgehammer. My legs got all busted up and they pain me a lot especially since that arthritis set up shop in my knees. The chair just makes things a little easier."

"Really? A sledgehammer?" Justin asked in disbelief.

Johnson shrugged. "Anyway, reason why I called you down here is I wanted to talk to you about something. Now I didn't say this to the police because – well, I don't know. You know why Gordon was locked up, don't you?" Johnson asked, gesturing over his shoulder with a thumb.

"I do." Justin nodded.

Johnson leaned forward in his seat. "Well, one day I'm sitting here at my window as I do sometimes and I see Gordon over there sitting on his porch. Now that's okay except for the fact that there were two young boys there playing around in the street. Well, the reason why I'm sitting there looking at Gordon is because he's paying extra special attention to these young fellows, if you catch my drift.

Boy, I shit you not that pervert gets to squeezing and yanking on his cock and he gets this look on his face what remind me of when I'm looking at a nice ass on a woman. Only thing stopped him from his perverted ways was he remembered himself and got to looking around to see if anybody done seen what he was doing. Pissed me off so bad I almost grabbed my shotgun."

Justin clenched his eyes closed. There were red bursts of rage exploding behind his eyelids. These were different than the white streaks of lightning rage that he had become accustomed to over the last couple days. He was almost blinded with rage.

"Well, when Lisa went missing," he could hear the old man saying, "I got this dreadful feeling in my gut, and when the police said that they found her little bike out in front of his place I damn near went and set that bastard's house on fire. Now hopefully, justice will be

310

served, but you explain to me how a little girl who rides up and down this street all the time just suddenly vanishes out of nowhere, and to top it all off, her little bike ends up in front of a pedophile's house and he don't know nothing about it. My ass."

Justin placed his head in between his legs and breathed in and out in deep breaths. *Detective Jones is going to have another missing person if he doesn't hurry up and find out what Gordon did with my niece.*

Larry sat up in his room alone and stared into space. A string of drool that had trickled from between his parted lips had attached itself to his shirt and slowly began to trail down and run along the inside of his forearm. *Stop it*, he told himself as he wiped his mouth with the back of his hand. *Stop thinking dirty, dirty.* He had to control his urges – that's what the counselor said. *He had to be empathetic to the boys that he had bad thoughts about.* He wouldn't look at the pictures and touch himself.

What had started him to think about those bad pictures anyway? Oh, yes. The detective had asked him to take a polygraph exam and he had started to think about the things that he had done that no one knew about. *That's why you started fantasizing about the pictures.* The lie detector might reveal other things that he didn't want revealed. No, he had told the detective, he wouldn't take it. It had been days since the girl had gone missing and Larry doubted that they would find her alive anyway.

He thought about his job. Larry had searched for employment for so long that when the janitorial service had called him he and his mother had been shocked. They never looked into his background and Larry had done his job and stayed out of the way. But that missing girl's uncle told Larry's boss, Norm, that he raped kids. Norm told Larry he had to let him go after that. Larry had known it was coming.

That girl's uncle was stalking him. He saw him some nights standing in the backyard staring up at his bedroom window. Dark stubble covered his chin and his appearance was always disheveled, but to Larry he had a vicious look about him. He wanted to mention this to Detective Jones but he feared retaliation from the uncle. *Them pigs gone stick together anyway*, his mother had said. Larry knew that his life was in danger.

312

October 9th, 1:02 p.m.

Justin punched the wall repeatedly as he screamed with rage. He kicked the TV until the glass broke and then punched the wall again. The veins in his neck bulged and his skin was on fire. *I tried to be good. I tried to be good for Rachael.*

He had found the DVD taped to the windshield of his car when he'd left that morning for the pharmacy to fill a prescription for Rachael. Intuitively, he had known what it was and his legs had threatened to give out from underneath him. He'd stumbled into the house and watched the two minute video on mute. Only a thumb appeared on the screen at first and then Lisa – his little Lisa in just her underwear and a blindfold. She looked asleep and Justin breathed a sigh of relief as he watched her little chest rise and fall. *She was still alive.*

Suddenly, a hand had reached out and grabbed ahold of one of her small ankles and parted her little legs and then the video cut out. Justin couldn't breathe then and struggled for breath as he tried to calm down. Tears of rage and frustration streamed down his cheeks and for the thousandth time his mind went to the little cabin that his parents had left to him and Rachael. It sat half a mile off of Rouge Lake. It was isolated and there was no one around for miles. Rachael wouldn't notice whether he was gone or not. She had had a nervous breakdown long ago and was popping pills like candy. It killed Justin to watch her give up. She was convinced that Lisa was dead.

That video was the straw that broke Justin and he sat on Rachael's couch and waited for night. As always, he thought of Gordon, and he was going to get Larry Gordon tonight. He had waited too long. *Wheels of justice my ass.* He punched himself repeatedly in the head as he thought about Lisa. Why hadn't he gone after Gordon when Mike had gone through Jones' files for him and found out that Lisa's glasses had been found in the alley behind Gordon's house?

They had been bent and broken, but Jones had never mentioned it to him. *Why wasn't that fucker locked up*, he had asked Jones long ago. Shirley Gordon had provided her son with an airtight alibi. She swore that Gordon had been home with her the day that Lisa had gone missing. Justin almost blew his top when Jones told him that Gordon had refused the polygraph.

314

Mike and Rich had been after him to let them help him grab Gordon but he had refused. He didn't think about calling them tonight either. He didn't want any help with this. That son of a bitch was going to tell him where Lisa was or he was going to hurt him. Justin himself had finally gone crazy. He couldn't wait any longer.

Larry's eyes snapped open and his heart started to pound. There was someone in his room. He was afraid to lift his head and look around. He knew who it was and he had known that he would come eventually.

"Get the fuck up." The uncle said, kicking the bed.

Larry sat up and swung his legs over the bed. He slowly turned and looked behind him. The uncle was standing on the other side of his bed.

"Get up and get dressed. If you make a sound I'll knock your teeth out. Understand?"

Larry nodded but he thought about screaming. The detective wasn't holding a weapon but he was bigger than Larry, and Larry didn't doubt that he would knock his teeth out. If he screamed though his mother would come running and maybe he would be able to make a run for it. Larry's eyes darted to his bedroom door. As if he knew what he was thinking, the detective came toward him with a sneer on his face.

"Put your shit on."

Larry hurriedly dressed and then thought about crying out again as the uncle handcuffed him and then threw a cloth bag over his head. He felt himself being led down the stairs and then into the cool air as he was pushed out of the house. *I should scream*, he kept telling himself, but he was afraid that the detective would hit him. *He's probably going to do more than that anyway.* As he was being led out the back door, Larry started to scream and then everything for him suddenly went black.

Justin had pushed Larry out of the house and into the backyard when the smaller man started to scream. Enraged, he punched him in the back of the head and Larry fell hard and his head struck the ground with a loud thump. Justin leaned over and picked Larry up and slung him over his shoulders like a sack of potatoes and then crossed the backyard to where he had parked his car on the street.

316

There was no one outside at that time of night, but Justin could care less if anyone saw anyway. He opened the trunk of his car and dumped Larry inside. Without looking around, Justin got behind the wheel and drove away.

Larry awoke in pain. He was on a floor – a cellar floor. He tried to move and then grimaced. He was still handcuffed. He looked up and noticed the uncle sitting in a chair watching him.

"Do you know me?" He asked Larry.

"I know who you are." Larry said softly. The other man's eyes were on fire. *He's gone mad*, Larry thought.

"I am Detective Justin Young. My niece is Lisa Young. She's only seven years old." Justin sat forward in his seat. "Where is my niece, Larry?"

"I didn't take her. I swear I –"

"You're a liar!" The crazy looking man screamed. Spittle flew from his mouth.

"I swear I don't know where she is." Larry started to cry.

"Larry, if you don't tell me where Lisa is I'm going to kill you. I promise you that. You'd better start talking."

Larry rested his forehead against the concrete floor. *What goes around always comes back around,* his mother had told him since he was a boy. "I swear, mister, I didn't touch that little girl." He watched as Justin got up from his chair without a word and removed his jacket. He stepped over Larry and went to the opposite end of the room. Larry heard a scraping along the floor and turned to see the detective dragging an axe behind him. *Are you fucking kidding me?*

"Please, mister. Please! Listen to me – wait."

Justin picked the axe up above his head and brought it down upon Larry Gordon. The man's leg was severed at the knee and Gordon let out a blood curdling scream. Sparks flew as the sharp blade of the axe hit the concrete as it went through the flesh and bone of Larry's leg.

"Tell me!" Justin screamed in rage.

Larry curled into a ball and cried in agony.

"Oh, no. Please." Justin began to laugh. The sound drove Larry insane and he began to scream.

Justin laughed louder until he tired of the man's screaming. "Shut
318

up before I cut off the other one."

"Please." Larry whimpered as he watched Justin look his leg over.

"Where is she, Larry?" Justin whispered to the bleeding man. He looked over to the drain in the basement floor. *That's where you're going, Larry.*

"Please. I didn't touch her. Please."

"Do you understand what's going on here, Larry? If you tell me where she is, you have my word that I will take you in myself. You'll do a little time in the pen but then you'll be right back out again to diddle little girls and boys to your fucking heart's content." Justin kicked Larry in the side and turned him over onto his back. " But if you don't tell me right now – today – where Lisa is, I'm going to cut you up in little itty bitty pieces."

Larry began to wail again.

"She's dead, isn't she? You made that video when you took her, right?" Justin asked him. He could hear his own voice breaking with grief.

"I don't know what you're talking about." Larry placed his hands together as if praying and pleaded with Justin to let him go.

I'll bet you made that video when you took her. I'll bet you killed her right after you were done with her, you sick bastard. Justin stood again and swung the axe wildly and severed Larry's other leg. The man screamed in anguish and went to grab for his leg but couldn't reach it.

Justin laughed. "Your leg is literally hanging by that small piece of meat, Larry. Do you see it?"

Larry lay on his back and cried.

"Here let's get those handcuffs off." Justin said politely as he leaned over Larry and removed the cuffs from his wrists.

"Just tell me, Larry. Is she dead?"

As hours passed and Larry bled to death, Justin's mood did a constant flip flop. The detective begged and bargained with Larry. He pleaded with Larry to no avail. Larry was in so much pain that he just stopped responding. Unconsciousness threatened to overtake him and he welcomed it because no matter what he said, the detective wasn't going to believe him anyway -- he was too crazed with grief and rage.

"Yeah, she's dead." Justin decided. *Son of a bitch*, he thought. *You killed her.*

320

He looked down at Larry. The screaming had been replaced with a whimpering that grated on Justin's nerves. *The son of a bitch is in shock*. He wanted to lift the axe and bring it down on the man's skull, but he held out hope that eventually Gordon would tell him where Lisa was. He tied the dying man up in the basement and left him there.

The next afternoon, Justin sat on Rachael's couch and once again removed the pictures from his pocket that he had taken from Gordon's house. He had found them taped underneath a dresser drawer when he had gone to the house the night before. He had searched the Gordon house before while Shirley and her son had been sleeping, but last night had been the first time that he'd thoroughly searched the other man's bedroom. While Larry Gordon had lain in bed, Justin had quietly searched through his belongings using a small penlight that he kept on him. The pictures hadn't surprised him, but he had been relieved to not find a picture of Lisa among them.

As he sat there looking at the pictures, Justin was not sorry for what he'd done to Gordon – not even slightly. He silently cried as he stared at the photos. *Whose child was this?* He'd make sure that the pictures got to the police.

He got up and undressed then put his clothes and shoes into a plastic garbage bag and then hid them under the kitchen sink. He would dispose of them later. Naked, he walked to the bathroom and got into the shower. He cried more as he ducked his head under the hot stream of water. Afterwards, he threw on a t-shirt and a pair of jeans. He crept to Rachael's bedroom door and peeked inside. She was asleep under the blankets. Her wastebasket was in its usual position by her bed and was filled to overflowing with tissues. Justin quietly closed her door again and went to the couch to lie down. He closed his eyes. This time he slept.

Monday, October 21st, 3:45 a.m.

"Wait, Molly. Look!" Kevin said pointing at the small child walking in the street alone.

Molly threw her cigarette butt out the window. Her mouth fell open and she blinked with surprise. It was a little girl. She was only wearing a t-shirt and a pair of panties. There were no socks or shoes on her little bare feet.

322

"Oh my god!" Molly said as she jumped out of her car and ran to the little girl. "Sweetie, how'd you get out here all by yourself? Where's your mom?"

The girl stared at her blankly. Molly knelt down in front of her. "What's your name?"

The small girl started to cry and Molly removed her jacket and placed it on her quaking shoulders. She picked the child up in her arms and carried her to her car.

Johnson sat in his vehicle and grasped the steering wheel tightly in his hands. He watched the chubby, brown haired woman pick Lisa up and take her to her car. He waited until they drove away and then turned his headlights on before starting his car and slowly pulling away from the curb. Lisa was safe. She would be home soon.

It had been past due time to let her go. He had been tired of drugging her with the morphine that the doctor had given him for the pain in his legs. He hadn't wanted to hurt Lisa – just use her to manipulate her uncle into doing what had to be done. Things had worked out perfectly as far as he was concerned. Larry had

disappeared and Johnson was absolutely sure that the young

detective had finally done something about him.

Johnson wasn't sorry. He had had to push him. They had a

responsibility as adults to protect children and Johnson told

himself that that's what he had done. Lisa had been a means to an

end. That was all. How else was Johnson supposed to get rid of

Larry Gordon?

That pervert deserved whatever had come to him. Sure Larry

hadn't done anything to Lisa Young, but Johnson was certain that

he had saved some other child from the danger that was Larry

Gordon. *You did the right thing, Johnson. Brilliant.*

Justin Young slowly climbed the steps of the cathedral. Once he

was inside, he removed his hat and looked around. He was alone in

the church save for one woman who sat in the front pew with her

head bowed. Her lips moved silently as she made her petition.

Justin stared at the large statue that stood upon the altar and bowed

his head in deference to the figure that represented a most holy

sacrifice.

He had begun to come to church after Lisa had been found. She had appeared out of nowhere -- had been found dehydrated and slightly drugged wandering along the side of the road. Her small wrists and ankles had been severely chaffed by whatever had been used to bind her, but otherwise, Lisa was physically unharmed. At first she wouldn't speak, not even to Justin or Rachael, and when she did, her traumatized mind was unable to recall anything of significance. They were just grateful that she was home alive and well.

What didn't make sense to Justin was the fact that Larry had been dead for several days before she appeared. *Where has she been all that time?* The doctors had been relieved to tell them that Lisa had not been molested. Justin couldn't make sense of it in his brain. Who would drug a child and hold onto them for weeks only to let them go? His mind would sometimes go to the crippled old man that lived down the street, but he would dismiss the thought. Nothing was left to grieve for except Justin being unable to escape the guilt that gnawed at him constantly. Though Larry had been guilty, he had not been guilty of hurting Lisa. He tried to convince himself that some other child had surely been saved from Larry, but the guilt always came back to haunt him. When he closed his eyes at night, all he could see was Larry Gordon pleading for his life. All he could hear when he closed his eyes was Larry's anguished screams as his limbs were severed. He had nightmares about Larry – his bloody hand reaching out to him, a desperate plea in his eyes as Justin swung the axe. He woke up most nights in a cold sweat.

Justin walked over to the confessional box and entered. He knelt and made the sign of the cross.

"Forgive me, Father, for I have sinned. It has been a month since my last confession. I want to confess the sin of fornication. I have lied. I have committed the sin of murder upon an innocent man…"

Justin waited for the priest's words of absolution and then exited the confessional. He didn't feel any better now than when he had entered – he never did. He would keep coming nonetheless. Justin donned his hat as he exited the church. It had begun to rain and he lifted the collar on his coat to protect his neck from the drizzle. He walked to his car with his head down. His tears mingled with the rain. Justin headed home.

326

"My Jesus, I place all my sins before you. In my estimation, they do not deserve pardon, but I ask you to close your eyes to my want of merit and open them to your infinite merit. Since You willed to die for my sins, grant me forgiveness for all of them; thus I may no longer feel the burden of my sins – a burden that oppresses me beyond measure. Assist me, dear Jesus, for I desire to become good. No matter what the cost, take away, destroy, and utterly root out whatever you find in me that is contrary to your Holy Will. At the same time, dear Jesus, illumine me so that I may walk in your Holy Light." – St. Gemma Galgani, A Prayer for the Forgiveness of Sins

*   *   *

"What a story." Susan said, yawning and stretching her body on the sleeping bag that she'd laid on the ground. Their fire was almost out and Paula got up to add more wood.

"The sun is just about to rise. How about another story before we hit the sack?" Isaac said.

"Okay, Isaac. It's on you." Paula said coming back to snuggle against Andrew.

A WESTERN

My papa is Daniel "Big" Kane. He's a white man. My ma is

Delilah, a black woman – dark as midnight. She's mean as a rabid

dog. The two of them would rob anything with pockets. I love them

very much. I am sixteen years old. My name is Fancy Kane.

California, 1849

Otis and Red sat on the outskirts of the town that evening. The

former was feeling good and carefree, the latter, ornery and

exhausted. It had taken them days to make the journey from Texas.

The horses had been pushed hard and they needed to be tended to.

The pair had disagreed about the route to take to get there. Red

wanted to take the desert trails, but Otis disagreed. The trails were

the perfect spot to get massacred by Indians. He argued with Red

to the point of exasperation, but ended up on the cattle trail onward

to Horsehead Crossing and farther still to the Chihuahua Trail.

"Hell, ain't nothing here." Red said, leaning over and spitting

tobacco juice onto the ground.

"I'm sure there's somewhere we can get room and board."

"We can find a place to make camp. I ain't in the mood for the bull

tonight. Let's get this thing done and head on home tomorrow."

328

Red snapped. He was feeling more ill-tempered than usual.

"Well, I want a bath, Red."

Red turned and looked at Otis and mimicked him. "I need a bath."

He turned and spit again. "Listen, Suzy, I told ya I ain't in the

mood tonight."

"Come on. It'll be fun." Otis argued. He badly wanted to

participate in mischief before he bedded down for the night.

"Bathe at the creek." Red turned without another word and rode

away.

Otis sighed and followed him. He'd been hoping to have some fun

with some unsuspecting, prejudiced white patron. He'd do the 'yes

massa' and 'no massa' routine then bathe and eat right off the fork

that was for the whites only. Too bad Red didn't like the cock and

bull.

Otis yawned and stared at his friend's back as he rode away.

William"Red" Killeen. Otis had been born on the Killeen

Plantation some forty years back. He and Red had been inseparable

ever since they were toddlers. When old man Killeen died, Red

sold off the plantation, slaves included, all except for Otis, that is.

329

They didn't have a home per se – more like several homely hideouts. They spent their days gunslinging and thieving. They were just all around trouble makers.

Red was a strongly built man. He had a shock of red hair and a beard that he never groomed. He chewed tobacco and drank whiskey to an excessive amount. He was meaner than tarnation and nobody could stand his company -- but Otis. Instead of making his money on a cotton plantation, Red preferred the grit of the road and the hardness of being a criminal.

Otis on the other hand, was lively and carefree. Where Red started trouble just to be mean, Otis started trouble simply because he was wicked. Plus, the act of burning some poor, dumb sap gave him such a terribly delicious feeling. He saw the world as a land that had riches free for the taking and he took what he wanted. He was a handsome, dark man who liked to keep himself groomed and clean. He'd never chew tobacco and ruin his beautiful teeth. Red could tease him and call him Suzy or pansy if he wanted. Otis laughed. If he had really been a pansy, Red would've shot him dead a long time ago.

They found a place to camp and Red started a fire while Otis went

330

off to the creek to bathe. When he came back to camp, he found Red on the ground lying on a blanket. His cowboy hat was pulled down over his face. That was his signal to Otis that he didn't want to talk.

"What you say, Red? How you think we gone make out tomorrow?"

Red didn't reply.

"I think we'll do all right. This is our biggest one yet, you know." He pondered as he absentmindedly brushed his beard. "I think I'll get me a wife after this."

"Humph." Came Red's reply as he rolled over.

Delilah had a bad feeling about today. She paced back and forth atop the new steed that Big had given her. Her horse, Dotty, was getting old and Big didn't trust her for the job this time. This horse was a big brown that Big had won from a German man in a card game some time back. This mare didn't seem skittish, but Delilah hoped that she didn't become spooked when bullets started flying. Big calmly checked his pocket watch as they sat atop the peak and

331

waited. He could see the small wagon train winding through the mountains and steadily making its way towards them. He looked over to Delilah who was sitting quietly next to him. As always, she was dressed as a man. Her duster carried the grime of days of hard riding. He knew that underneath her coat she carried a pistol holstered under each arm in addition to the two that were strapped to each thigh. Her pretty, dark brown face was half covered with a bandanna and her thick, wavy hair was plaited and wrapped with another bandanna. She was wearing one of his tattered wide brimmed hats. He saw how intently she watched the train with her cold, black eyes. Her gloved hands tightened on the horse's reins and she leaned forward in anticipation.

"Hold on, sugar." He whispered to her in his deep southern drawl. The train was carrying bags of gold nuggets and cash on it and Big sincerely thanked the driver for bringing the Gold Rush to his feet. He and Delilah might just retire after this one. He nickered to his horse and he and Delilah discreetly descended the rocky peak. The train was coming straight for them.

They tied their horses to some trees and then ran swiftly to hide behind boulders that sat above the road and lined the train's route

332

of travel. Things went just as they'd known they would.

"Dere they is." Delilah said pointing.

Big followed her gaze and counted the men waiting below. As the wagon train made its way toward them, Big watched as men appeared on horseback. As the wagons rounded the curve, more men appeared on horseback seemingly out of nowhere and blocked the train's travel. The wagon train driver was caught by surprise.

"He thought he was a secret." Delilah whispered to Big and then laughed to herself.

The shootout started right away. The driver knew that the posse planned to rob his train and him and his men refused to surrender without a fight. Big and Delilah watched men shoot and get shot, flee and give chase.

"Give up." Delilah could hear a male voice scream.

"You'll have to pry this gold outta my dead hands." The driver screamed from his hiding spot behind a wagon.

Delilah watched as a tall, lean black man snuck around and disappeared behind boulders that lined the trail. *What is he doing,* she thought as she popped the snap on her holster. She and Big were lying flat to the ground and she watched quietly, her eyes intent on the boulders as she searched for his dark face. She heard the gunshot first then his head popped into view. Her hand relaxed on her pistol. She watched as the top of the conductor's head flew off and he collapsed to the ground, his blood running into the sand and gravel. Ultimately, the wagon train was no match for the bloodthirsty villains.

The men dismounted and boarded the wagon train. There were screams that were followed by the *pop, pop* of gunshots and then nothing but the voices of the posse. Once they had robbed the train, the men quickly rode off carrying money bags and bags full of gold.

Delilah and Big ran back to their horses and mounted them, quietly winding their way through the terrain as they discreetly followed the men. They trailed the posse for hours before they stopped to make camp. Big and Delilah crept upon them silently and watched. Big counted ten white men, a black man and an Indian. They watched as the men split the loot and began to leave and go their separate ways. Delilah and Big were more concerned about the gold than the money, so they waited and watched to see who took

334

what. The men separated and went off in groups of two or three.

Big wanted more than one share of the booty so he didn't bat an

eye when the Indian left alone.

They waited into the night as five men remained drinking around

the fire. Delilah crouched and began to pull blades of grass from

the ground as she eyed the men. Particularly, she kept her eyes on

the grungy, red haired man. He amused her. She could tell that he

was up to something. She could hear the black man talking.

"And I tell you, Willy, I always been scared of cats. Never

liked'em. It's that sound they make. Creeps me the hell out."

The four men guffawed and laughed together as the red haired man

listened silently.

"What you gone do with all that loot, Willy?" The black man

asked, taking a drink from a flask.

"Well," Willy said, leaning back and pulling on his beard, "I

reckon I may as well start that ranch. I been meaning to do that

now for a while. I'm getting old. Need to stop all this nonsense."

"You know that's what I was telling Red here. He don't think we

got enough money though. What you think, Tom?" The black man turned to a burly, grizzled blonde man.

"I reckon I don't give a shit, Otis, that's what." He got up and dusted off his pants. "See you fellers later."

"Just a minute there, Tom." The red haired man jumped to his feet and walked with Tom towards his horse.

Big looked down the clearing to Delilah and smiled cynically to himself. He wondered if she knew what was going on. Things were going to turn out better than he had thought. He watched as Red removed a knife from his belt and stabbed Tom in the side. Caught off guard, Tom reached for his gun only to be grabbed roughly about the face to muffle his screams as the knife repeatedly pierced his back and ribs.

Delilah laughed quietly to herself as the knife was nonchalantly wiped on Red's chaps and then tucked away. He turned and walked back to the camp and sat down again. An hour passed before an intoxicated Willy finally got up to leave only to be followed and knifed in the back the same as his predecessor. The last man who remained at the fire was blessed with a bullet to the back of the head, and Delilah and Big watched as Otis and his red haired friend loaded five shares of gold and money and then rode away with the dead men's horses. Big quickly ran to where Delilah was hiding behind some redwoods.

"I can't believe them dead fools fell for that." Delilah said, disgusted at the red haired man's constant spitting.

"But I'm glad they did." Big said, excitedly hopping from foot to foot and slapping his hat against his thigh. "Let's go, sugar."

They stalked the men throughout the night as they headed for the trails. They made camp for the night and Delilah and Big quietly waited for morning.

Red opened his eyes as he heard the shotgun being cocked. In fact, that's what woke him up. He looked into the gray eyes of a large, black haired white man.

"Top of the morning to you, sir." He said as he rested the shotgun muzzle upon Red's top lip.

Red quietly assessed his situation. He saw movement out of the corner of his eye and looked around. Otis wasn't there. *At the creek splashing your nuts with water, Suzy?* There was a black woman there. Red's eyes widened with surprise. *Look at this bitch dressed like a gunslinger. Just when you think you done seen it all.*

Her gaze met his and she nodded to his left. He looked over to the horses and the loot then back at her. She removed the bandanna from her face and smiled. Red laughed aloud from his place on the ground.

"You're going to rob me? You and a woman?" He said, turning back to the man.

"Yes, sir. I was thinkin' on bustin' your teeth out with the butt of this shotgun afore I run off though. What you think?" Big mocked him.

Before Big knew what had happened, the man grabbed the barrel of the rifle and quickly moved it to the side. The shotgun blast startled him and the wooden log that Red had been resting his head on exploded. He kicked Big in the knee with the flat of his hard boots and moved away as the large man swung. The woman pulled a pistol and fired at him. She couldn't get a good shot at him as he and the bigger man tousled. Distracted by the woman, he caught a fist to the temple and fell to his knees but kicked a foot out as the large man came for him and caught him hard in the belly. Still slightly dazed, Red cocked his fist back and brought it up into the man's groin and then kicked him in the chin when he doubled over. Big fell to the ground unconscious.

Red staggered to his feet. The woman slowly removed her coat.

"I think I'm gone get me one of them guns as a souvenir." He mocked her and pointed to the guns that were strapped to her slim thighs. She didn't respond but eyed him directly as she circled him.

"You sure you wanna fight with me?" He asked her.

The woman was on him before he knew it. He did not expect the attack that came from her and found himself fiercely blocking blows. She was too fast. He grabbed her leg as a booted foot came straight for his head and threw her away from him, but she landed on her feet.

"Why don't you just shoot me?" He yelled at her, his arms held out wide.

"Cause ya meaner than tarnation and I wanted to whup on ya ass a little."

Red shook his head in disbelief. "If your man hadn't of relieved me of my guns, I'd shoot you in the gut."

"Hmm. I fixed ya friend up. He's hogtied naked by the creek."

Delilah gestured over her shoulder with a thumb.

"Is that right?" He glowered at her.

She saw the way he glanced worriedly over her shoulder. "That yo' boy?" She asked.

"I owns him but he come and go as he please."

"Oh, I see." She said sarcastically. "Well, I hopes an opossum come along and chew off his johnson."

"I reckon you 'bout the meanest bitch I ever come across." Red said, scratching his bearded chin.

"Sexy ain't I?" She placed her hands on her hips. "Control yourself, baby."

"Son of a –" Big said as he struggled to his feet. He picked up the shotgun and trained it on Red. "Put your damn hands up." He told him.

Delilah approached Red with rope. He waited for his chance then tried to grab her once she was close enough. Delilah drove the heel of her hand into his nose and Red fell to the ground unconscious.

"Well, I think you broke his nose, sugar." Big said to her as he stood over Red.

Delilah donned her coat and they walked to their horses.

340

"Honey, how you let him get the best of you like that?" Delilah asked as they rode away.

"There was something in my eye, babe." Big replied.

Fancy stood in the backyard of the cabin and stared into Waya's eyes. They were hidden between the sheets that Fancy had just hung on the clothing line.

"I missed you, Fancy." He told her.

"I missed you." She said as he pulled her into his arms for a kiss.

Her mother's voice startled them. "Fancy!"

Fancy and Waya jumped apart. Her parents were home. She had been so wrapped up in Waya that she hadn't heard the horses.

"Go Waya! Go now." She told him.

He hurriedly kissed her on the cheek then jumped the fence and ran toward the trees and towards the forest that surrounded her home. Fancy straightened her hair and dress and came from behind the sheets. Her mother was standing in the doorway with her arms crossed. A pipe dangled from the corner of her mouth and she watched as the young Cherokee boy disappeared into the forest.

"Oh, he just came to check on me, Ma. Squirrel couldn't make it out. She's big with the baby, you know."

Delilah looked her daughter over as she spoke to her. Squirrel was Delilah's good friend and kept an eye out for Fancy for her when needed. Waya was Squirrel's nephew.

"What he runnin' fo' then?" She asked her daughter.

Fancy looked at her feet.

"You come on in this house." Delilah told Fancy and stepped aside so she could pass. "You thinks I don't see what's going on but I do." She followed Fancy into the kitchen where Big was removing his boots.

"Ain't nothin' going on, Mama."

"That boy don't wanna do nothin' but lift your knees to your ears."

"Delilah!" Big exclaimed, shaking his head.

"You hush. Shoot, he'll trick her just like you tricked me. She got titties now and he looking at her." Delilah said to Big and he choked with laughter.

"Mama!" Fancy yelled, folding her arms over her chest. She glowered at her father.

"You crazy, woman." He said, wiping his mouth with the back of his hand.

"You mind what I say, girl." Delilah said, pointing a finger at Fancy.

"Yes, Mama." Fancy muttered.

"You love your mama, girl?"

"Yes, Mama."

"Good. Now come here and give me some sugar." She hugged her only child to her and lovingly stroked her hair. "I loves you, chile. Now go get ya papa some supper."

The following day Big took the girl to town. He insisted that Fancy sit up front with him as he drove the small carriage.

"Honey, you know you can get whatever you want today, right?" She nodded. He told her the same thing every time they came to town. Her mother would say the same thing to her before she left the house,

"Fancy, get whatever you want, chile."

Her parents tried to make up for being criminals by buying her whatever she wanted. When they were home, they tried to be normal for her. Delilah wore dresses and took care of the house. Big tended the land and took care of his family. They lived miles from anyone, so they hardly saw another body for long periods of time. They tried to hide the truth from her but she knew. As a child, she remembered sitting up at night and listening to them whisper together as they planned robberies. She would stand in the window cloaked under the darkness of the house and watch them hide money in one of the many holes in the yard. Squirrel had told her once in confidence that her mother and father had slowed down when she was born.

Even now, they only left her when there was a lot of money involved. She had promised herself that the next time one of them lied to her about a gunshot wound she would let them know that she knew exactly what they were doing. They smothered her mostly though. She never went anywhere without one or both of them being around.

She sighed sadly as she thought about Waya. He had asked her to marry him and she'd said yes. Her parents – particularly Delilah – would definitely be a barrier to their happiness. Fancy had asked Waya to wait for her until her seventeenth birthday which was only five months away. At seventeen, Delilah couldn't possibly refuse her. She had to prove to her mother that she wasn't "her baby" any longer.

Big stopped the wagon in front of the general store and they got out. Fancy wanted to get some material to make dresses for herself and Delilah. They entered the store together arm in arm.

Otis stood in the midst of the town and leaned against a building. He wasn't smiling today. His body was still chaffed from where the woman had bound him with the rope. How embarrassed he'd been when a bloody Red came to untie his naked, hogtied body. On top of that, they'd lost all their loot. He rolled his eyes when he thought about how kind the couple had been to leave them two horses. *They had probably laughed their heads off.* So this was what it felt like to be robbed blind.

He waited for Red to come back from the saloon. They were determined to find out some information on the couple. They wanted their money back. On top of that, their pride had been bruised. He leaned against the wall and looked around him. There was hardly anyone about. He watched a carriage pull up and a big, white man lead a pretty, laughing mulatto girl into the general store. *Must be his mistress*, he thought.

Red exited the saloon and headed over to him. He had two black eyes from the broken nose that the woman had given him.

"Find out anything?" He asked Red.

"Naw. We been to every saloon and every town up this way and nobody knows about'em. The trail they left points in this direction. I just don't get it." Red took his hat off and wiped the sweat from his face with a bandanna.

"What you thinkin'?" Otis asked.

"That they're long gone. We'll probably never see'em again."

Otis and Red mounted their horses and headed back toward Texas.

"Get everything you wanted?" Big asked his daughter as they rode home in the wagon.

"Yes, sir. I did. Thank ya." Fancy smiled at Big.

They pulled in off the road and Fancy went into the house while Big tended to the horses. Delilah stood in the kitchen humming to herself as she kneaded the dough for apple pies. She was making a

346

big dinner for her family and wanted to have a great dessert.

"Squirrel brought more apples, huh, Mama?"

"That she did. Put on an apron and help me, chile."

Fancy donned an apron and sat down to peel apples. Maybe this was a good time to talk to her parents about Waya.

"Mama," she started cautiously, "you ever think about having grandchildren?" Fancy exhaled a frustrated breath as she watched her mother's back stiffen.

Without turning around, Delilah continued to knead the dough, but said, "Why you askin' me about young'uns, chile?"

"Just wondering, Mama."

"You been letting that Injun boy under ya dress?" Delilah said carefully.

Big stood quietly in the doorway listening. He was going to get his shotgun if he found out that, that Cherokee boy had come and took liberties with his little girl while he was away. Fancy paused and took a deep breath.

"Waya asked me to marry him, Mama. I said yes."

Big exhaled a relieved breath but Delilah spun around and looked at Fancy with surprise.

"I'm almost seventeen years old, Mama. Most girls my age is hitched already."

"Fancy, what are you thinking?"

"I love him, Mama." Fancy said quietly, wringing her hands in her lap.

"You don't know nothing 'bout no love, girl."

"Delilah —" Big started.

"You hush now." Delilah said, pointing a finger at him in warning.

"Fancy, you ain't marryin' that boy and that's it." Delilah turned back to her dough. "Me and ya papa don't bust our asses 'round here so you can go run off and marry some good for nothin' boy."

"Waya is good, Mama. You'd know that if you bothered to talk to him."

"Is you sassin' me, girl?" Delilah spun around again.

Fancy defiantly returned her stare. "I love you, Mama, but I ain't gone be miserable just 'cause you are."

Big and Delilah gasped in surprise.

Fancy stood up from the table. Tears welled up in her eyes.

"Matter of fact, I don't know if it's that you're miserable or just plain mean. You won't even hear me out. I tell you this," Fancy said, pointing a finger at her mother, "I'm marrying Waya whether you like it or not. I'm damn near a grown woman and I ain't staying in this house with you for the rest of my life." Fancy stumped out of the kitchen and left the house.

"Can you believe that chile?" Delilah said to Big in disbelief.

"Yeah, I can believe her."

"So now you angry too?"

"You got a lot of nerve, Delilah. You remember how hard it was for us when we wanted to be together? You remember me almost getting my ass shot off stealing you from that wretched Arkansas plantation?"

Delilah started to speak but Big held a hand up to silence her. He was mad. She sat down at the table.

"You seem to forget, Delilah, that when two people love one another that it's hard to keep them apart. Now who are you to throw a stumbling block in front of that little girl and stop her happiness? If you don't give that girl some breathing room you gone lose her. I love you, Delilah, but I ain't gone lose my child for you. That girl run off and you gone answer to me." Big turned on his heel and walked away.

Delilah sighed and sat back in her chair. *So now she was the villain.* She shook her head. Yes, she remembered Arkansas. She almost got choked up thinking about it. She was just a child when she came to the Willens plantation. She had been sold away from her mother and siblings. She'd never known her father.

A morose child, Delilah had been cared for by a slave called Uncle Charlie. The old woman that took care of the orphaned black children on the plantation couldn't stand Delilah's ill-tempered ways. When beatings didn't work, she stopped caring for her all together.

Uncle Charlie had pitied her and kept her in his own cabin. With him is where Delilah learned to fight and shoot a gun. It was important to Charlie that Delilah knew how to take care of herself. Her small size worried him more than anything, and so he would wrestle with her into the night and teach her how to defend herself against a bigger, stronger opponent. He showed her how to pick a grown man's pockets without him having a clue. He made some money off her too. He and the other men would bet and jeer as she

350

beat on the older boys on the plantation when they got ideas in their head about the budding breasts on her small body.

She had been a small, muscular girl and tomboyish. Her smooth, dark skin and doe-like eyes were in complete contrast to the fire burning within her. She would hurl herself at a boy twice her size and knock the air right out of him and then proceed to pounding on him as he lay there on the ground. Charlie loved her like she was his own daughter.

When Delilah was sixteen, Big came to work on the plantation as an overseer. Delilah had beat the large, white man in a few games of poker and that's where Charlie noticed Big watching Delilah, but he didn't worry much. He knew that Massa Willens didn't allow no cavorting between whites and blacks on his land and he was confident that Delilah wouldn't disobey him.

Charlie caught the romance that budded between them too late.

"Where this pistol come from, Delilah?" He asked her one day. He'd been fixing the roof on their small cabin and had discovered the gun by accident. When he'd opened the oil cloth and found the small deringer tucked inside he had been taken aback.

"Ah -- um." Delilah was caught off guard.

"I say," Charlie's voice rose, "where a black girl slave get this nice pistol from?"

Delilah reached for the gun but he snatched away from her and held the pistol behind his back.

Charlie already knew where she had gotten it. "I thought you was smarter than that, girl. You been messing wit' that white man, ain't ya? I said ain't ya?"

"We gone run away together." She said quietly.

"I ought to knock the taste out ya mouth. And you believe every word he says to ya, right? Huh?" Charlie was almost beside himself with anger. "Ain't no good black men on this plantation? You got to go running after some white man?"

"Well, I tell you one thing," Delilah started vindictively, "at least I know with that white man ain't nobody gone sell off my children. Anybody ever sell off your children, Uncle Charlie?"

The look of sadness that passed over Charlie's face hurt Delilah's heart and she regretted the words that had come from her mouth.

"And on top of everything else, you got the nerve to be disrespectful." Charlie shook his head. "I'm ashamed of ya."

352

He laid the gun on her bed as he left the hut. Delilah would never forget the look of disgust on his face as he turned his back to her.

As she went back in time, Delilah sat in her kitchen and lit her pipe. She hit the table with her fist as she thought about how she'd awaken the morning following her argument with Uncle Charlie. The sun had been shining bright that day. She'd grimaced as her head hit the cabin floor. She peeked out from under an eyelid.

"Wake up, gal." Massa Willens was standing above her.

He turned his head and spit tobacco juice on the floor. Delilah had to stop herself from kicking him. She closed her eyes and swallowed to keep from retching.

"I say wake up, gal."

"I is woke, Massa." Delilah opened both her eyes and looked up at him.

"What this I hear from Charlie 'bout you running off?"

Delilah looked around the room. Willens was there with Wright, an overseer that had been there as long as she could remember. That's what worried Delilah – Wright. He'd take the skin right off your back. Charlie was standing at the door. He wouldn't look at her.

"What this I hear 'bout you messin' with Big Kane?"

Delilah knew that she was in trouble by the predatory way that Willens was staring down at her.

"Everybody on this plantation knows my rules. Now I set some of these rules in place for reasons. Pisses me off when somebody up and think that they gone do whatever they wanna do on my land." He scowled down at her.

"Massa –"

"Shut up!" He yelled and pointed a finger at her. "I been saying to you for the longest, Charlie, that Delilah mouth too smart. I been saying, Charlie, she getting too big for her britches. What you say? Naw, Massa, she don't mean no harm. Now look." Willens gestured towards her.

Delilah climbed to her feet. Charlie stood in the doorway with his back to them. Delilah looked at Willens. He was wearing a suit as usual – blue today. A gold watch hung from the pocket of his vest. He wasn't wearing a hat and his long, gray hair spilled over his shoulders.

"But I ain't gone play with her, Charlie." He turned to Delilah. Her eyes locked on the silver eyetooth on the left side of his
354

mouth. Charlie's betrayal stung.

"I just might've let you pass breaking a rule cause of Charlie, but you thought you was gone run off on me. Let me tell you something, gal -- you property, and I'm thinking on breaking your legs." He turned and spit on the floor.

"Naw, you thinkin' on breaking my spirit." She said defiantly.

Delilah fell onto the bed as he punched her hard. She closed her eyes against the pain that pounded in her head and wiped the blood from her mouth as she stood up again. Charlie left the cabin. She knew that he wanted her to humble herself, but she refused to bow to this repulsive white man. *You will not cry, Delilah.*

Wright came for her and she swung at him with all her might. Surprised, he jumped back and looked at her.

"I ain't got no quarrel wit' you, Wright, but if you touch me, I'm gone try and take ya head off."

"Hmm. I always did admire your spunk. Just wanted to say that before I take the whip to you." He said to her gruffly.

Those were the most words that Delilah thought she had ever heard him say. She pulled the pistol from the pocket of her dress and pointed it at them. She was very satisfied with their gasps of astonishment. Charlie must have forgotten to mention the gun in his haste to keep her on the plantation.

"Hold on, Wright. She only got one shot." Willens hooked his thumbs into the pockets of his vest and spit again.

"You are so nasty." Delilah spit at him in revulsion.

First, Willens stared at her with an incredulous look on his face and then he and Wright burst into laughter.

Wright leapt at Delilah and she fired the small gun. She heard his outcry as a bullet caught him in the shoulder. He growled and swung a big fist at her, but she ducked and he missed. While she was distracted, Willens hurled himself at her and she fell to the ground under him as the air whooshed out of her. Dazed, she reacted too slowly and his fist came down hard on her forehead. Delilah sunk into darkness.

When she came to again, her hands were tied on either side of her and raised high above her head. She could taste blood in her mouth and her eye hurt. Someone had pulled her dress down around her waist and her breasts were out for the world to view. She looked up to see what seemed like the whole plantation standing around watching her. She didn't see Charlie. Willens stood on the porch of the big house. Wright approached her with the bull whip in his hand. His left arm was in a sling. Delilah turned her head and spit blood onto the ground.

"Now how you gone whip somebody wit' my bullet in your shoulder?" She asked, smiling at him.

His cold, blue gaze didn't shake her. "Wrong arm."

"I'll bet you hit like a girl." She told him.

"You are one evil bitch." He told her.

Wright walked around the back of her and Delilah tried to swallow her fear into her stomach. She could see that some of the old women had begun to cry. The tears on their black faces angered her. She closed her eyes. *You will not cry, Delilah.* That's what her mother had told her as they were being torn apart. She heard the whip whistle as it cut the air and then pain exploded in her back and her legs gave out from under her. She bit her tongue to keep from screaming out loud. That's when she heard the first gunshot. People were running everywhere and she heard screaming. Wright dropped the whip and ran for the big house while Willens ran out of the house with a shotgun. There were three Indians and they were having a shootout with the white men on the plantation. Injuns! *You got hit in the head too many times.*

"I got ya, honey."

Delilah looked up and then laughed with relief. Big untied her wrists and half carried her as they ran to his horse. The Indians were right behind him whooping and hollering as they fled the plantation. Delilah's bloody back seemed to ache with every pound of her heart. Big could feel the weakness in her and he held her half naked body tightly against him as she was jostled around in his arms. The horses' hooves beat the ground beneath them as they fled Willens. Tears of joy burned in Delilah's eyes. *She was free!* She thought of Uncle Charlie and cried. They would never have a chance to say goodbye.

Delilah's daydream was interrupted by Big coming into the kitchen and sitting down across from her. She placed her pipe on the table and went over and sat in his lap.

"She'll always be your baby, Delilah."

Once again, he held her while she cried.

Fancy glowered at her mother's back as they began their journey. She rode in the wagon with her father and Delilah rode up ahead on her own horse. Her parents had to go to California to handle some business and had decided to take her along. *Horseshit,* she thought folding her arms across her chest. *She doesn't trust me to be home alone with Waya around. She's trying to keep us apart.* Fancy turned and frowned at her father.

"Are you in cahoots with mama?" She asked him bluntly.

Big rolled his eyes skyward. A week later and Fancy still wasn't speaking to her mother.

"Fancy, your mama ain't hurting you none. That darn boy will be there when you come back. Now hush." He told her with a huff. Whenever they camped, Fancy would be anti-social and avoid her mother. Delilah was determined to win Fancy back to her before she gave her permission to marry. Delilah thought about Waya. She had talked to him sometimes when she visited Squirrel – had watched him grow up in fact. He was a responsible young man, respectful. *He ain't sissified neither. Don't want no tender foots for grandkids.* Delilah nodded to herself as she puffed on her pipe.

She didn't want Fancy thinking that she was getting her blessing just because she had an attitude with her mother. *That boy gone have to come by the house so I can get an eyeball on him.* But she did as Big told her and gave Fancy some space.

They made it to California in good time. Big and Delilah derived pleasure from watching Fancy's eyes widen in surprise when she saw a china man for the very first time. He smiled at her and nodded as he went about his business. There were people everywhere and the bustle of the town was new and exciting for Fancy. They pulled up to an old, red wooden building and her mother and father dismounted. Delilah signaled for her to stay on the wagon as she walked over to her father and handed him a burlap sack. *I do not want to know what's inside.* A tall, white man in a poncho came out to speak with them and then Big followed the man into the building. Delilah went back to her horse.

Fancy turned her attention back to the street. Her eager mind was on overload and her head swung from side to side in excitement as she looked about. She looked down at herself and then gawked at the women who passed. Her mother had always insisted that she dress as a boy when they traveled anyway, but she was surprised to see so many women moving about in trousers and flannel shirts. *Just like the men.* Some even smoked like her mother.

Her father came back to the wagon and they headed for the mining camps. As they entered a settlement, Fancy stared about at the tents and was amused by the children that ran about. A stray dog limped by them with disinterest. Women stood over fires and stirred large pots in preparation for their evening meal.

They rode beyond the camps and Big stopped the wagon and he and Delilah dismounted. They hadn't planned on being away from home long and had traveled light. Fancy grabbed pots and utensils as Big started a fire. Delilah tended to the horses as they cooked a meal.

"Daddy, can we go back to that town?" She asked later.

"We'll pass through on our way out of here tomorrow." Big told her as he got up to get himself a second helping of stew. He stole a hunk of bread from Delilah's bowl as he passed. She kicked at him with a booted foot.

Otis ran as fast as he could back to the saloon. He was out of breath as he burst through the doors and over to the table where Red was playing cards.

"I gotta talk to you." He told Red.

"Yeah. Well, I got me a good hand here so it's got to wait." Red said as he concentrated on his cards.

Otis pulled up a chair and sat down beside him.

"You know that guy Ralph what work for that prospector they call Lee?"

"Yep." Red said nonchalantly as he gulped down the contents of his whiskey glass.

"Ralph do dirty work sometimes for this lawyer over there in town. Well, guess who Ralph say that lawyer just bought a bunch of gold from?"

Annoyed, Red exhaled and threw his hand in with three other men that sat around the table. A grizzled man who sat across from him scooped up his winnings.

"I ain't in the mood for no guessing games, Otis." Red got up from the table and went over to the bar.

"You don't care nothin' 'bout our gold being sold right up from under us?"

362

Red swung around and stared at Otis who had a big grin plastered

on his dark face. Red grabbed him by the front of the shirt.

"You telling me that ornery bitch is here with that giant feller?"

"That's what I'm saying. They laying right out there beyond them

camps." Otis picked Red up and danced about with him. They

laughed wickedly together as they sat down and made their plans.

As they rode home, Fancy couldn't stop herself from smiling. She

had gotten some souvenirs for Squirrel and her daddy had given

her a small gold nugget to give to Waya. She bit into a juicy peach

that they had bought as they passed again through the bustling

town. Delilah had promised to make some peach pies once they

arrived home. She was glad that she had traveled with her parents.

There was so much in the world that she didn't know about. She

would be sure to express to Waya how important it was to her that

they see a little of the world before they started a family.

When they arrived home, Delilah had a bath and laid down for a

short nap. Fancy and Big went back out again and headed to the

Cherokee village to invite Waya over for dinner. To Fancy's

irritation, he had gone out hunting and wasn't expected back to the following day.

They headed back, and on their way home, Fancy and her father chatted happily together. They didn't notice the two men who were following them until it was too late.

"Daddy, somebody just jumped behind that bush up yonder." Fancy pointed.

Big slowed the wagon. He heard the click of a gun being cocked. He looked to his left and saw the red haired man.

"What's going on, Daddy?" Fancy asked.

"Daddy?" Red said.

Big sneered at Red as the man clapped his hand to his mouth in mock surprise and then smiled.

"Where's my gold?" He asked Big.

"I'm sure we can work something out." Big slowly reached for his holster.

"Get ya stinkin' hands off me."

Big looked over to see Otis dragging Fancy from the seat of the carriage. She struggled to no avail, and he jumped from the wagon and started to run towards Otis. The last thing he heard was a gunshot and Fancy screaming his name before he sunk into unconsciousness.

Delilah stood in the kitchen again kneading dough. She heard the horses as they pulled in off the road and smiled to herself. They were back already. She paused and listened. Usually Fancy and Big chattered incessantly when they returned from trips together. That was strange. She didn't hear her daughter talking or Big laughing. Maybe that Cherokee boy was with them. Had she heard a wagon or just horses? *Naw, it's way too quiet.* It was almost sundown and Delilah had one lone candle lit on the table. She swiftly went to it and blew it out. She'd bet that any minute Big would be saying to her "you're crazy, woman". He'd call her paranoid and they'd laugh, *ha ha,* but for now it was better to be safe than sorry.

She pulled her pistol from the holster that hung from a chair in the kitchen and crept into the sitting room. She dropped to the floor in a crouch. A man was on the side of the house. *And it ain't Big.* She could see the top of his hat as he moved cautiously around her home. She aimed for his head. He stopped to listen and she saw his face. Delilah slunk into the shadows. Her back hugged the wall behind her. She wanted him to come into the house. She edged her way against the wall and over to peek out of the window. Big was on the ground lying motionless. *Where's Fancy?*

She swiftly turned and pointed her gun towards the kitchen. He was in the house. She could see him through the mirror that hung on the wall opposite the kitchen. She aimed for his head again. He rounded the corner and she shot him. He flew into the wall, dropping his gun. She shot again and he leapt back into the kitchen. Delilah kicked his gun away and crept along the wall barefoot -- her dress hiked up past her brown knees. She listened then slowly, cautiously peered around the corner.

A brown arm snaked out and grabbed her by her hair and drug her into the kitchen. They struggled there on the ground and Otis drew his fist back to punch her but was met with a knee in the groin. Delilah crawled away and reached for her gun but was drug back again towards him. She allowed him to drag her onto her back and then lifted her hips and threw her legs over his shoulders and around his dark neck and began to apply pressure with her strong thighs.

In a panic, Otis struggled to his feet, lifting her body from the ground as her legs locked around his throat. Delilah stood with her hands planted firmly on the ground and then deftly twisted her body and flipped Otis hard enough that he tumbled into the wall. She jumped up and ran to the cast iron stove and grabbed two knives from a block of wood. *First rule, you gotta be quick* -- she could hear Uncle Charlie say.

As Otis tried to get up, Delilah hurled her body at him, knocking him back into the wall. He hit his head and fell hard into the wall behind him. She fell upon him as he landed on his back and threw her body down beside him, wrapping her left arm around his neck and pressing the blade of the knife into his jugular.

"You bastard, where's my chile?"

Otis laughed and began to struggle again but jerked to silence as Delilah pressed the point of the blade to his throat. Her face was so close to his that he could kiss her.

"I ain't seen no child. I seen me a pretty mulatto girl though."

Delilah nicked Otis' neck with the sharp knife and blood trailed down to the collar of his shirt.

He gritted his teeth as she whispered harshly in his ear, "If you don't tell me where that chile is, I gone cut ya from here," she pressed the tip of the blade in her left hand into the hollow of his throat, "to here." She pressed the tip of the blade in her right hand into his scrotum.

"Give me my money and you can have her." She didn't respond and he looked at her.

"You kill my man?" Delilah asked him suddenly.

"He breathing."

"Tell me where she be." She trailed the knife along his groin and he stiffened.

"I ain't telling you nothin'. You get our money together and meet us tomorrow afternoon at the Yosemite Saloon. That's the only way you gone see that gal again."

"Why shouldn't I cut your head off right now?" She asked him.

"If I don't show up then Red gone hurt that gal and you know it. Now get off me!"

Delilah held the knife to his throat as they both rose to their feet.

Otis cautiously took a step backwards toward the door and another

368

until he was on the back porch. He turned tail and ran and Delilah watched him as he jumped onto his horse and rode away. She ran out the front of the house and went to Big. He groaned as she turned him over. As he lay there on the ground, she frantically searched his body with her hands looking for the source of the blood. There was a bullet wound in the back of his right shoulder. "Can you walk?" she asked him.

With her help he staggered to his feet. He leaned upon her as she helped him into the house and led him into the sitting room and made a pallet for him on the floor in front of the fireplace. After starting a fire, she helped him out of his clothes. As she removed the bullet from his back, he told her what had happened on the road with him and Fancy. Delilah got him drunk on whiskey until he passed out into a deep sleep. She then sat at the kitchen table and oiled her guns and thought about Fancy and hoped that her baby girl was all right.

Too riled to sleep, Delilah re-plaited her hair and then sat in her favorite chair and waited for morning. When the sun rose, she dressed for the road and then went out to saddle her horse.

As she had strapped her holsters on, she thought about the gold that was hidden in a secret compartment in the roof. *They weren't getting one damn nugget. How dare they terrorize her family?* She promised herself that she was done slinging guns after today. If she escaped with her family intact, she was going to retire. She went back into the house and pulled on her coat then tied a bandanna around her neck. She would have to ride west. The Yosemite Saloon was in a town that was frequented by outlaws. Those two boys planned to kill her – shoot her down in cold blood. They meant to lure her to a place where no one would bat an eyelash when she fell. She knew this because it was the same thing that she would do.

"Where you going?" Big asked her as he struggled to sit up.

"I'm going to get Fancy."

"I'm riding." He rose to his feet.

"You're bleeding too much. Lie down, Big."

"You ain't going alone, woman." Big hurriedly dressed and they left the cabin.

They looked down on the town before entering. It seemed quiet around the saloon. It was the middle of the day and people were in the streets going about their business. Big went down first, pulling another horse behind him. She had stuffed some money bags with stones and paper and packed them onto the horse beneath a blanket. Delilah looked around at the people as they entered the town. They openly gawked at the tall, black, gun-toting woman who was dressed in men's attire.

She followed Big to the saloon where he dismounted and walked in. Delilah waited outside. Big exited the saloon red faced and glowering. He was followed by a sinister looking Otis who mockingly tipped his hat at Delilah.

"Is that the gold?" He approached the bag ridden horse, but Delilah stepped in front of him, blocking his view.

"Where's Fancy?" She asked.

Otis whistled loudly and then pointed behind them. Big and Delilah turned to see Red walking towards them with Fancy out in front of him. He had a gun pointed at the back of her head. People gasped and moved out of the street as they turned to watch. Big shook his head as deputies crowded the doorway of the marshal's office. Delilah smiled. She was so proud of Fancy. *She ain't crying one drop.*

Red stopped in the middle of the street and hollered to Otis. "You got it?"

Otis turned to Delilah and Big and raised his eyebrows. Delilah nodded and Otis went to the horse and peeked beneath the blanket. He whooped and waved his hat at Red then led the horse away.

"Now let her go." Big screamed to Red.

Red aimed at him and fired before pulling Fancy with him as he ducked behind a building. Delilah ran towards the building but was almost trampled as Red rounded the corner on a horse and nearly ran her down. She could see Fancy thrown over the saddle in front of him. Delilah raced back to her horse and jumped on it, giving chase to the fleeing men who had her daughter. She could hear Big coming up behind her. He went after Otis, shooting at the man as he gave chase. Otis expertly maneuvered his steed in an attempt to elude the gunshots.

Delilah rode hard after Red. Her long coat flapped in the wind. She aimed her gun at his back then cursed, not wanting to hit Fancy. She shot at the air above his head and he ducked, steering to one

372

side and then the other as she pulled the trigger again. She re-holstered her weapon and gave chase. She screamed at him to stop. There was a cliff up ahead. Red turned back to look at her. *What was he doing? Did he not know?* Delilah began to panic. Suddenly, the horse reared and threw its front legs in the air as it skidded to a stop. Red and Fancy were thrown hard to the ground. Delilah quickly jumped from her horse and ran towards them. Red staggered to his feet and grabbed Fancy as she tried to run past him to her mother.

"Let her go, Red." Delilah screamed as she came toward him. He threw Fancy to the ground behind him and challenged her. "Or what?"

They stood perfectly still then – Red and Delilah -- sizing one another up. Red held his hands to his side as did Delilah. She noticed the involuntary twitch of Red's right hand as he watched her. *Don't move, Fancy.* They held each other's gaze. Red smiled and Delilah exhaled a strained breath and waited.

He reached for his gun first and Delilah pulled her pistol and threw herself backwards as she pulled the trigger. She felt his bullet go *whish* past her face. Fancy screamed and Delilah watched as Red fell to the ground, a bullet hole in his forehead. She lay back on the ground and stared at the sun as she caught her breath.

Fancy crawled to her mother and worriedly looked her over.

"Are you hit, Mama?" She asked Delilah as she ran her hands over her mother's body.

"Naw, chile." She told her, swatting her hands away. She grabbed Fancy by the chin. "Did they hurt ya?"

"I'm all right, Mama."

Her father found them there standing on the bank hugging and crying.

"Did you get'em?" Delilah asked him.

"I got him." He nodded.

They rode home in silence. Fancy rode with her father.

"So I hear you getting married." Delilah said as she lit her pipe.

Fancy looked over at her mother and nodded.

"Congratulations, chile." Her mother said, placing her pipe back in her mouth.

Fancy laughed as Big looked down at her and winked.

374

COCKY

The jig was up. He paused on the concrete as they surrounded him.

He was outnumbered. Groucho Roach turned tail and ran, leaving

Cocky on the sidewalk to face the gang alone. He shook his head.

The Roaches were known for being yellow bellies.

The Ant Hill gang had him trapped. Mellow Ant leapt from a blade

of grass and onto the sidewalk. He and Cocky had beef going way

back. He had been waiting for this day for a long time. He flexed

his muscles and prepared to strike.

"Well, if it isn't Cocky Cockroach." He said in his high pitched

voice as he approached the huge roach.

"Let's throw down, Mellow. Me and you." Cocky said, jabbing a

leg at the nefarious carpenter ant.

Mellow balled up his fists. "I've been waiting a long time for this,

Cocky, ever since you and your cock-eyed brother, Rocky

Cockroach, robbed my family on the way back from the picnic

table."

"Took you long enough, chump." Cocky smirked at Mellow.

The two bugs circled one another warily.

None of the insects were prepared for the scoop of double chocolate chunk ice cream that fell from above and exploded in their midst. A child giant shrieked and then reached its hand down and picked the ice cream scoop up and examined it. Mellow Ant, who was stuck in the sweet treat along with other members of the Ant Hill gang, screamed aloud as the child giant picked them off with a fat finger and then wiped its sticky hand off on its jeans, smashing the ants with a swipe of its large hand. The scoop was then placed back atop a waffle cone and licked with pleasure. Cocky lay there in the grass and wiped ice cream from his eye. When the giant ran away to play with the other human offspring, Cocky got up and sped off down the sidewalk. He could feel his little legs begin to stiffen as the ice cream dried on him, and he needed to hurry and find water.

He counted himself lucky. Had that been Rory Wasp and his gang, Cocky wouldn't have had a chance. Even the human offspring were terrified of Rory.

Cocky swiftly headed home.

THE END

www.ingramcontent.com/pod-product-compliance
Lightning Source LLC
Chambersburg PA
CBHW061306170626
46817CB00001B/68